About the Author

Claire Boston discovered her passion for romance and suspense when she discovered her mother's stash of Nora Roberts novels at the age of eleven. Born in Western Australia, Claire has always believed every love story deserves a happily-ever-after—especially when the journey is rugged, dangerous, and set under the vast Australian sky.

Claire's romantic suspense novels often find her characters caught between danger and desire: resilient heroes and heroines who must battle both external threats and their innermost fears. Whether it's a small coastal town shaken by crime, secrets buried in the outback, or a past that refuses to stay silent, Claire creates worlds where love is worth the risk.

She fuels her imagination through her desire to learn: new cultures, interesting vocations, and remote landscapes all become threads in her stories. When she's not writing, Claire can be found travelling with her husband, dabbling in crafts, or curled up on the couch immersed in a book.

Claire's novels have been nominated for the Romantic Book of the Year award, and the Vivian Award. Through all her stories—whether set in the Australian bush or halfway around the world—Claire celebrates communities, found families and love's power to heal.

Also by Claire Boston

Romance

<u>The Texan Quartet</u>
What Goes on Tour
All that Sparkles
Under the Covers
Into the Fire

<u>The Flanagan Sisters</u>
Break the Rules
Change of Heart
Blaze a Trail
Place to Belong
Take a Chance

<u>Stand Alones</u>
Love Me Do

Non-fiction
<u>The Beginner Writer's Toolkit</u>
Self-Editing

Romantic Suspense

<u>The Blackbridge Series</u>
Nothing to Fear
Nothing to Gain
Nothing to Hide
Nothing to Lose
Shelter
Shield
Harbour
Protect

<u>Retribution Bay</u>
Return to Retribution Bay
Trapped in Retribution Bay
Escape to Retribution Bay
Secrets in Retribution Bay
Beached in Retribution Bay
Adrift in Retribution Bay
Wrecked in Retribution Bay
Captive in Retribution Bay

<u>Squadron 6</u>
Rescuing Mila
Guarding Zoe

<u>Lilydale Cottage</u>
Repairing Dreams

Repairing Dreams

Lilydale Cottage Book 1

Claire Boston

BANTILLY
PUBLISHING

First published by Bantilly Publishing in 2025

Copyright © Claire Boston 2025
The moral right of the author has been asserted.

All rights reserved. This publication (or any part of it) may not be reproduced or transmitted, copied, stored, distributed or otherwise made available by any person or entity, in any form (electronic, digital, optical, mechanical) or by any means (photocopying, recording, scanning or otherwise) without prior written permission from the publisher.

This is a work of fiction. Names, characters, businesses, places, events and incidents are either the products of the author's imagination or used in a fictitious manner. Any resemblance to actual persons, living or dead, or actual events is purely coincidental.

Repairing Dreams: Lilydale Cottage

EPUB format: 978-1-922916-16-7
Print: 978-1-922916-17-4
Large Print: 978-1-922916-18-1

Cover design by EmCat Designs
Edited by Ann Harth
Copyedited by Teena Raffa-Mulligan

Chapter 1

Ding, ding, ding.

The speed of the incoming messages on Chelsea McGinnis's phone made it sound like a child bashing a xylophone. Her gut clenched as she lunged for it. Nothing good came this fast at this hour of the morning. She spotted the name, *Aria Simpson,* and her heart went into overdrive.

No, no, no.

What had Aria done?

Her fingers shook as she clicked on the link Ellen, her manager at the advertising company, had sent her.

Nausea swept through her as she read, and she sank onto her unmade hotel bed. Last night's event had launched Aria as the ambassador for Tours Australia. The post was of the influencer posing with two Indigenous Australian women who had danced at the launch and were still wearing their traditional dress and face paint. The photo itself would have been fine, but Aria's words put a stake right into Chelsea's heart.

After all these years they still haven't embraced modern makeup or clothing. Indigenous ladies, follow me for tips.

Followed by a laugh emoji.

Chelsea closed her eyes and her hands trembled.

There was no coming back from this. All her hard work cajoling the self-entitled prima donna to do what they needed for the campaign was obliterated in one careless, ignorant post.

Months of effort getting Aria to agree to the role at the client's request, and then thousands of dollars spent touring Aria around the country and filming her, had all been wasted.

No way could they use her as a spokesperson now.

Chelsea scrolled through the comments; some thought she was funny, others were horrified and angry at her disrespect.

Toni, the elder pictured with Aria, would be furious. She had spent months negotiating with Tours Australia to have her cultural tours included on their program. She was a proud and business savvy woman and this would be a kick in the teeth.

Chelsea had known Aria Simpson wasn't the right person for the role. Model and influencer, now with her own range of makeup, Aria had always been opinionated and potentially divisive, but the client's representative was a fan and believed she would attract the younger demographic. As if the younger demographic had the funds to take Tours Australia trips.

Her phone vibrated in her hands as a call from Ellen came through.

Shit.

Taking a deep breath, she answered it. "Ellen, what do you need me to do?"

"Get Aria to write an apology and delete the post."

"She's not going to." It was one thing Chelsea had learnt after spending every day for two weeks in the woman's company—Aria always thought she was right.

"Then you post it. Fix this, Chelsea. Your promotion is on the line."

Before Chelsea could comment, Ellen hung up.

Shock made her breathless. How was this her fault? She'd spoken against Aria when her name was first raised.

But if Chelsea was associated with this, no one would want her working on their campaigns. She couldn't afford to lose her promotion because rent on her outer-suburb apartment in Sydney was more than half her pay.

Chelsea inhaled deeply, pushing the panic aside for another time. Fixing things was her superpower. She slipped on her shoes, twisted her chocolate brown hair into a messy French twist and then called Toni. The elder deserved an apology first.

Toni answered on the first ring. "What are you doing to fix this?" Her tone wasn't aggressive, but it was insistent.

"I'm going to speak to Aria," Chelsea said. "I'm so sorry for her disrespect."

"It's not your fault. That girl wouldn't know respect if it hit her over the head."

The tension in Chelsea's shoulders lessened. She'd really liked Toni's outlook on life and her dedication to her culture. "I'm hoping to get her to post an apology."

Toni snorted. "Good luck with that."

Chelsea smiled. "I'm certain Tours Australia will post an apology and I'll keep you up to date with what's happening."

"Thanks, Chelsea. I know how hard you worked on this." Toni hung up.

Chelsea exhaled. If only the rest of the people she had to deal with were as understanding as Toni. She checked her appearance in the mirror by the door, tucked a stray hair behind her ear and then knocked loudly on the hotel room next to hers. It was only seven o'clock, but Aria should be awake as she was flying to Italy today for a fashion show.

While Chelsea waited, she checked the time the damning post had gone up. One a.m.. Aria had been drunk when Chelsea walked her to her room around midnight after the event ended. Aria had wanted to keep partying, but Chelsea had convinced her it would be wise to get a good night's sleep before her long-haul flight from Sydney to Milan.

Chelsea pounded on the door again. She should have let Aria go out. Then Aria might have been too busy to post to social media.

Aria opened the door, her red hair a tangled mess and her eyes bloodshot. She wore a hotel robe and behind her every bottle from the mini bar was empty on the floor. The scent of alcohol suggested not all the liquid had gone into Aria's mouth.

Yep. She definitely should have let her go out.

Aria screwed up her face. "What are you doing here? I thought we were finished."

If only. Chelsea gritted her teeth. "You posted something to social media last night." She held up her phone so Aria could see.

Aria squinted at it. "Yeah." She grinned. "Pretty smart, right? I just found a whole new demographic for my label."

Chelsea opened her mouth and then closed it again, trying to find the right words. How could she phrase this so it didn't get Aria's back up? Your post was… insensitive, ignorant, clueless. No, she still needed Aria to post an apology. She cleared her throat. "There are many people who find your comments offensive."

"Haters gonna hate." Aria walked back into her room and Chelsea followed her, trying to reason with her.

"Can you see how derogatory it might seem to those in our Indigenous community?"

"It's not like it isn't true. They need to stop being precious snowflakes about the past and move on."

Chelsea had no words. She bit her tongue and clenched her hands. This clueless, self-absorbed, entitled cow deserved all the backlash that was coming to her. But right now, she held Chelsea's job in her hand, so Chelsea had to play nice.

"The management of Tours Australia is quite upset as are the elders you disrespected. This could ruin the campaign we've been working so hard on. It would help if you could post a statement apologising for your comments. I'll even write it for you." She opened the note-taking app on her phone and started writing.

"That's their problem. I've done my bit and been paid for it." She flopped on the bed and turned on the television. The morning news was doing a story on her post.

Shit.

Aria laughed. "Look how upset they are. Bunch of woke hypocrites."

"Please, Aria," Chelsea begged. "I know it's trivial to you, but this impacts me too. I would appreciate it if you posted what I write."

"How does it impact you?"

"Because you've been my responsibility throughout this campaign. What you do reflects on me and I'm trying to get a promotion."

Aria switched off the TV. "That's stupid. You can't control what I say." She stood and walked towards the bathroom.

"Aria, please." God, she hated begging this woman who had made her life hell for a fortnight.

At the doorway, Aria turned. "If they sack you, it'll give you the opportunity to go out on your own. Forge your own career not dictated by others. It'll be good for you. I gotta shower." She shed her robe and left Chelsea staring at the closed door.

Chelsea rubbed her arms as a chill swept through her. She battled the nausea swelling in her stomach and inhaled slowly.

Memories flooded her of all those years watching her mother struggle to make ends meet, the uncertainty of where they would live when their lease was up, or the company her mother worked for had gone through sweeping redundancies. Seeing how stressed her mother was as she tried to find work during an economic downturn.

Chelsea had worked hard for her independence and to ensure she wasn't vulnerable to the influence of others, but this post could ruin everything.

She had to get Aria to post the apology.

Otherwise she was screwed.

***

An hour later, after writing the apology and again begging Aria to post it, Chelsea slammed the door closed on the car that was taking Aria to the airport. The sound was like an axe on a chopping block. She had failed.

She dragged her own suitcase down the footpath of the Sydney Central Business District and into the skyscraper where she worked. Viral Posts Media took up an entire floor of the building and when the elevator dinged, Chelsea walked into the bright reception area where she was greeted by the receptionist, Meg. A large vase of colourful lilies sat on the desk, bringing cheer to the area, and a faint floral scent was enhanced by the oil diffuser hidden behind the reception desk.

"Oh my God, Chelsea," Meg said. "Everyone is going crazy in there. Did you get Aria to retract her statement?"

Chelsea shook her head as her stomach rolled again. "No." She looked around. "Can I leave my suitcase behind your desk?" She didn't want to walk into the main office dragging it behind her, and there was no room in her small cubicle for it.

"Sure."

Chelsea walked through the glass doors of Viral Posts

Media. Her colleagues sat in cubicles, the walls of which were high enough that she couldn't see their faces. Quickly she strode down the corridor on her four-inch heels towards Ellen's office.

Ellen's personal assistant looked up as Chelsea approached and gave her a sympathetic smile. "Chelsea. I'm to send you straight to Harold's office."

The managing director. Chelsea swallowed hard. "Right."

She pivoted towards the corner office. By now people were rubber-necking from their cubicles as she walked past, some smirking, some wincing in sympathy. She kept her shoulders back and her head held high. She had done nothing wrong. It was ridiculous to think she could gag a celebrity, particularly one like Aria.

Harold's personal assistant said, "Go right in. They've been waiting for you."

Nerves danced in her stomach. She could do this. Chelsea smoothed down the front of her sleeveless navy dress and knocked on the door before cautiously pushing it open. Harold sat behind his desk with Ellen and Vivian, the client from Tours Australia, across from him.

The tension in the room was palpable. Vivian glared at her and Harold frowned in his impatience. Only Ellen's expression held a hint of sympathy.

"You took your time," Harold said.

"My apologies. Aria wasn't in a rush to get to the airport this morning."

"Did she post the apology?" Vivian demanded.

Chelsea clasped her hands together. "I'm sorry, she refused to. I offered to rewrite it to suit her, but she doesn't believe she has anything to apologise for."

"This is unacceptable," Harold said. "She was your responsibility. Why did you let her post it?"

Let her? She glanced at Ellen, who shrugged as if there was nothing she could do. Right. No support from that front. "Unfortunately her social media is out of my control. She posted it last night after I left her in her hotel room."

"What are we going to do?" Vivian asked. "We can't use anything we've just filmed." She glared at Chelsea again.

Chelsea had been considering options. "We have a lot of scenery footage we can still use," she said. "We could use a different celebrity to voice over it." But it would cost a lot more to get the celebrity on camera and take them to all the places they'd taken Aria.

"I'm sure we'll be able to salvage a lot," Ellen agreed.

"I'm going to be crucified," Vivian moaned. "Whose idea was it to use Aria?"

Chelsea raised her eyebrows, but a shake of Ellen's head kept Chelsea's lips pressed firmly together. Vivian had been the worst kind of fan-girl when she'd met Aria at the airport on her arrival.

"My management is not happy," Vivian continued. "I want whoever it was fired."

Some of the tension left Chelsea's shoulders. It hadn't been her decision, and she had it on record that she'd opposed the idea. She'd be safe.

"Now we know Aria's stance," Harold said, getting to his feet, "we can rework the campaign and come up with a solution." He gestured Vivian towards the door.

"I need this before midday," Vivian demanded.

"We'll get it to you," Harold assured her as he walked her out of his office.

Less than four hours to rework something that had taken weeks to put together. Chelsea looked at Ellen. "What now?"

"Now you need to work some magic." Ellen stood. "Let's go."

Chelsea followed her boss out of the room, the tension returning ten-fold.

She received the unspoken message loud and clear.

This was all on her.

Four hours later Chelsea watched the new ad and smiled, the tension of the morning finally dissipating. She'd done it. "You're a genius, Kylie," Chelsea said to the video editor who'd reworked one ad in record time. "I owe you big time."

"Dinner's on you next time I'm in town," Kylie agreed and hung up.

Chelsea checked the time. Two minutes to midday. She saved the video to the folder along with the updated proposal outlining how to restructure the campaign without Aria. She rubbed her temple where an insistent throbbing had taken up residence three hours ago.

"Are you done?" Ellen walked into her cubicle.

She nodded, pressing print on the proposal. "I've redone one ad with a voice over by rock star, Kent Downer."

Ellen's eyebrows raised. "How did you arrange that?"

Chelsea smiled. "I have contacts." It was good to remind Ellen she had value. Her boss didn't need to know Kent had married one of her friends from primary school. She pressed play on the ad Kylie had reworked.

Kent's Texan drawl was recognisable on the video and at the end he did a shot to camera standing in his living room wearing an Akubra hat, suitcase in tow as if he was about to embark on one of Tours Australia's tours. The video quality was excellent.

"This is fantastic," Ellen said.

Chelsea grinned as she fetched the proposal from the nearby printer. "We'll need to arrange payment to Kent for his work." Aria had never been a great representative of Australia, whereas Kent's transformation from goth rocker to guy-next-door rock star after his secret identity had been revealed was perfect.

"How much?"

She named a very reasonable price. Kent hadn't wanted any money, but she wasn't letting her boss have him for free. "Is Vivian coming back here for the presentation?"

"Harold and I are taking it to her," Ellen said. "Get some lunch and I'll let you know how we get on when we return." Ellen took the proposal and walked away.

Chelsea watched her go. She liked her boss, but Ellen was very career focused, and willing to blame mistakes on others rather than admit they were her own fault.

Chelsea lowered herself into her chair, enjoying being back in her space. She'd been excited about touring around Australia for the campaign, but then she'd had another project which had kept her in Melbourne for a month, and she hadn't been at her desk for about six weeks. She watered her small pot plant. It was looking sad, its leaves wilted.

"Chelsea, I'm getting souvlaki for lunch," Jo called from the cubicle next to hers. "Do you want one?"

"Yes, please." She transferred money into Jo's account.

"Crisis averted?" Jo asked in a murmur, coming to stand at her cubicle.

"I hope so." She swallowed two headache tablets. Right now, all she wanted to do was crawl into bed and sleep for twenty-four hours, but her inbox was already full of emails asking her to comment on Aria's post, and she needed to update Toni on the progress.

Maybe Aria was right. Maybe it was time she did something else, something she had more control over.

She shook away the thought. She had a steady, well-paying job she enjoyed… most of the time, a tidy apartment and a good relationship with her family. She was grateful for what she had. It wasn't right to wish for more. Life had taught her how hard it was when she didn't have stability.

She wouldn't risk her security on a whim.

With a sigh, she got to work.

"Chelsea, can you come into my office?"

Chelsea glanced up at Ellen's voice and checked the time. She'd been working solidly for three hours. Ellen and Harold must have spent a lot of time smoothing the waters at Tours Australia.

She followed her boss into the office and Ellen closed the door with a click.

Chelsea stiffened. Ellen only ever closed the door for performance reviews. This wasn't a good start. She pushed through the unease as she sat down. "How did it go?"

"Tours Australia were pleased with the proposal. We've pulled down everything from last night's launch and issued a statement distancing Tours Australia from Aria's comments. We'll release the first video in the new campaign by the end of the day."

"That's great. Did they agree to the rest of the celebrities?" She'd put together a list of celebrities who could do voice-overs for the remaining campaign. They were all people she'd worked with before and who she believed would do it.

"Yes." Ellen paused, a deep frown on her face.

Chelsea waited, knowing there was more to come.

"There's one more thing," Ellen said. "Tours Australia have requested you no longer work on this campaign."

Chelsea jolted. "Why not?"

Ellen glanced at her desk before sighing and meeting Chelsea's gaze. "They feel as if you didn't choose the right celebrity endorser."

Chelsea gaped as disbelief coursed through her body. "But Vivian insisted on Aria." And she had the documentation to prove it. Chelsea had worked so hard on this account. They'd set a ridiculous deadline for the work to be completed and because they were a big client, Viral Posts Media had bent over backwards to make it work.

She was exhausted trying to please Vivian.

"Vivian is also extremely influential in town. If she doesn't recommend us, no one will touch us."

Chelsea bit her lip to stop herself from saying her stepfather also held a lot of clout. It wasn't a card she was willing to play. She exhaled, thinking of the positives. It would give her more time to work on her other accounts. "So I'll hand the account over and continue with the rest of my work?"

"I'm sorry, Chelsea. Tours Australia stated they wouldn't recommend Viral Posts Media while you work here. I tried to talk Harold out of it, but they're our biggest client." She cleared her throat. "I must advise you that your employment at Viral Posts Media is now terminated."

Chelsea shook her head. "You can't do that. I've done nothing wrong. I've worked my butt off for this company for the past five years." She'd been the one to win them the Tours Australia account.

"I'm truly sorry," Ellen said. "I'll write you a good reference."

This couldn't be happening. "Effective when?"

"Immediately. I'm to escort you from the premises."

Chelsea studied her boss for any signs of a joke, but she stared back, sad but unruffled. "I could report you to the Fair Work Tribunal."

Ellen nodded. "But you won't. You're not that kind of person and you won't get another job in the industry if you do."

She was right, but Chelsea had bills to pay. Her brain whirled as she considered options, pushing down the panic that wanted to take control. "I want a redundancy package," she stated. "My four weeks' notice plus my accrued long-service leave, annual leave, and my sick-leave paid out." It wouldn't be a lot, but it would be enough to tide her over. It also gave her the option of saying she wasn't fired. Not that word wouldn't spread fast in this industry.

Ellen stared at her for a long moment and then gave a small smile of approval. "I'll get HR to organise it now. Why don't you pack your things?"

Chelsea got to her feet, her movements stiff. This was really happening. She blinked as tears threatened to form but straightened her spine and returned to her cubicle.

She tapped her finger rapidly on her thigh and then clenched her hand to stop it. It wasn't the end of the world. There were plenty of other agencies in town. Not all of them would believe she was tainted. She'd have a job in no time.

She took three slow breaths as she considered her next steps.

There wasn't anything personal on her work laptop. She opened the desk drawer and pulled out her stash of tea bags and snacks, putting them into a reusable shopping bag she kept in her purse. She fetched her coffee from the freezer in the kitchen and retrieved her mug. Then she returned to her cubicle and went through the other drawers.

Her favourite fountain pen and her personal organiser went into another bag and then her hand hovered over the framed photo on her desk. Aunt Maggie, a ten-year-old Chelsea, and her mother at Lilydale Cottage. Happier times. It was taken before her mother met Chelsea's stepfather. They'd gone to visit her mother's aunt, Maggie, at Lilydale Cottage like they regularly did, and the photo was taken in front of the bed of pink and red roses that were blooming so beautifully.

Those days at Lilydale were the best. An escape from everyday life where Chelsea could run through the gardens and play with her friend Lauren, who lived down the road. It was before she was old enough to get a part-time job to help with household expenses.

She'd adored Aunt Maggie and had written her letters

every month when they'd moved from Rockingham to Sydney and could no longer visit on weekends. Aunt Maggie had insisted emails were too impersonal.

A jolt of longing passed through her. What would it be like to return to Lilydale? Would it be the same without Aunt Maggie there?

Tears threatened to overflow and she sniffed, tucking the photo into her bag. Chelsea had been devastated when Aunt Maggie died last year.

"Are you OK?" Jo poked her head over the cubicle wall.

Chelsea swallowed hard so she could speak. "I've been made redundant."

Jo's eyes widened, and she hurried around the wall to hug her. "That's not fair."

Chelsea sniffed again and cleared her throat. "It's been nice working with you." The words came out as a whisper and she turned to check her drawers again. She had everything that was hers.

"At least Aria got what's coming to her," Jo said.

Chelsea frowned. "What do you mean?"

"The fashion show dropped her." Jo grinned. "They saw her post and said they didn't want to be associated with those kinds of opinions. A bunch of the other brands she normally models for are also distancing themselves."

"That's great." It gave some measure of comfort that Aria was dealing with the ramifications of her comments, but right now Chelsea had bigger concerns.

Ellen returned holding a contract and Jo made herself scarce. Chelsea reviewed it and then signed the bottom and handed her key card to Ellen.

Ellen walked her to the elevators. "I'm sorry, Chelsea. I wish you all the best."

Chelsea nodded, unable to speak. This was it. She was no longer employed. She grabbed her suitcase, managed a smile at Meg before she stepped into the elevator.

It wasn't until the doors closed and the elevator descended that she let the tears fall.

Chapter 2

Ethan Ward knew it would be bad news the minute he walked into the major's office. He did his best to hide his limp and pretend the constant ache in his pelvis wasn't there, but he wasn't fooling anyone. His team leader, Sergeant Damien "Dobby" Dobson, gave him a sympathetic smile.

Ethan saluted Major Hammond, a humourless man who only cared for the army.

"The army has denied your request to return to work at this time," Major Hammond said.

Ethan Ward stared down the man. "With all due respect, sir, I'm ready to come back."

"You're still walking with a limp, Corporal. You'll be a liability."

Ethan growled his displeasure. "I've been in rehab for months now. I'm going crazy." His team had been deployed several times without him and not being there for them, not being part of the action, was killing him. He was letting them down.

"Then I suggest you see a psychologist," the major said. "We'll reassess in a month. Dismissed."

Ethan glanced at Dobby, who gave a slight shake of his

head. Yeah, there was no arguing with the major. He saluted again and left the room, frustration almost overwhelming him. What the hell was he going to do for another month? He'd read a million books, worked religiously on his physio and finished half a dozen video games.

He missed his team mates, the excitement of the mission and the cameraderie they shared.

A feeling of helplessness swirled up inside him, battering him about like the wave of the tsunami had. He was doing everything he could to get back, but it wasn't enough. Just like his fight against the water had been futile.

His chest tightened as he paused at the entrance of the building and took several deep breaths to calm the anxiety inside of him.

He slammed his hand against the door frame. Damn it! He should be over this fear by now.

His therapist said it was a form of post-traumatic stress disorder, but that was rubbish. If he was going to get PTSD it would be for being shot at, or tortured, or due to any one of the horrific things he'd seen on the job over the years, not because he'd been tossed about by a wave.

He was stronger than that.

He'd had to be.

Dobby joined him and Ethan pushed through the anxiety, standing straighter, breathing slowly.

"I've tried everything I can think of." Dobby clapped Ethan on the shoulder. "Why don't you get away—have a proper holiday?"

Ethan stared at his friend in disbelief. Neither of them was good at downtime. They had to be moving, doing something active.

"Yeah, I get it. Is there anyone you can visit?"

He'd been raised in a bunch of foster homes and had no family. All his friends were in the army and due to be deployed soon. Perhaps it was a sad indication, but his life was the army. No one else had given a toss about him. No one except Chelsea… he pushed the thought away. He'd made his decision a long time ago and wouldn't, no, didn't, regret it.

"What about the woman you write to?"

Trust Dobby to remember the one person connected to Chelsea. "Aunt Maggie?" Not technically his aunt, but everyone called her that. She'd been the closest thing to family he'd had during his final years in foster care. A woman who had made him feel as if he was worth something. It had been spending time with her and hearing about her fiancé who had died in the Vietnam War, which had inspired him to join the army and aim for the Special Forces.

Not that she'd been happy about his choice.

He hadn't seen her in over a year. There hadn't been enough time between deployments, and he hadn't written since before the accident, not wanting to admit he'd been hurt, not wanting her to worry.

When was the last time she'd written to him? He frowned. Maybe last Easter.

Perhaps he should check on her. He exhaled and brushed his hair out of his face. "All right."

Dobby patted his back. "Keep working on the rehab. If anyone can make it back after what you went through, it's you."

Ethan grunted. He didn't want to imagine a life where he couldn't be in the army. It had been his saviour. He'd given up the one person he'd ever loved for it. His sacrifice couldn't be for nothing.

He exhaled, his mind working on a new plan. A month. Plenty of time to head to Honeybrook and visit Aunt Maggie. She'd be getting on in age and perhaps he could help her around her beautiful garden. "Fine. Talk to you later."

He drove home to his small apartment close to the

base. His pelvis ached as he climbed the front steps. Of all the bones to break…

No point whinging about it.

Inside he took stock of his life. Almost thirty years old and he might be headed for an early retirement. After over a decade in the army he knew nothing else. The few photos he had around the place all featured his army team mates, the most recent from Squadron Six, the Special Forces SAS elite team.

Aside from that, all he had were the usual trappings of the male bachelor; huge eighty-inch television, gaming console and comfortable couch. His kitchen bench had a couple of stools underneath it, and he ate his meals there. The small balcony contained a table and chairs for when mates came over, and he had a spare bedroom where they could crash if they drank too much.

Not much, but it was all his.

After a childhood moving from foster home to foster home with only a backpack to call his own, it was a lot.

He sighed and pulled a beer from the fridge.

Why was he getting maudlin? It was like Dobby said, if anyone could pass the medical, it was him.

Perhaps it was because thoughts of Aunt Maggie dredged up thoughts of the girl he'd given up.

He opened a nearby drawer and pulled out an old, worn photograph taken at a local fair during his last summer in Honeybrook. He looked happy standing with his arm around the girl he'd fallen in love with.

Ethan squeezed his eyes closed. The day had been beautiful and warm. He and Chelsea had borrowed Aunt Maggie's Landcruiser and driven to the neighbouring town. He'd spent time at the army stall where he'd enlisted. It was his way out, his opportunity to take control of his life. He'd get somewhere to live and could earn a living. Then he and Chelsea could get married and live happily ever after.

He snorted, shoving the photo back in the drawer and shutting it.

Still naïve despite all the shit life had thrown at him.

Reality had shoved him back where he belonged quickly enough.

Ethan wandered back into the lounge and sank onto his couch. There was no doubt in his mind he'd made the right decision by breaking up with Chelsea, but that didn't mean it hadn't hurt.

He shook his head, as his heart twinged. Surely he'd accepted his decision by now.

Dobby's partner, Mila, had offered to look up Chelsea on social media for him, but he'd told her not to bother. He was too afraid he'd see she was married. Though he still hadn't forgotten how Mila had told him he was an idiot for leaving Chelsea without telling her why.

It had made sense to him at the time.

Aunt Maggie never mentioned Chelsea when she wrote, maybe because she'd known how hard it had been for him to leave.

But Chelsea McGinnis was the first and only woman who had truly seen him.

He wished the idea of her happy with a family didn't cause an uncomfortable twinge of jealousy and sorrow in him.

Ethan sipped his beer. No point wondering. She wouldn't care what had happened to him after he'd broken her heart.

He shook his head. That was all in the past. Time to consider the future. He wouldn't bother calling Aunt Maggie before he went. Part of him was a little concerned she'd tell him not to come, and then he'd have to fill another month with only his thoughts and physio for company. Better to surprise her and offer to help her in the garden like he had when he was a teenager. It had to be getting too much for her these days. Sixteen acres of gardens had been a lot over a decade ago when they'd both been a lot younger.

He smiled, feeling optimistic for the first time since the incident.

Lilydale Cottage was the closest thing he'd ever had to a home. Though he'd been an employee, Aunt Maggie had never treated him as such, and he'd spent a lot of time working next to her in the garden, either in a Zen-like silence, or chatting about school or a fundraiser she was organising.

Peaceful. Safe.

It would be nice to see her again.

Early the next morning, Ethan passed the wooden sign welcoming him to Honeybrook. His chest tightened and then relaxed. The two years hc'd spent here hadn't been too bad in the scheme of things. His foster parents hadn't wanted an almost adult male in the house, but there'd been a mix-up in the paperwork, which got his age wrong. The social services worker had talked fast to convince them to keep him, and he'd promised to help around the house. All he'd wanted was a place to finish school.

Perhaps it was the offer of free labour which had convinced them, because they'd agreed, and he'd taken over all the chores.

Then his foster father had volunteered him to help Aunt Maggie in her garden and Ethan had been ticked off but said nothing.

It turned out to be the best thing to have happened to him.

Aunt Maggie always had fresh, home-made biscuits and slices and a pot of tea for him mid-morning, and slipped him payment for his work. She'd even arranged for him to open a bank account so his foster parents didn't know about it. Neither of them was certain that his foster father wouldn't take Ethan's money from him.

Ethan turned off the main street and wound his way through to the edge of town where Lilydale Cottage was located.

He slowed as he caught his first glimpse of it and his instincts went on high alert.

Something was very wrong.

Waist-high brown weeds had replaced the beautiful green lawns he'd mowed, the lake in the middle was dry and the garden beds were dead and choked with weeds.

He accelerated, his heart beating rapidly. Hedges hadn't been trimmed, and no annuals had been planted. The pagoda close to the road was covered in leaf litter and the paint was peeling.

Everything was out of control.

Aunt Maggie never would have let it fall into this level of disrepair.

He pulled into the drive and leapt out of the car, his breath coming fast. As he pounded up the steps of the front porch, he noted more peeling paint and sagging gutters.

His knock was like three sharp cracks of a pistol.

No noise from inside.

"Aunt Maggie!" He peered through a grimy window. Inside the furniture was just as it had always been – her roll-top desk in the corner, two slightly hard sofas in a floral print cover, and the wooden coffee table that had always contained a tray of biscuits. A thick layer of dust covered it all.

He wanted to be sick.

How long had it been since he'd heard from her?

She always sent a Christmas card, but last Christmas he'd been in hospital after the incident. There hadn't been a card in his pile of mail when he'd got out, but he hadn't realised, too caught up in pain and rehab.

He'd written to her around Easter last year and sent her a bilby Easter egg because she'd always had a soft spot for chocolate and native animals. Easter reminded him of the egg hunt she'd organised for him each year, knowing his foster parents wouldn't have bought him any chocolate. He'd appreciated the thought and although he'd been almost an adult, he enjoyed feeling like a kid searching for the eggs around her garden.

She'd replied to his letter, thanking him and telling him about life in Honeybrook. She hadn't sent him any photos of the garden though. Normally she would.

Was that because she'd been struggling to maintain it?

Had she become ill and gone into a home? Was she sick? Anything else was too much to consider. He should have contacted her before now.

Who would know what had happened?

His heart raced and his chest squeezed as if trying to stop the racing. He gasped for breath and closed his eyes, going through the breathing exercises his psychologist had taught him.

When he could breathe normally again, he glanced across the road. The simple brick and tile house belonged to the Education Department and teachers came and went, but Aunt Maggie had always welcomed the new ones with a cake.

He exhaled and crossed the road to knock on the door.

A short, plump woman answered it and she took a step back, her eyes wide when she saw him.

Ethan shifted back and tried to relax his tense muscles, knowing his broad almost six-foot frame could be intimidating. He smiled. "I'm sorry to disturb you. I was driving through town and decided to visit Aunt Maggie." He gestured over the road. "I haven't heard from her in a while and it looks as if the place is abandoned."

The woman put her hands to her lips, her expression sad. "I'm so sorry to tell you this. Aunt Maggie died last year."

He stepped back as grief hit him, his throat tight, eyes

stinging. "How?"

"She fell off a ladder," the woman said. "My husband found her, but by then it was too late."

He wanted to shake his head to deny it, but there was no point. He gritted his teeth as the grief threatened to overwhelm him. She'd been his family, and he hadn't known she was dead. What kind of person was he?

"How did you know her?" the woman asked.

"I did garden work for her when I was a teenager," he answered. "She was always kind to me."

"Are you Ethan?"

He blinked and nodded.

"She spoke about you. She was ever so chuffed by the bilby chocolate you sent her last year. I'm surprised none of the family told you about her death."

Chelsea. She would have been devastated. Maggie had been her surrogate grandmother. "Is Chelsea in town?"

The woman shook her head. "No. I met her and her mother, Sabine at the funeral, of course. Maggie left the house to Sabine, and Sabine said she would hire someone to upkeep the gardens while she decided what to do with it, but I guess she didn't get around to it."

Ethan had never been impressed by Chelsea's mother. She'd left Chelsea with Maggie for an entire summer while she toured Europe with her new husband. Chelsea had been struggling with the fact her stepfather didn't want her to join them, and hadn't enjoyed moving to Sydney. She'd been vulnerable, and Ethan had done everything he could to make her feel wanted.

The woman cleared her throat. She stood patiently in the doorway while he processed the news. What the hell did he do now? "Would it be all right if I looked around the garden?" He didn't want her calling the police and getting him arrested.

The woman smiled. "I'm sure no one would mind. There's been a property developer scoping out the place as well."

He raised his eyebrows.

"Wants to build a retirement village from what I hear," the woman said. "It would be such a travesty to see the property turned into units, but I guess all of Maggie's hard work is disappearing as it is."

A possessive feeling swept through him. The garden had been Maggie's life. He couldn't bear to see it reduced to nothing. "Do you have Sabine's phone number?"

The woman shook her head. "I should have got it at the funeral, but I didn't think of it. I believe she and Chelsea live in Sydney."

He nodded. "Thank you for your help."

He returned to Lilydale Cottage and circled the house. The little pergola in the private garden still stood, its white paint starting to age and peel. Underneath it sat a round wooden table with four bench seats where he'd spent many break times drinking tea and eating biscuits with Aunt Maggie.

This amount of deterioration couldn't have happened in under a year. When was the last time he'd actually visited Lilydale?

It must have been three years ago when he'd been coming back from training down south and stopped for a couple of nights on the way back to the city.

Not good enough. Aunt Maggie had needed help with the upkeep when he was younger. He should have made sure she was still getting help.

Though she was stubborn.

He would have expected Sabine to help her aunt. She'd married a wealthy man and, from what Chelsea had told him, Aunt Maggie had helped them both when Sabine was a struggling single mother.

Ethan ran his fingers over the wooden table, the rough grain grounding him. He pushed through the small gap in the overgrown hedges and underneath the large peppermint trees which formed a cool canopy between the public garden and the three cottages which Aunt Maggie rented out as holiday accommodation.

He inhaled deeply, enjoying the protection from the hot autumn sun.

The hammock still hung between two trees, its olive-green canvas dirty, but the thick ropes still seemed to be in good condition. Sturdy enough to hold two people. Though he'd been lighter then, and Chelsea was only small.

Sometimes they'd snuggle in tight together. Other times they'd lay head to toe, both content to read their respective books through the heat of the day.

He smiled at the memories and continued.

Ground cover and grass covered the path that wound its way through the section of the garden Aunt Maggie had opened to the public.

Here there were myriad memories of the work he'd done; water fountains he'd cleaned were now dry and filled with leaf litter, a Balinese pagoda where he and Chelsea would take a break and talk about life now contained only a mouldy mattress, and a few ponds were now unrecognisable but he knew where they should be. And of course, the replica of the Sydney Harbour Bridge spanning the dry harbour lake.

His heart ached at how quickly the weeds had taken over and turned this once beautiful, tranquil space into an eyesore. Aunt Maggie would be devastated.

He was tempted to track down Sabine and give her a piece of his mind.

Ethan stopped in front of the sculpture of Cupid. The red and pink rose bushes surrounding it hadn't been pruned in some time and the flowers desperately needed dead-heading. He plucked off a couple, rubbing the soft petals between his fingers and inhaling the sweet scent.

He'd given Chelsea a single red rose from this garden

on the day he'd told her he loved her.

His throat closed over. This wasn't right.

He spun around and strode to the garden shed behind the house. There were no locks on the door and the metal protested as he forced it open, pushing the rust on the hinges to give way. Inside was dusty and dim, but the secateurs hung above the bench right where they always had. He grabbed them and the nearby weeding bucket and headed back to the roses.

It had been over a decade since Maggie had taught him the correct way to prune roses, but it wasn't something he'd ever forgotten.

He got to work.

An hour later, the sun was sinking to the horizon, and he finished pruning the last bush. He stepped back and wiped the sweat from his forehead. The bushes were stalks now, but they looked much better. He glanced at the weeds choking the roots and gingerly knelt on the ground, his pelvis twinging.

The weeds came out easily and each section of clear dirt made him feel lighter, as if he was achieving something.

A willy wagtail hovered nearby, watching his progress, and darted forward to eat an insect he'd disturbed by weeding. It chittered its thanks and flew away.

Ethan smiled. The bird life in the garden had always been a source of entertainment and joy. The magpie warble or the kookaburra's laugh early in the morning, the crows coming throughout the day to see what was happening, the blue wrens flashing their colour during mating season and the cheeky willy wagtail always looking for the easy meal.

Lilydale had been a place of peace.

The sun touched the horizon as he pulled out the last weed. He rocked back on his heels, ignoring the ache. Done.

It wasn't much, considering the sixteen acres of gardens, but it was a start, and it felt damned good.

He sighed. What was he doing?

This wasn't his place, but he still couldn't bring himself to leave. It was the first place he'd found a home, a sense of belonging, love.

He couldn't just let it go.

Ethan dumped the weeds in the bin and returned the equipment to the garden shed. He had to find somewhere to sleep, and then he could track down Sabine and ask about her plans for the place.

His gaze caught on the old barn. It used to be filled with hay when Aunt Maggie had a horse and a few rescue animals. He smiled. He and Chelsea had had some epic make out sessions in the barn.

Ethan rubbed the ache in his chest.

This place was bringing back too many memories, painful with their bittersweetness.

Wandering over, Ethan peered inside the barn, using his phone torch to illuminate the dark space. It still smelled of hay, though he couldn't see any in the large area. To one side, Maggie's ancient yellow Landcruiser was parked gathering dust. That thing had been old when he'd been a teenager, but she'd always sworn she didn't need anything new.

Next to it was room to park his car and he could camp in here easily enough. He'd brought camping equipment in case Maggie wasn't home.

He closed his eyes as the grief swept over him again.

He couldn't explain this urge not to leave the property. It was almost as if by leaving, he was abandoning Aunt Maggie.

He'd done it once for his own good. He couldn't do it again.

Ethan opened both barn doors and walked back towards the front of the house. A side gate led into the property and he opened it, wincing again at the squeak. He glanced across the road but didn't see the neighbour. He didn't think she'd call the police or care if he stayed.

He drove onto the property and into the barn, shutting the gate and doors as he did.

Tonight he'd camp here, make a plan, and tomorrow he'd put it into action.

Somehow he would make this right for Aunt Maggie.

Chapter 3

The cheerful tune of *You Are My Sunshine* jolted Chelsea awake, and she almost fell off her couch. She brushed her hair back and fumbled for her phone, which was on the coffee table. She answered the call, willing her brain to work. "Hi, Mum." Why had she been asleep on her couch?

"Chelsea, I just saw all the furore about Aria Simpson. Weren't you working on something with her?"

Everything rushed back; the uproar, being fired, spending several hours that afternoon searching for a new job, but none of her contacts wanted anything to do with her. Not after Aria. She'd hung up from her last option and cried until she'd fallen asleep. "Yeah."

"Are you all right?"

Chelsea closed her eyes at the concern in her mother's voice. They'd always been a team of two until Ezra came along. Since then Sabine's attention had been divided and Chelsea had worked hard not to be upset about it. But whenever Chelsea needed her, her mother was always there. She took a deep breath. "No. I've been fired."

"What for?" Her mother's outrage soothed some of

Chelsea's hurt.

"Because I was responsible for Aria. The entire campaign had to be reworked, and our client wanted someone to blame."

It still burned that despite her redoing the campaign so it would require little extra cost, she was the fall guy.

"I'm so sorry, baby. What are you going to do?"

That was the million-dollar question. "I don't know." She wandered into the kitchen to pour a glass of water. The mail caught her eye. Not much considering she hadn't been home in over a month, but all of her bills came electronically. She'd dumped the mail on the bench when she arrived home but hadn't opened any of it.

Now she flicked through the envelopes. Some advertising for the upcoming election, a letter from a charity she usually supported and a letter from her real estate agent. She slid her finger under the fold to open it. "No one is hiring." Her eyes scanned the letter and her stomach swirled with nausea. No. This couldn't be happening. "Shit." She sank into the nearest chair.

"Don't swear, Chelsea. You'll find something."

"No, it's not that." But it was partially. She breathed slowly three times to make the nausea disappear, but it didn't. This was her worst nightmare. Unemployed and, "I just got notice on my apartment. The owners are selling and I have four weeks to vacate." After a childhood watching her mother scramble to make ends meet and moving from house to house when the lease was up, she'd thought she'd found stability for herself.

She rubbed at her hot skin and her fingers curled around the letter. No, screwing it up wouldn't make the problem go away.

Finding somewhere to rent in Sydney was difficult at the best of times, but if she was unemployed, it would be impossible.

"Oh, no. Can they do that?"

She blinked, bringing her attention back to her mother. "The lease is due to be renewed, so I guess they can." Jobless and homeless in one fell swoop.

"When it rains, it pours. You can always come home for a while if you can't find somewhere."

Some of the tension decreased even as Chelsea winced. "Thanks, Mum." It was the last place she wanted to go. Her stepfather wouldn't like it, and as much as she loved her much younger brother and sister, she didn't want to live with them. The house overlooking the ocean had never felt like home, despite its luxury. But it was a backup plan, and she was lucky to have that.

The photo she'd removed from her office caught her eye.

Lilydale Cottage had been her only real home.

She sighed and reread the letter. The date at the top caught her eye. It had been sent three and a half weeks ago.

No, no, no. She had three days to pack and vacate. Surely the real estate agent should have called, or emailed, or something.

She gazed around her apartment. She didn't have a lot, but it would still be difficult to get it done.

"I know!" her mother cried. "It's perfect and the other reason I called. You could go to Lilydale Cottage for a couple of weeks. Take a break and let all the fuss die down before you look for work."

Chelsea frowned. Odd that her mother should mention Lilydale when Chelsea had been thinking about it. "I'd love to, but I can't afford to go." Not when she had to spend all her time searching for work and an apartment. The cottage was across the other side of the country, and it still hurt that Aunt Maggie was gone. She wasn't sure she could face going through all her things.

"I'll pay for your flight and costs, of course. I had a call from a property developer who is interested in buying the land. I rang to ask your opinion. I know the place meant a lot to you."

Her mouth dropped open but before she said anything, her mother continued, "If we sell, we'll need to clear out the house. You could fly over, talk to the developer and pack Aunt Maggie's things. By the time you return, no one will remember Aria Simpson."

Lilydale Cottage.

The desire to return was almost overwhelming. It was her safe place. Spending time in the gardens would give her space to relax and plan what to do next. Hopefully they wouldn't remind her too much of the boy who'd broken her heart.

"Chelsea?"

"Sorry, Mum. I was thinking about it." She glanced around the house. "How long will it take to pack Aunt Maggie's things?" Excitement warred with anxiety. She could get away, escape Sydney and its stress, and take some time for herself, but her employment status and living situation wouldn't be fixed by ignoring it. She couldn't be so irresponsible.

"She was a bit of a hoarder, so two or three weeks I'd guess."

"I'd like to go, but without a job, I can't get a new apartment." Her words came faster as the panic threatened to take control.

"Oh, baby. Take a breath and calm down," her mother soothed. "I will always be here to support you. I understand you like your independence, but you're not alone."

Chelsea took another three breaths and tried to calm her thoughts. Her mother might always be there, but Ezra would make her feel like an imposition. It wasn't anything overt, but little subtle comments when her mother wasn't around.

She wouldn't let that happen. Her brain clicked over into problem-solving mode.

Perhaps she could stay at Lilydale until she found a job. Sure, it was an entire continent away from where she was looking for work, but she could do video interviews. At least she'd have her own space.

And she could always search for a job on the west coast. She didn't have as many contacts there, but perhaps they wouldn't care about the Aria Simpson fiasco.

"I need to pack up my apartment." She couldn't leave before she did. "Can I store some things at your place?" Their large shed should have room for her bed and couch until she found somewhere else to live.

"I'll get you a storage unit. Ezra won't mind paying for it."

She heard the underlying implication Ezra wouldn't want her things cluttering up his shed and ignored the stab of disappointment.

"How about I come over tomorrow while Miles and Amelia are at school to help you?" her mother continued.

Chelsea smiled. "I'd like that, Mum." They had little time together, just the two of them. "I'll see you then."

A little mother-daughter time would settle her. She glanced around her house and then checked her watch. If she was quick, she could make it to the hardware store before it closed and buy packing materials. Relieved she had a short-term goal to focus on, she grabbed her keys and headed out the door.

Three days later, Chelsea picked up her hire car at Perth airport and drove an hour and a half south to the small town of Honeybrook, nestled at the base of the Darling Scarp. She smiled as she passed the wooden welcome sign, and the stress of losing her job, packing and moving all her belongings into a pathetically small storage unit released. This had always been home to her. The place both she and her mother could get away and forget about their troubles.

A safe place away from the mountains of bills.

She drove down the main street and her smile faded. So many shop fronts were vacant, stores closed, and there was little movement even though it was the middle of the day.

Her favourite lolly shop was still there, but it looked as if it had halved in size.

Was Honeybrook suffering the fate of so many small towns in Australia? Was it dying?

Aunt Maggie hadn't mentioned anything in her letters and the last time she'd been here was for the funeral and she hadn't been paying attention to anything but her grief.

Chelsea turned down the street which led to Lilydale Cottage. She had the number of the groundskeeper her mother had hired but hadn't got a hold of him to tell him she was coming. She'd see him soon enough.

She rounded a bend and the house appeared in front of her. The quaint two-storey building with its wrap-around verandah and balcony had always appealed to her. It was old, built in the early nineteen hundreds back when Honeybrook had been a milling town and the start of the push south to find more farming land.

She parked next to the house and got out, stretching and twisting to view the beautiful garden.

She froze, her mouth dropping open.

Chelsea sucked in a breath, the inhale painful as she scanned the grounds.

What had happened? Where were the manicured lawns and tidy paths which tempted you to explore further? Where were the flowers and the bushes and the plants?

She stumbled towards the wooden fence and leaned against it as she took in the yellow weeds choking the grounds, the unpruned hedges and the vines which spread as far as they could reach. Her throat closed over. This couldn't be real. Her mother had someone maintaining the garden.

She fumbled for her phone and dialled Sabine, fighting back the tears.

"Chelsea, did you arrive safely?"

Chelsea swallowed hard and tried to keep the anguish out of her voice. "Yeah, flight was fine." She cleared her throat. "When was the last time you heard from the groundskeeper?"

"Darren? He emails me every month with photos of the property."

How was that possible? "Hang on. Let me put you on video call." Her finger shook as she pressed the button and then held the phone up to show her mother. "Is this what his photos looked like?"

Her mother gasped. "No. Is it all like that?"

"I haven't been around the back yet." Didn't have the strength. "Do you have Darren's address?"

"I'll text it to you," her mother said. "I can't believe this. He seemed so trustworthy." Her voice shook, and Chelsea understood how upset her mother was. "He must have taken photos on the first day and then done nothing."

Her phone dinged as the message came through. "I'll check the whole garden and then visit him. I'll call you tonight."

"All right. Watch out for snakes."

Good point. The long grass would be a haven for them, particularly as the block butted up against bushland. She debated dragging her suitcase inside and changing, but her steps took her down the side path to where the main path through the garden started. The flat sandals she wore had been comfortable plane footwear and weren't the best for this walk, but she didn't care. Slowly she walked the path from memory, not really watching where she was going. Her eyes were all for what was left of the garden.

The food garden held fruit trees laden with rotting fruit or needing a good prune, the vegetable patches were a mess of weeds and the banana passionfruit vine which had grown over a pergola was dead.

She closed her eyes as her heart squeezed. Memories of all the times she'd run down the path to pick one of the delicious fruits flooded her. She'd pluck a couple, then hurry to sit under a shady tree, or swing in the hammock and read her book while slurping on the fruit.

Blinking away the tears she continued, weaving her way through the native plant garden with its sweet scents from a flowering grevillea. These at least appeared healthy, being plants which were endemic to the region, but they needed pruning and the garden beds needed weeding.

She ran a hand over the railing of the replica Sydney Harbour Bridge and it came away dirty. She'd always found the bridge such an odd structure in the garden but had spent many hours playing on it. It wasn't until the last summer she'd spent here that Aunt Maggie had told her about its significance. The real bridge was the last place she'd seen her fiancé. They'd kissed for the last time, but he hadn't wanted her to come to the port to see him board the ship to Vietnam. He'd promised to meet her at that exact spot when he returned at the end of the war.

It was a promise he hadn't been able to keep.

The bridge still looked structurally sound, but she wouldn't test it yet. Instead she continued along the outer path where her footsteps slowed as she reached Cupid's garden.

Someone had pruned the roses and cleared the bed of weeds. It was so strange in a garden otherwise choked to death.

Was it the one garden bed Darren had actually tended?

She gazed at Cupid in the centre. She'd once thought he was her own personal deity, the one who had finally given her a man who loved her and made her feel worthy of love.

An image of when she'd first met Ethan flashed into her mind. He'd been taller than her, skinny, with shaggy brown hair and suspicious brown eyes, as if not one to trust easily.

Then an image of him on this very spot, looking down at her with eyes that promised forever and handing her a red rose as he told her he loved her.

She'd been a fool.

Perhaps they'd both been fools to believe a love at that age could last.

Shaking her head, she quickened her pace to get out of the sun. There were more parts of the garden she needed to assess before she visited Darren.

The shade of the peppermints welcomed her, and she smiled at the hammock still strung between the trees. Another place she'd spent many a warm afternoon. It had been an excellent place to spy on the cute gardener Aunt Maggie had hired to help her before she'd got up the courage to speak to him.

Too many places here reminded her of Ethan. Perhaps it was best to demolish it all and wipe away those memories for good.

No.

As quickly as the thought came, she dismissed it. This place had been Aunt Maggie's life, her homage to her fiancé and the life they were going to have together.

She couldn't let it die.

But her steps through the rest of the garden showed it would take a hell of a lot of work to bring it back to its former glory.

More than the two weeks she'd given herself to sort through Aunt Maggie's things.

Anger grew as she tripped in some long weeds. This blatant disregard for someone's life work wasn't acceptable.

Darren had better have a good excuse for what he'd done, though she wasn't certain anything less than his death would be good enough.

As the fury in her grew, she stalked back to the car and went to see a man about a garden.

Chapter 4

Ethan let out a breath and shifted back behind the barn as Chelsea disappeared around the side of the house, pleased that righteous indignation had replaced her grief. A moment later her car engine started, and she drove away.

His heart thudded an uncomfortable beat he refused to acknowledge.

She was the last person he'd expected when he'd heard the car pull up. Thank goodness he'd taken a drink break from where he'd been pruning the oleander hedge behind the barn, otherwise she would have caught him.

Ethan rubbed his chest and slipped back into the barn to process the new situation.

He'd almost called out to her when she'd first arrived, seeing only a glamorous stranger with perfectly put up brown hair, a slimline skirt which hugged her hips and a lacy top that was both modest and kind of sexy. But then she'd noticed the garden, and the way her hand had flown to her mouth was such a Chelsea gesture that the jolt of recognition had made him temporarily immobile. Damned if she didn't look as beautiful as she always had, though so much more sophisticated than the teenager he'd known.

So much more out of his league.

When his brain kicked into motion again, he'd followed as she wandered the grounds, knowing the path she would take, but making sure he kept out of sight. He felt her emotions from her gestures; a clench of her hands, the gentle brush of a leaf, the way she'd hugged herself when she'd seen the banana passionfruit vine was gone.

She'd spent a long time staring at Cupid's garden. Had she been thinking about their time together?

His heart twisted. If she had, it wouldn't be with fond memories. He'd broken her heart.

He should go.

Now, while he had the chance.

No good would come of speaking to Chelsea McGinnis again. Especially when she'd clearly made something of herself.

She was probably married with a bunch of kids.

But as his head listed all the reasons he needed to move, his feet refused to listen.

She would be back, of that he was certain.

He'd been building up a head of steam this morning while he'd fought the oleander hedges back into shape, thinking about what he would say to Sabine when he found her number. But then he'd overheard Chelsea's side of the phone call.

Chelsea and her mother hadn't intended to neglect Lilydale Cottage. He couldn't be angry at them.

Darren was another story, and someone he might visit later if he could get the address.

He walked back to where he'd been gardening, gathered his equipment and returned it to the shed, but he still couldn't bring himself to leave.

Lilydale was the only good part of his childhood.

He couldn't see it turned into units.

Though he had no right, he wanted to speak to Chelsea, ask her if there was anything he could do to help, find out whether she intended to sell Lilydale to a property developer.

Find out whether he could afford to buy it.

A stupid idea. He wouldn't be able to maintain the property while he worked with Special Forces. He wouldn't have enough time. But that knowledge hadn't stopped him reviewing his finances last night. Maybe he could pay someone dependable to maintain it and when he finally got out, he'd have somewhere to live.

Foolish dreams.

Ethan scanned the barn. He'd already packed his things into his car, ready in case someone discovered him and asked him to leave. He could be gone in less than a minute.

He jangled his keys in his pocket.

Leave already.

Closing his eyes, he sighed. He'd done everything to forget about Chelsea, but one glimpse of her had brought all the memories back to him.

The first time he'd met her was when she'd arrived to spend the summer holidays with her aunt. He'd known she was coming, because Aunt Maggie had talked of nothing else for weeks. It was her great niece's first visit since they'd moved to Sydney two years before, right before Ethan had moved to Honeybrook.

Ethan had heard Chelsea's joyful laugh from across the garden. He'd been weeding around the pond and he'd looked up as she ran down the path to the banana passionfruit vine, wearing a summer dress, her brown hair flowing out behind her. So beautiful. He'd ducked down so she wouldn't catch sight of him, not wanting someone so lovely to catch him in his grubby work clothes.

Kind of like he'd done today.

He'd avoided her for the first couple of days, but she'd caught him unawares on her third.

He'd been pruning the oleanders like today and she'd run around the corner, heading for the hen house, when she'd spotted him.

Though he'd braced himself for derision, she'd smiled a little shyly and said, "You must be Ethan. I'm Chelsea. Nice to meet you."

He'd grunted a response or something equally mortifying, and she'd continued to the hen house.

A Casanova he wasn't.

The fact he'd been surprised she'd been nice to him was proof of how low his expectations were. But it also encouraged his fantasies about one day having an actual conversation with her.

Ethan shook his head and pushed away the thought. He wasn't a lonely teen anymore. He had plenty of friends and confidence in himself.

Still, if he left now, Chelsea might not invite him back.

She had every right not to want to see him.

When had he become such a fool? All it would take was one phone call to the police and they'd turf him out, or arrest him for breaking and entering, and trespass.

As he unlocked his car, he heard an engine idling in the distance. Was Chelsea back already?

He moved to the barn door as the telltale squeak of the side gate opening was followed by the slam of a car door.

A moment later a black Porsche bumped along the road, heading towards the barn. Ethan shifted back, peering through the gap as the car drove past. The man inside wasn't someone he recognised from his time living in the town, but maybe he was the elusive Darren.

He waited a moment until the car stopped and silence filled the air. Footsteps crunched, moving away from the barn, and Ethan widened the gap to peer out.

Tall guy, grey business suit with smooth lines showing he wasn't carrying concealed, neat hair, polished shoes which probably cost a fortune. He held his phone up as if he was taking a photo and avoided all the thigh-high weeds with an expression of disdain on his face.

Definitely not the gardener.

No visible weapons, and the man didn't move like someone who had training. In fact, the man was oblivious to his surroundings.

Who was he?

It clicked into place. The property developer. He'd probably driven in here because he hadn't wanted to get his clothes dirty.

Perhaps Chelsea was in town to negotiate a deal with him. But then why would she want Darren's number if it was all going to be bulldozed anyway?

More likely the guy was using the opportunity to plan what he would do with the land and didn't realise she was around.

Another car engine and the businessman spun around, his muscles tight. Ethan shifted back, so he wasn't spotted, but could still see.

This car didn't drive past but instead stopped. Chelsea was back.

Ethan clenched his hands, waiting to see what the businessman would do.

The man glanced at the car and back towards the house. Yeah, Chelsea will hear you if you drive out. Ethan smiled at his conundrum, even though he shared it.

From here the front door of the house was visible as Chelsea lugged an enormous suitcase up the steps and stuck a key in the lock. She hip-bumped the section of the door that always stuck and went inside.

Ethan shook his head. Aunt Maggie still hadn't fixed the door. She'd rarely shut it, preferring to keep the fly screen locked rather than the solid wooden door.

Chelsea's bedroom was on this side of the house. Ethan imagined she would go there automatically rather than using Maggie's bedroom.

The man was still prevaricating.

Ethan lifted his gaze to the balcony and sure enough, Chelsea came to the window, frowned and then struggled with the catch as she lifted it up. "Excuse me. Can I help you?"

The man glanced up and smiled. "Hello. You must be Sabine Longmeyer. I'm Johann Meuller."

"Sabine is my mother. I'm Chelsea. What are you doing in my garden, Mr Meuller?" Her tone was more refined but brooked no nonsense.

Her garden. Ethan grinned.

"My apologies. I've been in discussions with your mother about buying this property." He looked down a bit bashful. "I guess I was getting ahead of myself, but I do want to get started as soon as possible."

Chelsea raised her eyebrows. "We haven't agreed to sell yet."

He winced. "I'm sorry. My last discussions with your father implied you would be selling."

"My father?" Her tone was deadly.

Ethan winced. Chelsea rarely spoke about the man who had sired her. It was a particularly sore topic.

"Mr Longmeyer..."

"My *step*father," Chelsea said. "And he has no say in whether we sell."

Johann started to speak, and Chelsea waved him off.

"Remove your car from my garden and then come to the front door. I won't continue to yell at you like this." She closed the window and disappeared.

Johann swore, staring death after her, his posture stiff. Ethan reevaluated his danger level. This man, when angry, could be a threat.

Ethan tensed, ready to act if necessary, but the man strode back to his car, and a moment later he backed it down the track and out of sight.

Ethan exhaled. Could he get closer without being spotted? Johann wasn't a man used to being told no, and Ethan didn't want him near Chelsea, particularly when he believed she was alone.

Hearing the gate squeak, Ethan crouch-ran over to the house. Chelsea wouldn't spot him through the ground-floor windows if she was going to the front door. He moved along the wall, waiting until Johann climbed the front steps before he got into position at the corner.

"I must apologise again for my impertinence," Johann said. "I didn't realise you were here."

Ethan rolled his eyes. Not much in the way of apology.

"I assume Sabine has spoken to you about my proposition?"

"Mum mentioned someone was interested in buying, but that's all I know," Chelsea replied.

"What a mix-up. My colleague didn't mention the property was jointly owned."

A pause. "Mum won't sell unless I agree to it," Chelsea said.

"Ah, then Sabine *is* the sole owner?" Johann's smug tone made Ethan clench his hands.

Another pause. "That is correct."

"Perhaps she hasn't shared the negotiations with you because she thought you'd object," Johann continued, confidence returning in every word.

Ethan wanted to shove Johann's glee down his throat. How dare he belittle Chelsea? But perhaps her relationship with her mother wasn't as close as it once had been.

"Don't presume you know about my relationship with my mother." Though Chelsea's words were firm, there was a hint of a waver in them.

Ethan exhaled, willing himself to calm.

"I've had a long day. If you access this property again without permission, I will call the police." The door shut, a double thud as Chelsea hip-bumped it closed.

Ethan bit back his cheer and watched Johann stalk down the stairs back to his car. He'd played his cards badly. The man didn't know how close Chelsea and her mum were… or at least they had been.

Maybe time had changed that.

But one thing he knew, Chelsea wasn't giving up Lilydale without a fight.

And he'd do what he could to help her.

***

Chelsea stalked away from the door, her throat tight and hands shaking. The nerve of the man. She fought the urge to scream as doubts assailed her.

Surely her mother wouldn't sell Lilydale without Chelsea's approval.

If Johann had spoken to her stepfather, then there was every possibility Ezra had implied they would sell. He wasn't a sentimental man, particularly not in relation to things which mattered to her, or if it was a way to earn more money.

She squeezed her eyes closed to stop the tears.

When her mother had first started dating him, Chelsea had hoped he would become the father she'd never had, but he hadn't been interested in a teenaged child who would be an adult soon. He'd tried to send her to boarding school, but her mother had put her foot down, so he'd had to wait a couple of years until she went to university and then he'd paid for her to stay at one of the colleges. Her mother thought it would be a wonderful experience for her, but Chelsea had known Ezra wanted her out of the house, particularly with her mother pregnant with his first child.

She knew when she wasn't wanted.

But she also recognised Ezra and Sabine adored each other and she wasn't impeding her mother finding happiness.

Old hurts battered to get out, but she kept them caged as she took three deep breaths and walked into the kitchen for a glass of water, relieved they had kept all the utilities on.

She reached for a metal cup with a sailboat on the side from the top kitchen cabinet and paused. The metal cups had been for children, because they were childproof and Aunt Maggie hadn't wanted the risk of broken glass around the house and garden.

Grief swept over her and she braced her hands on the sink, head bowed. Aunt Maggie had died too soon. She'd been so fit and healthy it had never occurred to Chelsea that she would have to deal with losing her. Chelsea had been planning to visit her next holiday, but she'd been a month too late.

Tears dripped onto the metal sink and she sniffed and straightened, pressing her hands against her eyes. She poured a glass of water and sipped. There would be time to cry later. Right now she needed to figure out her next steps.

She scanned the kitchen. Too many memories of

baking with her aunt or sneaking in to pinch a biscuit.

She hadn't been prepared for this—for the memories this place would raise.

In the three days since she'd been fired, she'd been so busy packing her entire apartment and searching for work that she hadn't considered what it would be like being back here.

It was far too quiet.

Aunt Maggie had liked to play classical music on her record player. She'd always said it soothed the plants and encouraged them to grow.

Chelsea wandered into the living room where the roll-top desk was open and the two sofas were covered in a layer of dust. She lifted the perspex lid covering the record player. The Best of Tchaikovsky was already in there. Perhaps Aunt Maggie had been listening to it on the day she'd fallen from the ladder.

Gritting her teeth against the pain, she placed the needle into position and music soon filled the room. She closed her eyes as Swan Lake played.

First step was to review the house, catalogue Maggie's things, and estimate how long it would take to pack. Next would be to call her mother and get a straight answer from her about the property. Then she'd get groceries and track down Darren, who hadn't been home when she'd dropped around earlier.

She opened the note-taking app on her phone and moved her way through the house, making a list.

Chelsea left Aunt Maggie's bedroom to last. It felt like such a breach of privacy to go through everything she had held so dear.

The photo of her fiancé still sat on top of the dresser in pride of place. Aunt Maggie used to brush her fingers over the frame every morning before leaving the room.

The rocking chair she'd found on a verge pickup and had reupholstered in a floral fabric. It was where she'd sit and read on a winter's day. A small table next to it to rest a cup of tea, also upcycled from an op shop.

A bunch of photos and paintings on the walls of different gardens and of Chelsea and her mother with Aunt Maggie.

Her mother hadn't been kidding when she'd said Aunt Maggie was a hoarder. There was so much stuff, but Chelsea had little use for any of it, and she would guarantee Ezra wouldn't want her mother bringing much of it into his house.

She went into the kitchen and filled the kettle. No, that wouldn't work. She had no milk. They'd cleared out the pantry and fridge of perishables after the funeral, knowing they wouldn't be back soon. She plugged in the fridge and then sat at the kitchen table to call her mother.

"Did you get hold of Darren?" Sabine asked.

"He wasn't home. I'll go back after five." She checked the time. Still an hour. "I ran into Johann Mueller though."

"The property developer?"

"Yeah. He'd driven into the back garden and was taking photographs." Annoyance replaced the sadness.

"That's cheeky of him."

"He said Ezra had implied the sale was imminent, so he was preparing." Chelsea bit her lip, waiting for her mother's response.

"I'd be surprised if Ezra had spoken to him, but I'll ask. He knows I won't sell Lilydale without your permission. It was our second home." Her mother's voice broke and the turmoil that had plagued Chelsea for the past hour dissipated.

She let out a shaky breath. "Thanks Mum. I was a little

worried. Could you send me a copy of the proposal?" She wanted to know exactly what Johann wanted.

"Of course. I should have sent it earlier. How are you doing, being there again?"

She sighed, scanning the room. "It's tough. There are so many wonderful memories here."

"The best," Sabine agreed. "Aunt Maggie was a hoot."

Chelsea smiled. "All her colourful overalls are hanging in her wardrobe still."

"Because you can never have too many pockets," Sabine said.

Chelsea nodded, smiling at the words Aunt Maggie used to repeat. "I recommended overalls to a colleague of mine who's a documentary film maker. She was complaining about not having enough pockets, and now she wears nothing but them."

"Aunt Maggie would be thrilled to hear it." Sabine laughed and then sighed. "I wish I could be there for you, baby."

"It's fine, Mum. The kids need you."

"You're my kid, too," she said. "No matter how old you get, I'll always want to look after you."

A lump formed in Chelsea's throat and she swallowed it down. It had been hard adjusting, having her younger siblings take up so much of her mother's attention after it just being the two of them for most of her life. "I'll be fine, Mum. It's nice being back. I might weed some of the garden beds around the house, and it will give me space to figure out what to do next."

"I still can't believe they fired you. I've told Ezra his company isn't to use them for anything."

Chelsea chuckled at the outrage in Sabine's voice. "Thanks, Mum. Listen, I still need to get to the shop. I'll call you in a couple of days after I've got my head around everything."

"I doubt it will take you long to have a plan," Sabine said. "But call me if you need anything."

"Love you, Mum."

"Love you more."

Chelsea smiled as she hung up, comforted by her mother's assertion she would have a say in what happened to Lilydale.

She couldn't wait to tell Johann.

Smiling at the thought of his reaction, she grabbed her keys and headed for the shops.

Chapter 5

After failing to get in touch with Darren again, Chelsea headed back to Lilydale with her groceries. She spent an hour cleaning the kitchen and dining area so it was free of dust before making an omelette for dinner and then settled at Aunt Maggie's roll-top desk. This was where Aunt Maggie had paid her bills and kept her affairs in order. There shouldn't be many sentimental things here. Chelsea couldn't bear to start anywhere else. Not with the emotions swarming around her in every room she entered. She needed an easy win to begin with.

She lined the bin with a bag and opened envelopes, reviewing the contents and sorting them either into the needs-further-investigation pile or tossing them in the bin.

Then she opened the top drawer and tears welled in her eyes blurring the vision before her. Her throat tight, she picked up the pale purple writing pad with its border of irises and ran a finger over the cover.

This was where her aunt had sat to write all the letters she'd sent to Chelsea. Receiving a purple envelope in the mail had always made her drop everything and sit down to read her aunt's letter. Perhaps she'd send Miles and Amelia a letter while she was here. They might think it was cool—or old-fashioned.

She placed the paper in the keep pile and closed the drawer, jiggling it to get it to go in. No fancy rollers on this desk, just wood on wood.

The second drawer contained two small boxes side by side. Chelsea opened the first and gasped. It was full of envelopes. She recognised the matching stationery from writing pads she'd bought to write to Aunt Maggie. Her heart ached as she slowly flicked through the familiar envelopes, seeing her penmanship go from that of a child to the script she now used.

Aunt Maggie had kept all of her letters.

She blinked to keep the tears at bay.

Her hand trembled as she replaced the lid and put the box on the keep pile. One day she might reread them and discover what younger Chelsea had deemed important to tell her aunt.

The second box was also full of letters of a similar age to Chelsea's. She opened the first one and scanned the contents.

Her mouth dropped open as she read the words and then noticed the signature.

Ethan Ward.

She flicked through the envelopes and saw the same handwriting on each one.

Why had Ethan corresponded with Aunt Maggie?

Why hadn't Aunt Maggie ever mentioned it to her?

She closed her eyes as an image of the boy she'd loved flashed into her mind. Shy and angry at the world until you earned his trust. Then his warmth and kindness came out.

Of course he would have written to Aunt Maggie. She'd treated him as a person, not a burden, and he'd often told

Chelsea he owed Aunt Maggie a lot.

She checked the dates. The last one was dated over a year ago. Did Ethan know Aunt Maggie had died?

He hadn't been at the funeral.

She hadn't known to contact him—though she would have asked her mother to do it.

Chelsea opened the last letter and scanned the contents. He'd joined the army straight out of school, but he mentioned little about it in his letter. Probably wasn't allowed to.

He sounded happy though. She heard his voice in her head as she read his words. There was no mention of a wife or children, and she scowled at the flutter of relief that passed through her.

He had left her.

Why should she care what he did now?

But a part of her did care. She'd loved him intensely, and it had taken years to stop hoping he would realise he'd made a mistake and come back for her. No one else had understood her like he had.

Tap… tap, tap, tap. The soft knock on the front door had her glancing up. This is what thoughts of Ethan did to her. It sounded like his knock.

She exhaled to calm her racing heart and shook away the fancy as she approached the door, switching on the porch light. It was probably Darren coming to explain himself.

She opened the door wide and her breath left her body.

Thick dark hair, a little messy with an oleander leaf in it, brown eyes the colour of jarrah bark, and beneath a well-maintained beard was a mouth which turned up at the edges as if uncertain about his reception. She blinked to clear the apparition as her gaze lowered further. Broad shouldered, tight muscles underneath his black T-shirt, cargo pants that didn't show the shape of his legs.

Surely she couldn't conjure someone just by thinking of them.

"Hey, Chelsea."

The same smooth tone she'd heard in her head while reading his letter. "Ethan?" Her head spun and she reached out to grab the door frame to steady herself but somehow missed it. She tripped, falling towards the floor, but before she hit it, Ethan's strong arms encircled her and he helped her over to the sofa.

"Sit."

He pressed her into the seat and she was too stunned to protest, but her body heated where his touched hers. She blinked rapidly again as he crouched next to her, concern in his gaze. "I'll get you some water."

He strode into the kitchen, knowing exactly where the glasses were. Of course he did. He'd practically lived here when he'd been in Honeybrook.

Her fingers brushed his as he handed her the cup. She sipped the cool water, allowing it to refresh her mind. "Thanks."

Right, so he was definitely in front of her and not a figment of her imagination. Joy and love filled her, followed quickly by anger. He'd broken her heart. "What the hell are you doing here?"

He looked down at her for a long moment. "I came to visit Aunt Maggie."

All at once her shock and anger dissipated, replaced by empathy. "Oh, God. No one told you she died."

He cleared his throat. "The neighbour did when I arrived."

What a horrible way to find out the woman he considered a surrogate aunt was dead. "I'm so sorry. I had no idea you kept in touch with her. If I had, I would have contacted you." She moved past him to the roll-top desk and picked up the box she'd discovered. "I found this just now." She handed it to him. "We didn't go through her things after the funeral. Everything was too raw."

With a slight frown, he opened it. Grief crossed his face as he stared, not saying anything. His fingers brushed each letter, the only movement he made.

His stillness cried out to her. He was only ever this still when he was sorting through his emotions. She'd seen it twice; once when she'd told him she loved him, and the second, when he'd read the letter to say he'd been accepted into the army.

Chelsea longed to comfort him the way she used to. "She kept all of mine as well."

He glanced at her, tears glistening, and she couldn't keep her distance. Yes, he might have hurt her when they were young, but he was hurting now. She took the box from him, placed it on the couch, and then wrapped her arms around him.

He stiffened and then he hugged her back.

She closed her eyes as his body trembled. This would mean so much more to him. He'd spent his entire childhood being passed from foster family to foster family, no one wanting him. Aunt Maggie was the first person who had cared. And she had cherished his letters enough to keep them all.

She rubbed his back, feeling muscles which hadn't been there before, and his arms cocooned and protected her like they always had. The two of them had needed each other that summer. She'd felt vulnerable about her place in the family with her mother pregnant with Ezra's first child, and he'd been anxious about what he would do when he aged out of foster care.

Two souls coming together when they'd needed each

other most.

Perhaps that's all they had ever been and Ethan had been right to break up with her.

She pushed away thoughts of the past and focused on now. He smelled the same; a potent combination of grass and sweat. Her cheek rested on his, and she had a strong urge to kiss it.

Chelsea stepped back, shocked by the strength of her emotion. Not appropriate.

"It's my turn to get you some water." She strode into the kitchen, her insides scrambling; one portion wanting to go back and kiss him, and the other portion reminding her he'd broken her heart. If he'd wanted to be kissed by her, he wouldn't have left her.

Handing him the water, she moved across the room and tucked a few stray hairs behind her ears.

Damned if he didn't look good. He'd grown a beard, but it was trimmed short and had been soft against her cheek. He'd never reached six feet, possibly due to the malnutrition he'd suffered as a child, but he was stocky now, pure muscle. The cargo pants he wore reminded her of the army, as did the black T-shirt that clung to his chest. His hair was messy and she noticed the leaf again.

Her eyes widened. "You weeded Cupid's bed."

He nodded. "I arrived yesterday. When I saw the place… I had to do something."

She understood completely. "I'm waiting for the groundskeeper to call me back."

"Darren."

Chelsea frowned. "How did you know?"

He rubbed the back of his head. "I heard you talking to your mum." He looked a little sheepish. "I spent last night in the barn. Thought I'd do some more work in the garden while I was here. I was going to track you down, find out what you were doing with the place. The neighbour mentioned a property developer was sniffing around."

Staying in the barn? Surely it wasn't in a liveable state. But if he'd been on site… "Did you see Johann when he was here?"

Ethan nodded again. "Heard most of your conversation."

"You eavesdropped?" How did she feel knowing he'd been here all along? Sure, there were plenty of places to hide, but it was kind of creepy.

"You've got to admit, Chels, it's awkward. I shouldn't be here and you've just arrived. I wanted to give you time to settle before I made myself known. This place has a lot of memories for us both."

She hugged herself. No one called her Chels, but him. It was another tie leading back to their past.

But damn it, he had a point. If he'd arrived before she'd discovered his letters, she might have been ruder than he deserved.

She rubbed her eyes.

"Are you going to sell?" Ethan asked.

"I don't know. I only heard about the offer a couple of days ago." It had always been so easy to confide in him. He listened in his quiet way and made her feel like the centre of his world.

But that was then. Who knew the man he'd become?

"I can't bear the thought of the garden turning into units," Ethan said.

"Me neither, but the garden's ruined anyway."

Ethan hummed. "I could chip away at it." He shrugged. "I've got a month's leave, and I was coming to help Aunt Maggie anyway."

Such a nice gesture. But she couldn't decide now. She was still struggling with his reappearance in her life. "Let me consider it. I want to hear what Darren has to say for himself."

"Can I go with you?" Ethan asked. "I'd like to hear it myself." His eyes flashed with anger and for the first time she saw the lethal military man he'd been hiding.

Definitely not the boy she used to know.

She pressed her lips together and nodded. Backup might be useful. "How about seven tomorrow morning?"

"All right. I'll leave you be. I'll be in the barn if you need me."

He was gone before she said anything.

Did she want him camping in her barn? It was oddly comforting after the way Johann had reacted. She might not know the man Ethan had become, but he wouldn't hurt her.

What she needed was to sleep on it. Give herself time to process everything.

Because out of everything; going through Aunt Maggie's things, dealing with Johann, and the destruction of the garden, the one thing that shook her most was Ethan Ward walking back in her life.

Because the pull towards him was still so strong.

And her heart wouldn't survive a second round of rejection from him.

***

Ethan stepped out of the barn and scanned the surroundings. The sun was still low in the sky giving everything a dawn glow, birds chirped and flew between bushes and the lights in the house were on.

Chelsea was up.

He kept his eyes forward, away from her bedroom window. If she was still as organised as she'd been as a teen, she'd be downstairs already, but he didn't want to invade her privacy more than he already had.

His pulse increased as he approached the house. It was ridiculous. He'd approached buildings containing armed hostiles with fewer nerves than he had today. He'd barely slept, replaying his conversation with Chelsea in his head. She'd been shocked, and perhaps a little angry until she'd realised no one had told him about Aunt Maggie. Then her compassion had come through and she'd hugged him. He'd never thought he would hold her in his arms again, and he'd savoured every single second.

She still smelled like cherry blossoms.

God, he'd missed her. He'd pushed thoughts of her far away, but he'd never been able to eradicate them. They'd always popped back in times of great emotion; loneliness, fear, happiness. When he'd been hit by the tsunami late last year and the wave had swallowed him, his one regret had been pushing her away.

Which was why he hadn't given her the chance to ask him to leave last night.

She might not be as welcoming this morning, now she'd had time to process everything. She might order him off her land like she had the property developer.

As he came around the side of the house, she was sitting on the cane sofa on the front porch, waiting for him. Today she wore navy blue slacks and a white shirt with three-quarter length sleeves. Perhaps she wanted to look business-like for their meeting with Darren. She cradled a mug in one hand, and there was a travel cup on the table beside her.

Chelsea had always been better at mornings than him. She gestured to the second mug. "I wasn't sure whether you had coffee."

He smiled, his heart expanding. She'd thought of him. When they were younger, she'd always made him coffee.

He'd arrived at Lilydale at dawn to work in the garden before the day turned scorching. Aunt Maggie and Chelsea would join him, and Chelsea always provided the coffee. In those days it had been instant coffee because he'd been yet to discover the delights of proper fresh espresso coffee.

"Thank you." He reached for the cup.

"It's a flat white."

"I didn't realise Aunt Maggie got herself an espresso machine."

Chelsea laughed. "She didn't. I brought my travel kit. I could never convince her instant coffee tastes crap."

Her laugh was a melody sweeping over him. It had been enough to cheer him, even on his darkest days. He sipped the fine liquid and closed his eyes. "I'm going to have to get one."

She pushed off the sofa, leaving her mug on the table. "Shall we go?"

She didn't wait for his answer and he followed her to the compact white hire car, carrying the travel cup. On the drive they passed his foster parents' place. The lawn was yellow and far too long, and the garden beds were full of weeds.

He'd spent hours in the garden ensuring it was up to his foster-parents' standards.

Chelsea glanced at him. "Did you stay in touch?"

He shook his head. "They couldn't wait to be rid of me. I don't know if they still live in town."

"Did you keep in touch with Josh?"

"No." Josh had been his only friend, but Ethan had wanted to leave Honeybrook behind him. "What about you and Lauren?"

"Not really. I read her posts on social media sometimes, and I saw her at the funeral."

The two girls had been good friends, and he'd been

jealous of the time they spent together because it meant he had less time with Chelsea.

Selfish.

She pulled into the driveway of a brand-new modern brick and tile house. The garden had a freshly planted look, which came with many display homes. Darren might not have been working at Lilydale, but he was putting Sabine's money to good use.

They got out of the car and Ethan pounded on the door, letting out some of his anger.

Chelsea raised her eyebrows. "That was a bit excessive, wasn't it?"

"Just wanted to make sure I'd wake him."

After waiting a couple of minutes, he pounded again. "I suspect he's avoiding us." The front door had a security camera, the type where you could access the feed from your phone. Ethan glared at it. "Darren, if you aren't at the door in thirty seconds, we'll contact the police."

Immediately there were sounds from inside. He grinned.

The door opened and a twenty-something man stood there. They'd obviously woken him because his hair was dishevelled, his T-shirt was on inside-out and his eyes were bleary. "What do you want?"

Really? This was how he was going to play it?

"You're Darren Whaley?" Chelsea asked.

He nodded, scratching his crotch.

"I'm Chelsea. I left you a couple of messages yesterday. My mother is Sabine Longmeyer."

She waited for a response, but all Darren did was nod.

"Sabine has been paying you for the past year to take care of the gardens at Lilydale Cottage."

"That's right."

Ethan clenched his hands at Darren's nonchalance.

"Then why haven't you been doing it?" Chelsea asked, keeping her tone pleasant.

"It's a big garden. It's hard to keep on top of it."

"That's no excuse to do no work," Chelsea replied, her voice sharpening.

"Well now, there didn't seem to be any point when it was going to be demolished for the retirement village." Darren's gaze darted away and then back to Chelsea.

Ethan's muscles tightened. "Who told you that?"

Darren shuffled back, and his flash of fear was intensely satisfying.

"The developer."

"When did you meet him?" Chelsea asked.

"He came to Lilydale the first week I started."

Chelsea frowned. "Mum only got the proposal a week ago."

Ethan smelled a rat. "What exactly did Johann ask you to do?"

Darren's brief widening of his eyes told Ethan he was on the right track. "Nothing."

That rang true. Ethan thought about it. "Johann asked you to stop work on the garden?"

The man paled, and he glanced at Chelsea and back at Ethan. "Ah, well…"

"How much did he pay you?" Chelsea's whole body tensed.

Darren backed further away, reaching for the door. Ethan slapped his hand against it to stop Darren from closing it. "I suggest you answer Chelsea's question."

"I'll call the police if you hurt me," Darren said.

"Please do," Ethan replied. "While they're here they can arrest you for theft and destruction of property."

"How much did he pay you?" Chelsea repeated, the warmth gone from her tone.

Darren closed his eyes. "Fifty thousand. He said no one would want to buy it with the garden destroyed and he'd get a bargain."

The bastard.

Chelsea exhaled noisily, a sound that told Ethan she was on the verge of tears.

"What are you going to do?" Darren asked, glancing between them.

"I don't know." She stalked back to the car, her eyes already glistening.

Ethan turned back to Darren. This arsehole had made Chelsea cry. He curled his hands into fists but kept his anger at bay.

Darren shifted back another step. "She won't have me arrested, will she? I did nothing wrong."

Anger grew inside him. "How much was Sabine paying you?"

The man swallowed. "Four thousand a month."

"So you've stolen forty-eight thousand dollars from her?"

He nodded.

"Then I suggest your first step is paying it back." Let him hurt for a change. Ethan wasn't sure what else they could do to make Darren pay for his greed.

"I don't have forty-eight grand."

"Get a mortgage on your lovely new home. You have a week." Though it would be immensely satisfying to punch Darren in the face, it wasn't worth the potential arrest and disciplinary action he'd get if he did.

Ethan spun on his heel and joined Chelsea at the car. He had no problems making threats. If Sabine received the money back, she could hire people to do the job Darren was supposed to have done.

Chelsea sat there, staring at nothing, taking long, slow

breaths.

"We'll fix this." He didn't know how, but he would.

There was no way he would let Aunt Maggie's passion be destroyed or let Chelsea down a second time.

Chelsea nodded and drove home.

Her silence was deafening and Ethan knew she was barely holding herself together, so he didn't speak.

Instead he began to plan.

For the first time since being caught in the tsunami, Ethan was glad he had another month's leave.

He was going to need it.

Chapter 6

Chelsea found it difficult to breathe, her chest tight as she drove back to Lilydale. The nerve of the man! Both of them. Thinking her mother would sell because the garden had been left to die.

She gripped the steering wheel tighter to stop her hands from shaking. Aunt Maggie's garden had been destroyed because of some greedy bastard who didn't understand the history of the place.

Tears burned her eyes and her throat ached, but she would not give into them. Not with Ethan here. It would make her too vulnerable to him.

She shouldn't have allowed him to come with her. This was her business, and he'd opted out of having anything to do with her years ago.

She swallowed hard, focusing on the road ahead of her through her blurry vision. Thank goodness the road wasn't busy.

Her one take-away from this morning was they were not selling to Johann, or any subsidiary he might be associated with.

But she had no clue what to do with Lilydale.

The enormity of the task came into view as she turned the corner and saw the overgrown mess of the garden. She bit back a sob as she pulled into the driveway and the tick of the engine was loud in the silence.

Chelsea shoved open the door and strode towards the house, taking big gulps of air to keep the angry tears at bay. Hopefully Ethan would take the hint and head back to the barn while she pulled herself together. At the front door, she struggled with the key and with a groan of frustration, she stepped back to stop shaking.

Ethan gently took the keys from her and unlocked the door. "How are you feeling?" Without looking at her, he hip-bumped it open.

Damn it. She didn't want him to see this. Taking another deep breath to control the quaver in her voice, she said, "Furious." She swallowed hard. "Devastated." And glad he wasn't watching her, which gave her the ability to pretend he wasn't witnessing her melt-down. She headed for the kitchen to put the kettle on.

"I told him he has to repay the money."

Surprise made her glance at him. "We both know this is about more than the money." The sympathy on his face made her turn away again.

"Yeah, but it will help if you do want to restore the garden."

She heard his unasked question. Did she want to restore it? It would take her time to find a new job and somewhere to live. "I have to think about it."

"What are you doing today?"

Why wouldn't he leave her alone? She wanted to throw herself on her bed and cry for a couple of hours for all she had lost—Aunt Maggie, the garden, and Ethan—but that's not the way she worked. "I'll start sorting through the house." No matter the final decision, she would have to remove all Aunt Maggie's personal effects.

The kettle boiled and with surprise she noticed she'd prepared two mugs for tea. She exhaled slowly as she turned to him, finally getting her emotions under control. "Do you want one?"

"No, I'm good." Ethan favoured his left side as he moved to the door. "Do you mind if I keep working in the garden?" He shrugged a little self-consciously. "I'm enjoying it."

She debated asking him about his injury. It was none of her business. But perhaps she had a responsibility if he was gardening for her. "What happened?" She nodded to his side.

"Broke my pelvis," he said. "I'm on medical leave."

She frowned. "How?"

He grimaced. "Got caught in the tsunami last year in Asia."

Her eyes widened. From the footage she'd seen, it had been horrific. "Were you on holiday?"

He shook his head.

Why could he ask all the questions and not elaborate on hers? "The army?"

Ethan smiled. "I can't answer that question."

"Why not?"

"I'm Special Forces. I can't talk about my work."

Fear gripped her heart. Special Forces were the best of the best. She knew he'd be exposed to danger in the army, but Special Forces were an entirely different league. They were sent to the riskiest situations.

A part of her was proud of him. He was dedicated. Another part was terrified. "Should you be gardening with your injury?"

"I'm meant to get regular, light exercise."

She snorted. "There's nothing light about the amount of work at Lilydale."

"I know my limits."

Did she want Ethan hanging around? It was another question she didn't have an answer for, but at least he understood his work might be for nothing if she sold the place. "It's fine. Tell me if you need any equipment or help."

"I will. I'm really sorry this all happened, Chelsea." His dark eyes captured her soul, sending her sympathy and understanding in one look.

She ducked her head as the tears threatened again and busied herself pouring the tea she didn't want. "I'll see you later."

It wasn't until he closed the door that she let out a deep breath. She had enough on her plate without adding her complicated emotional reaction to Ethan. They'd broken up a decade ago, but he had a magnetism which still drew her. It had been that way since the first day she'd seen him.

No. Pining after Ethan was not on her to-do list.

Shaking her head, she pulled out her phone and checked her action plan for the day, crossing off 'Speak to Darren'. Next was to sort through the rooms. She'd start with the two bathrooms. There shouldn't be anything sentimental in them, and they would be an easy win— which was what she needed right now.

Because Lilydale was proving to be far more challenging than she'd expected.

***

Sweat dripped down Ethan's back as he hacked at the bougainvillea by the side gate, picturing Johann's face as he did so. The audacity of the man to pay someone to destroy Aunt Maggie's life's work. And he'd made Chelsea cry.

She did her best to hide it from him, but she'd barely held it together.

When they were younger, he would have gathered her in his arms and held her while she'd sobbed, but he no longer had the privilege. He'd had to pretend everything was fine while all he'd wanted was to comfort her.

That and wrap his hands around Johann's throat and choke him.

Letting out a deep breath, Ethan stepped back and put the hedge trimmer down. He was still seething after several hours of hard work. He knew better. He couldn't let his emotions rule him. What he needed was a plan. Chelsea had already agreed she wasn't selling the property to Johann and for that, Ethan was supremely grateful. But the man wasn't likely to give up. Not if he'd been working on this plan for over a year. Why was that?

Ethan took out his phone, searched Johann's name and found a profile on a social media site. The company he worked for was a multinational and did a lot of retirement villages and other types of development. So why Honeybrook? And who had he been planning this with? Ethan glanced at the house.

It wasn't his business. Not really. But damned if he didn't feel a sense of ownership over this property, this place. He owed it to Aunt Maggie to make sure her pride and joy wasn't turned into a bunch of buildings with postage stamp backyards. He shuddered.

There wasn't anything special about the land, or about Honeybrook either. Though the location was a good one; only a short drive from the capital city for those who wanted to retire in the country, but have all the perks of the city nearby.

He wandered away from the bougainvillea and towards the cottages on the property. During high school he'd fantasised about asking Aunt Maggie if he could move into one and leave his foster family, but he'd never got up the nerve. It would have hurt too much if she'd refused, and he'd figured if she'd wanted him here full-time, she would have asked him herself.

Grass had grown up the steps and wrapped itself around the wooden posts. He tested each step before he put his full weight on it, and they held. The door was locked, but he peered through the grimy window. The interior looked the same as it had a decade ago. A small open plan living area with kitchen, table, and sofa, and then a corridor branching down to two bedrooms and a bathroom.

He scanned the ground. A paved path used to wind its way between the three cottages and there was parking behind each one. He spotted the crushed gravel path and followed it around the back.

The parking area was clearish, though the grass was encroaching across the gravel ground.

A thorough clean, and tidying the worst of the overgrown grass, and the cottages could be reopened, assuming there weren't any leaks. The view wouldn't be as pretty as it once had been, but it would be an income for Chelsea and her mother.

He shook his head.

What was he doing? This was none of his business. He'd barely said anything to Chelsea, but he still couldn't bring himself to leave.

His phone rang and for a second he thought it might be Chelsea, which was ridiculous as she didn't have his number. Dobby's name flashed on the screen. "Yeah?"

Dobby chuckled. "You make it to Honeybrook?"

"A couple of days ago."

"Was your aunt happy to see you?"

Ethan closed his eyes. "No, she died."

Dobby sucked in a breath. "Mate, I'm sorry. What happened?"

"She fell off a ladder. Her family didn't realise I kept in touch with her, so they didn't tell me."

"Shit. That sucks. You doing OK?"

What could he say? "I guess." He glanced around the garden. "I showed you photos of the place, didn't I?"

"Yeah. Gorgeous gardens."

He took a photo and texted it to his friend. "This is what it's like now. Apparently the heirs hired someone to maintain the gardens, but a property developer paid him to let them die so he could get the land at a cheaper price."

Dobby swore. "That's criminal. What are you doing?"

Dobby knew what he'd been through. "I can't leave it like this."

"What about the new owners?"

"Chelsea arrived the day after I did. She's pretty shocked, but she hasn't decided what she's doing yet."

"Your Chelsea?"

Ethan closed his eyes. "She's not mine."

"You know what I mean."

He did. "Yeah, that Chelsea."

"How did she react?"

"She was still in shock." Which was probably a good thing. He wasn't ready for a conversation about how their relationship ended.

In the background, he heard a female voice asking something.

Dobby laughed. "Hang on a second. I'm putting you on speaker. Mila heard me mention Chelsea, and she wants to know what's happening."

Ethan smiled. Dobby's partner, Mila, had helped him through his recovery and had made him tell her about

Chelsea. She'd told him the way he'd left was criminal. "Are you being nosy, Angel?"

A snort. "No, just following up our therapy sessions."

He rolled his eyes. She wasn't a therapist. "What do you want to know?"

"What happened?"

"It was awkward. She'd just found all the letters I'd written Aunt Maggie over the years and realised no one had told me she'd died."

"Was she sympathetic or angry?" Mila asked.

"Sympathetic."

Mila made a happy sound, but before Ethan could ask her what she meant by it, Dobby asked, "Where are you staying?"

"I'm camping in the barn on the property."

Another happy squeal from Mila. "Then she can't be holding a grudge."

Or hadn't quite processed his presence yet. "I'm free labour. She said I can tidy the garden while she decides whether they're selling."

"How big's the property?"

Dobby's interest made him frown. "You looking at buying?"

A pause which went on for a good long while before Dobby said, "I'm considering a few things."

Ethan's eyebrows rose. "What things?"

Dobby sighed. "I'm getting to the age where command wants me to go into a more leadership position."

Leadership was code for desk job. "You'd hate it."

"Yeah, but I can't deny I'm getting older. I need to consider what I do post army."

Ethan leaned against the porch post. "You thinking about getting out?" It wasn't something Ethan had considered, not even with his injury. The army was the only place he felt as if he was worth anything. He glanced towards the house. There and in Chelsea's arms.

"I'm playing with options. One of those is going into security."

"So why the interest in the property?"

"We'd need somewhere to train."

Interesting. Aunt Maggie had mentioned she owned the land behind the garden, but he hadn't paid attention. "It might be a decent size. I can ask Chelsea."

"Can't hurt," Dobby said. "Let me know how you go. I can come down on the weekend and help."

"Ooh, definitely," Mila agreed. "I want to meet Chelsea."

Mila and Chelsea would get on well together, but he was slightly concerned about what Mila might say to her. "Thanks, mate. I'll call you."

Retirement wasn't an option he'd considered, but if Dobby was serious about starting a security business, Ethan could help him set it up. He'd still be working with his teammate and doing the type of work he enjoyed.

And maybe he'd finally be able to call Lilydale his home.

He shook his head. He was getting ahead of himself. Dobby might not leave.

But that didn't stop him from considering it as an option for himself…

He stared at the main house. It was mid-morning, so he'd find something to eat and take a break at the garden table where they'd always sat.

And maybe he'd see Chelsea.

He ignored the nerves in his belly as he walked back to the barn.

Chapter 7

By mid-morning Chelsea needed to get away. So much for the bathrooms being easy. She'd found the rubber duck and other bath toys she'd played with as a child tucked away in the back of one cupboard. She'd loved bath-time as none of the rentals she'd lived in had had baths. It felt so exciting to splash around at night after spending hours in the garden.

As she'd grown older it had been completely decadent to soak in the bath reading a book. She'd looked for an apartment with a bath in Sydney but it had been beyond her budget.

Then there was the poem hung above the sink about keeping the bathroom tidy. To this day she often recited it in her head when she cleaned her own bathroom.

In the end she'd cleared out both bathrooms as fast as she could, keeping only toiletry supplies which were still good, and the rubber duck.

Then she'd cleaned both top to bottom, getting rid of dust, grime and old soap scum. Removing all traces of Aunt Maggie.

The thought was enough to have her hauling the bags downstairs, needing fresh air and distance from the house.

She didn't have enough bags to justify a run to the nearest op shop, but she didn't care.

At the front door she paused, hand braced on the wall, head hanging, giving herself a second to breathe. In the background, the hedge trimmer which had been buzzing most of the morning fell silent. Ethan was another issue she refused to think about.

Unable to stop her curiosity, she glanced out the window, but she couldn't see what Ethan had been up to.

Perhaps if she was fast, she could get to her car without running into him.

Which reminded her she had to check where Aunt Maggie's car was. She'd only hired the car for a few days so she could figure out how long she would be here, and had been planning to use Aunt Maggie's car for the rest of the time.

She opened the door and the warmth of the day flowed in, making her pause.

At this time of day, Aunt Maggie would have had tea and biscuits ready and be taking them out to Ethan so they could have a break. Often they'd sit at the table under the pergola in the shade and talk about what needed to be done, or their plans for the afternoon.

It had been a soothing ritual and had given Chelsea the opportunity to speak to Ethan before they had started dating.

She smiled at the memory of her nervous teen self, and how massive her crush on Ethan had been.

She shook her head. Chelsea wasn't Aunt Maggie, and she hadn't decided whether she wanted to spend more time with Ethan. He jumbled her insides and brought back memories she would rather have forgotten.

But perhaps she should offer him a glass of water. It was autumn, and the sun still had an occasional bite to it.

Her gaze shifted to the wild garden. Johann had been in it for the long game if he'd contacted Darren a year ago. But the question was, why? Why wait so long to make an offer? Anybody could have expressed interest in the meantime. They could have sold it to a local.

Perhaps he'd tried to buy the property straight after Maggie's death. They wouldn't have considered anything then, too caught up in grief by Maggie's unexpected passing. She would have to ask her mother.

There were also the permissions he needed. Had he been in discussions with the council about the retirement village? She needed to know more. Perhaps she'd drop by the council while she was out.

Then she'd call her mother and discuss the situation.

She glanced at the bags by the door. She'd heard glass break when she'd dropped one of them, and if it cut the plastic, she didn't want anything leaking into the hire car. She headed for the key hooks inside the pantry and scanned the bunches of keys until she spotted the one with the Sydney Opera House key ring.

Grabbing the bundle, she headed to the barn and hesitated outside the open door. Ethan stood next to a white four-wheel drive, drinking from a large water bottle. His shirt was darker in spots from sweat and his skin glistened.

She swallowed, ignoring the shot of lust which swept through her body. As she debated whether to come back later, he spotted her and smiled. "Taking a break?"

Chelsea held up the keys as she struggled to find words and ripped her gaze from him. "Looking for Elsie." Aunt Maggie had a habit of naming inanimate objects. The LandCruiser was parked further inside, next to Ethan's car.

"I'd be surprised if she starts, but I've got jumper leads if you need them."

Chelsea nodded and then screwed up her nose. "Should I take it to a mechanic before I drive it?"

"Aunt Maggie always kept it well-maintained, and it's been sitting out of the weather. I can check it over if you want, but it should be good to get you around town."

He moved closer, and she hurried towards the car, not wanting to be near while he looked so sexy. She unlocked the door and slid behind the steering wheel, slotting in the key.

It was a manual, and she hadn't driven a manual car since she got her licence. She put it into neutral, already second-guessing using the car. Then she turned the key.

Silence.

Ethan smiled. "Battery's dead. If you wait there, I'll get my cables."

No. She didn't need the extra stress of gears while he was watching. Sliding out of the car, she said, "Don't worry about it. I'll do it later. Glad it's still here."

"If you leave me the keys, I'll fix it. Are you heading out?"

She tossed him the bunch. "To the op shop."

"Have fun." His smile sent warmth through her and she ignored it as she hurried back to the house. She would not be distracted by him.

By the time she arrived at the op shop, Chelsea had tucked all her emotions away where they belonged. She recognised the older woman volunteering behind the counter with her dyed brown hair and floral blouse.

She searched through her memory for a name. "Mrs Britza," she greeted. "It's lovely to see you again."

The woman frowned as if trying to place her.

"I'm Chelsea McGinnis. Maggie McGinnis's great-niece."

The woman pressed a hand against her heart. "Have you come to clear out Maggie's things?" She gestured to the bags Chelsea held.

The pang of grief was never far away. Chelsea nodded. "Yes. I arrived yesterday."

"We were all disappointed when you didn't keep up Maggie's garden." She peered over her glasses, judgement in the stare.

Chelsea refused to feel guilty. "Actually Mum hired Darren Whaley as groundskeeper, but he took the money and did nothing." Word would spread about Darren's actions, and he deserved all the censure.

Mrs Britza raised her eyebrows. "Is that so?"

Chelsea debated for a moment before saying, "Yes. A property developer paid him fifty thousand dollars to let it die." Hopefully Johann would have opposition to anything he tried to do in the town. She smiled. "I'd better get back to it. There's still a lot of work to be done."

"Of course, my dear. Tell me if you need a hand. I'm sure there are many people around town who would be happy to help. Maggie was always there for us."

Chelsea remembered the times when she'd help her aunt bake food for fundraisers or to feed volunteers who were fighting fires or searching for missing people. "Thank you."

She took a deep breath as she walked outside into the fresh morning air, shaking off the judgement. She retrieved her phone from her pocket and looked up the location of the council building. Next stop was to get some answers.

The sliding doors slid open with a ding as Chelsea walked towards them. A woman who looked to be in her forties manned the reception desk. She smiled as Chelsea approached. "Can I help you?"

"I'd like to speak to somebody in the planning department."

"Do you have an appointment?"

"No. I was hoping they could answer some questions about the process of developing land in this area."

The woman clicked keys on the keyboard. "Leyton's in a meeting. I can take your details and get him to call you?"

Chelsea hesitated. She wanted to watch the man when she questioned him, analyse his reaction. "Perhaps I can make an appointment." A blonde woman about Chelsea's age came out of an office as the receptionist said, "Name?"

"Chelsea McGinnis."

"I thought it was you!" the woman from the office declared.

Chelsea turned. The woman's blonde hair was styled short, and she wore a charcoal grey skirt suit with a white shirt bearing the council logo. But it was her wide grin which sparked a memory in Chelsea. "Lauren?" She grinned in surprise.

"Yeah. It's been ages." Lauren stepped forward to hug Chelsea as if they'd seen each other yesterday.

Chelsea hugged her friend back. Lauren had lived down the road from Lilydale Cottage when they were kids and they used to play together. Chelsea had confessed her crush on Ethan to Lauren, and Lauren had created opportunities for her to see him, such as inviting him to go swimming with them at the Honeybrook lake.

Chelsea had seen her briefly at Maggie's funeral, but they hadn't caught up. She hadn't realised Lauren still lived in town.

"What are you doing here?" Lauren asked.

"I'm packing Aunt Maggie's things."

Lauren's face fell. "I'm so sorry. We all miss her dearly."

Chelsea nodded. Maggie had been an integral part of the Honeybrook community.

Maybe Lauren could answer Chelsea's questions. "What do you do here?"

Lauren laughed. "I'm the mayor."

Chelsea's eyes widened, and she grinned. "Congratulations. How long?"

"It's my first month," Lauren admitted. "I'm still getting my head around everything."

"Perhaps you can help me." Chelsea explained what had happened with Johann and Darren, and Lauren's mouth dropped open.

"I haven't seen or heard anything about a retirement village." She turned to the receptionist. "Have you, Robyn?"

Robyn shook her head. "Only the rumours around town."

Lauren walked towards her office. "Come in and I'll look it up."

Chelsea followed her into the office with dark blue carpets and a window overlooking the main street. A large jarrah desk sat in the middle with a computer monitor on it and several wooden bookshelves lined the walls. "Has the council done any business with Johann before?"

Lauren typed on her keyboard. "Let me check."

Chelsea sat in the seat across from her.

Lauren frowned as she read whatever was on her computer screen. "The company was involved in the sports complex development about eighteen months ago. It was completed around the time Aunt Maggie died."

Interesting. Chelsea would have to go through Aunt Maggie's correspondence and check whether she had any dealings with the company. "Could someone on the council have implied it wouldn't be difficult to get approval for the village?"

"Maybe," she said. "Leyton was their contact. He shouldn't have, but Honeybrook has been struggling for a while now." Her shoulders sagged. "A retirement village would have attracted people to town."

Chelsea squeezed her hand. "I noticed a lot of shops were closed on Main Street. Is that what you mean by Honeybrook struggling?"

Lauren nodded. "The only people moving to town are teachers getting posted here," she said. "All our generation moved on the moment they hit adulthood. Josh and I are the only ones left. Do you remember him? He was a friend of Ethan's."

"Yeah. Did you two ever get together?"

Lauren laughed and waved her hand. "No, nothing like that. We both had our reason for staying." A frown flickered on Lauren's forehead. "If the annual fair doesn't attract people back to town, I don't know what to do."

Chelsea perked up. "I used to love the Honeybrook fair," she said. "Does it still get the crowds?"

"Not even half," Lauren admitted. "People seem to have forgotten we're here."

Chelsea grinned. "Do you need help with publicity? When is it?"

"I would love help," Lauren said. "But we don't have the funds to pay anyone."

"I'll do it," Chelsea said. "I'm… on holiday at the moment. Publicity is what I do." She wanted to help this town, which had been a home to her. Aunt Maggie would want her to.

"Are you sure? Anything you could do would be amazing."

A small part of her brain told her she was procrastinating, finding an excuse not to make decisions about her future and Lilydale, but she ignored it. "All I need are the dates, any photos or video you have of past events, and a list of special events you've got planned for this year." Excitement shimmered at the thought of working on something worthwhile. "It won't take me more than a few hours to come up with some promotional pieces." She gave Lauren her email address. "Send them to me. I should have a plan within twenty-four hours." They swapped phone numbers, and then Lauren stood. "I have to get to a meeting. I can't thank you enough." Her goodbye hug held a hint of desperation in it.

"Honeybrook has always had a special place in my heart. I want to help."

Lauren grabbed her laptop. "We should catch up over dinner. I'll call you later."

"I'd like that." She couldn't remember the last time she'd gone to dinner with a friend. In Sydney she'd had colleagues more than friends, and she hadn't kept in touch with anyone from high school.

All she had were Lauren, and Libby from primary school, who now lived in Texas with her rock-star husband.

How sad was she?

By the time Chelsea arrived back at Lilydale, the weight on her chest had lessened. She had more information about Johann and his company, and she had a job. Sure, it wasn't a paying job, but she could point to it to show others not everyone had lost their faith in her ability.

She entered the house, inhaling the scent of roses beneath the still musty scent from the house being locked up for so long. She closed her eyes. Aunt Maggie's scent.

She opened a couple of windows to draw the mustiness out and reviewed her list. The laundry could be next. Another room which hopefully wouldn't be too sentimental.

She stood at the entrance of the room and her gaze caught on the coats hanging on the hooks by the door; one was Aunt Maggie's pink raincoat, one was her dark blue it's-freezing-cold-outside gardening coat, and the last was her pale green it's-hot-as-hell-but-I-need-to-cover-up coat.

Tears pricked her eyes. She could hear Aunt Maggie's no-nonsense tone and remembered when Aunt Maggie had bought her a purple gardening coat of her own. She'd thought it was the best thing ever and had worn it until it fell apart.

Aunt Maggie would never wear these coats again. Chelsea sniffed and swallowed hard. Her eyes roamed the room. Maggie's spare set of secateurs, one of half a dozen pairs Maggie kept spread around the house and garden in case she spotted something that needed pruning. The garden had been Aunt Maggie's life. Aside from the cabins she'd rented out as bed and breakfasts, she'd drawn income from the garden by charging a gold coin donation for people to wander through it and hosting weddings on the grounds. She hadn't been rich, but she'd always said she had enough for what she needed.

The last time she'd written to Chelsea, she'd mentioned she was considering converting the barn into a group space where people could hold workshops or meetings. Chelsea had offered to do the promotional material for her if she went ahead with the plan.

It would have brought people to the town.

Chelsea considered the idea. Could she bring Aunt Maggie's idea to fruition?

She'd never loved Sydney the way her mother had. This

had always been home to her, unlike all the rentals they'd lived in before Ezra. There was nothing stopping her from moving back to Western Australia permanently.

The thought was shocking and unexpected, but she didn't shy away from it.

There was a hell of a lot of work ahead, and success wasn't guaranteed but bringing Lilydale back to its former glory held a lot of appeal.

Her mother owned the property, so Chelsea wouldn't be homeless, but it would take time to earn enough income to survive. She'd need to pay utilities and for food, and all the repairs.

Her heart raced as she remembered the nights when she'd gone to bed hungry and the times they couldn't visit Aunt Maggie because there hadn't been enough money for fuel.

She exhaled slowly as her phone dinged with an incoming message. Lauren.

Have sent you what I can find. Thanks for your help.

Chelsea glanced at the laundry and then down at her phone. The promotional work would be easier.

The laundry could wait.

And perhaps if she did a good enough job with the fair, she'd find more contract work to supplement her income.

It was something to think about.

She fetched her laptop and in minutes she was immersed in her new project.

Reviving Honeybrook.

Chapter 8

By the end of the day, Chelsea had a decent promotional plan put together. It had taken her a little more time to search for the relevant websites, social media, magazine and newspaper sites around Perth that she could use to promote the upcoming fair, but she remembered a few from her teen-aged years. She sent Lauren a text to say it was ready and ask when she was free. While she waited for an answer, she called her mother.

"Chelsea, how was your day?"

Chelsea smiled at her voice as she sat on the couch. "Interesting. I ran into Lauren."

"Oh, that's wonderful! Is she still living in Honeybrook?"

"Yeah, she's the mayor. I'm helping her promote the Honeybrook Fair."

"How fabulous. Tell her I said hi."

"I will." Chelsea looked outside at the dry, dying garden and her mood plummeted. "I also spoke to Darren."

"What did he have to say for himself?"

"Johann paid him fifty thousand dollars to let the

garden die."

Her mother sucked in a breath. "How dare he!"

Her outrage soothed Chelsea. A small part of her had worried her mother had known and was using the destruction of the garden as an excuse to sell.

"Johann has been planning to buy the property since even before Aunt Maggie died." Chelsea had gone through the proposal her mother had sent her and noticed the creation date was before Aunt Maggie's death.

"That's no excuse for what he did."

Chelsea nodded. "I understand it's your choice, but I'd really prefer you don't sell to him."

"Absolutely," Sabine said. "He and his company can go to hell. The greed of the man…"

She heard Ezra speaking in the background and her mother explained what had happened.

"No, this isn't business," Sabine said. "Lilydale is Chelsea's home."

Chelsea's heart ached. Ezra wouldn't understand their sentimentality. He'd never gone without, never been abandoned by all their family except Aunt Maggie, had never been uncertain where he would live next.

Without Aunt Maggie they would have struggled far more than they had.

"No, I won't sell to that man since he's been so underhanded," Sabine continued, talking to Ezra. A pause and then, "We can discuss it later." The bite in her mother's tone made Chelsea smile. Sabine turned her attention back to Chelsea. "What are your plans now?"

A good question. "I've gone through a couple of rooms," she replied. "Taken some stuff to the op shop. There wasn't anything you wanted to keep, was there?" Probably something she should have asked earlier, but they'd taken a few things when they'd been here for the funeral.

"No, I've got everything I want."

"Then I'll keep going through the rooms."

"What about the garden?"

She pursed her lips, uncertain about her mother's reaction. "Actually, Ethan's doing some work on it."

"Ethan? Not the Ethan who worked in the garden during high school." She sounded shocked. "Didn't he join the army?"

"Yeah. He's on leave and came to visit Aunt Maggie. He didn't know she'd died."

"Oh, the poor man. I had no idea he kept in contact with her."

"They wrote regularly." It was sweet.

Sabine chuckled. "Aunt Maggie and her letters. She always insisted it was far more personable than email."

And she was right. Chelsea might have saved her emails in a folder if they'd emailed, but she never would have gone back and reread them. Not like she had with her letters.

"Didn't you have a crush on Ethan?"

Chelsea cringed, wishing her mother had forgotten. "Yes." It had been more than a crush, but by the time her mother had returned from Europe, he had already broken up with her, so Chelsea had played it down.

She'd dreamed of marrying him—maybe not immediately, but someday after completing university and getting a decent job.

As a teenager she'd believed something about her deterred the male gender since her father wanted nothing to do with her and Ezra had just tolerated her.

But with Ethan she'd believed she'd found someone other than her mother and Aunt Maggie who loved her.

She'd thought they could build a home and family that

neither of them had had growing up.

She'd thought wrong.

"Is he married?"

Chelsea rolled her eyes. Every now and again, her mother would bring up her single status or introduce her to a colleague who was age appropriate and single. "I haven't asked." She glanced out the window. They hadn't covered anything personal. She wasn't sure what to say to him.

"Maybe you should. Is he still good looking?"

He'd aged well, like a fine wine. No, more like a whisky or rum, something with more punch to it. "I guess."

That chuckle again. "There's no need to rush back to Sydney. You should take a proper holiday after this."

She wasn't ready to voice her idea she might not return to Sydney at all. "I might not have a choice if I can't find a job." She wouldn't ask Ezra to help her and her funds would only last a couple of months, but the idea of staying here longer soothed her.

"You said you were working for the council. It's a start."

Chelsea didn't mention it was a volunteer job. Her phone beeped with a text from Lauren.

I can meet you for dinner?

A great idea. She could get out of the house and forget about everything. "I've got to go, Mum. I'm meeting Lauren for dinner."

"All right. Keep me up to date."

"Will do. Love you." She hung up and sent a text back to Lauren. *Sure. Where?*

The pub. It's the only place. Six-thirty?

How sad. There used to be a couple of small restaurants in town. *See you then.*

She had an hour to get ready, but after she packed her

laptop into its bag, her footsteps drew her to the door. She hadn't heard Ethan working in the garden since midday and she was curious what he was doing.

OK, she was also curious to talk to him and find out about his life.

It was the neighbourly thing to do.

Heading towards the greenhouse, she spotted the neatly trimmed oleander hedge. The branches from it were over by the compost heaps, as were a bunch of branches from a bougainvillea.

The grass was flattened around the cabins, and she followed the path to examine the buildings. They needed a good clean and the outside could do with a wash, but they looked structurally sound. The biggest task would be taming the nearby garden.

Aunt Maggie had a ride-on lawnmower and various other equipment to tidy the grass, so perhaps she should ask Ethan to mow it.

But was it her place to tell him what to do? He was here because of his love for Aunt Maggie.

She wandered to the next cottage and then the last one as uncertainty filled her. It was too big a property to manage from interstate, particularly if they couldn't trust the person who was managing it.

Was it too much work for Chelsea to do on her own?

Aunt Maggie had struggled when the garden was healthy and she had a regular clientele.

Ezra would hate to spend money on something he would consider a money pit, and it wasn't fair to ask her mother to hold on to it for sentimental reasons.

But selling this place felt like the final nail on Aunt Maggie's coffin, and Chelsea's past life. Her happiest memories had been here; the barn was where Ethan had kissed her for the first time, the grassed area over there was where she and Lauren used to set up the sprinkler and run under it to cool off on hot days, and Aunt Maggie had given her that garden bed to do what she wanted with. The first bit of land which had been truly hers and couldn't be taken away.

Now it was barely visible beneath the weeds.

She sighed as she turned in a slow circle, surveying what was left of her childhood memories.

If she was honest, she'd never been happy in Sydney. The only thing keeping her there was her mother and siblings, and she didn't see them often. Their schedules never seemed to line up.

But Honeybrook was a little too far away from the city for a comfortable daily commute, and Chelsea wouldn't have much free time after work to deal with a garden this big.

She was foolish to even consider keeping Lilydale.

Her steps took her towards the barn and she hesitated outside. The door was closed, but she hadn't heard a car leave, so she assumed Ethan was still around.

She couldn't keep ignoring him. Taking a breath, she knocked on the wooden door and called, "Ethan?"

The door opened almost immediately. His cargo pants and T-shirt were damp with sweat and covered in streaks of dirt. His hair was flat and damp as if he'd been wearing a hat, but somehow when he smiled, he looked sexy, not grungy.

A memory flashed into her mind of her stripping off his shirt on a similarly warm day and helping him wash off the dirt under the hose.

"You don't need to knock. It's your place."

She swallowed hard, pushing the thought away. "You might have been changing." Which brought images of a clean, dry Ethan only half dressed, which was equally arousing. Not appropriate.

He shrugged. "I'm used to a lack of privacy, but if you don't mind, I'll set up a hose as a shower."

Heat rushed her cheeks as the memory came back stronger. She cleared her throat. "Don't be silly. Use the bathroom inside." The words were out of her mouth before she considered the impact of Ethan being in her space. Particularly a wet, naked Ethan.

It had been far too long since she'd been with a man if she was lusting after the one who'd broken her heart.

Still, one of the nicest things about a hard day's work was the long soaking shower afterwards, and she appreciated his help.

"Are you sure?"

She nodded slowly, not at all certain. "I'll get you a key to the house." Or perhaps a cabin would be more sensible. But she couldn't rescind the offer now.

"Thank you."

His sincerity spoke to her, and she didn't like the way her insides warmed. She changed the subject. "The oleander looks good."

"Thanks. Have you spoken to your mother about Johann?"

A sliver of annoyance slipped through her. It was none of his business. "Yes. She's agreed not to sell the property to him."

He tilted his head. "So, what will you do with it?"

She shrugged. "I don't know. I wasn't planning to stay here…" The way he looked at her, as if he was hanging on to her every word, reminded her too much of their past, of how it had been so easy to confide her hopes and dreams in him. She pressed her lips together as the old hurt flooded back.

He shifted, placing his hands in his pockets but opening

his chest in a friendly, non-threatening stance. "Where are you living at the moment?"

The temptation to tell him her worries was far too strong. Far too dangerous. She couldn't lose her heart to him again. It had taken her too long to recover the last time. "I've come from Sydney." She checked the time. "I need to go. I'm having dinner with Lauren. I'll drop the key by before I go." She strode back to the house, her chest tight.

She knew nothing about him anymore. He could be married or in a serious relationship, and if she let herself care, she would be devastated all over again. He was the only man she'd ever loved.

But he hadn't loved her. He'd abandoned her like her father had. Hadn't cared enough, like Ezra.

She hadn't been good enough.

She had to remember.

But it was so hard to when he looked at her with those eyes that promised he understood who she was to her core.

Apparently she was a sucker.

Annoyed, she strode into the house and locked the laundry door behind her.

The symbolic gesture made her feel stronger. She was in control of her life and her emotions.

It took only a short time to get ready for dinner. She checked she had the printed copy of her proposal for Lauren in her bag as she went downstairs. A few nerves danced in her stomach. What if Lauren didn't like it? What if she really wasn't good at her job and that was why Viral Posts Media had fired her?

She closed her eyes, gave in to her insecurities for three deep breaths, and then let them go like her therapist had taught her.

On the way out, she grabbed the spare key from the hook in the pantry, locked the house and then hurried back to the shed, tapping on the door before she walked in.

Ethan sat in a camp chair, reading a book, looking at home with a beer in his hand. There was no sign of the uncomfortable teen he'd been, always expecting to be told to leave.

Her heart ached as she remembered the conversations they'd had about books they enjoyed. He'd introduced her to the fantasy genre, and she'd introduced him to romance. The one he held was a romance by one of her favourite authors. She bit her tongue to stop herself from asking if he was enjoying it. "Here." She thrust the key at him.

He looked up and his eyes widened as he slowly scanned her from head to toe. Her body warmed at his slow perusal. "You look amazing."

Heat suffused her cheeks. Hardly. She just didn't have many casual clothes. Most of her wardrobe consisted of business clothes, with a few pairs of tracksuits for lazing around home in winter. She ignored his comment. "I'll be a couple of hours if you want to use the bathroom before I get back." And she hoped he would. The last thing she needed was to know he was wet and naked only a room away.

The image seared into her brain.

She turned and strode towards the door.

"Have fun. Say hi to Lauren for me."

She waved her acknowledgement but didn't turn around. She needed to get out of there.

And figure out what to do about the far too appealing Ethan Ward.

Chapter 9

Only a couple of older men sat at the bar with beer in front of them when Chelsea arrived. The mix of round and rectangular tables which spread out across the wooden floor were empty. Was it an indication of how the town was dying, or simply because it was a Tuesday night and no one was going out to dinner?

She ordered a glass of white wine at the bar.

"You just passing through?" the bartender asked as he handed her the wine. He was an older gentleman, around his sixties, with quite a bit of grey in his hair, but his smile was friendly and his eyes twinkled as he spoke.

She couldn't help returning his smile. "I'm not sure." She sipped her wine while she decided how much she should say. Honeybrook was a small town where everyone knew your business, but this could be a good way to discover whether anyone had expressed an interest in Lilydale Cottage lately. "I'm Chelsea, Maggie McGinnis's great niece. I'm sorting through Lilydale."

The man frowned. "I heard what Darren did. It's such a shame to see Lilydale that way."

She nodded, surprised he had already heard the gossip. "It was devastating, if I'm honest. Aunt Maggie would have been horrified." She swallowed past the lump in her throat.

"She would have been," the man agreed. "I've a mind to ban Darren from the pub."

"Don't let me stop you," Chelsea said, her tone a little grim.

"What are you doing with the place?" the man asked.

Wasn't that the million-dollar question? "I'm not sure yet. It's a big property for anyone to manage. I don't know how Aunt Maggie did it by herself all these years."

"Maggie was one in a million." The man mopped liquid from the counter.

"Yeah, she was." Chelsea blinked away the tears. The pub door opened and Lauren walked in.

"Hey, Chelsea," she called. "I'll have a wine too please, Alex."

The bartender grinned. "Yes, mayor."

Lauren rolled her eyes as she sat on the stool next to Chelsea. "I hope I haven't kept you waiting."

"No, I needed to get out of the house."

"I can't believe you've put together a proposal already. I'm dying to see it." She took the glass Alex handed her and gestured to a table against the wall. "Let's go through it over there."

Alex raised his eyebrows. "You two know each other?"

"Childhood friends," Lauren replied. "She kept me sane during the holidays."

Chelsea followed Lauren across the room to the table furthest from the bar.

Lauren lowered her voice. "Alex is a terrible gossip and I don't want word to spread about what we're doing. If people get their hopes up and it doesn't work, it will be devastating."

Suddenly the pressure hit Chelsea. She hadn't considered what might be riding on the success of the fair. As her heart raced, she sank into the chair and busied herself getting out her laptop.

"You look fabulous by the way," Lauren said.

"Thanks." The truth was, she was overdressed. The two men at the bar wore dusty jeans and well-worn jackets. Perhaps she should return to the op shop tomorrow and find something more appropriate for cleaning out Maggie's house.

"Let's order before we start," Lauren said. "I'm starving."

The menu had all the usual pub meals and Chelsea chose the chicken schnitzel.

She opened the PowerPoint presentation she'd created and handed Lauren the print copy. "I thought it might be good to appeal to people's nostalgia," she began. "Many adults would have come to the fair as kids, and now they'll have children of their own. If we can play into that, we might attract people." She'd mocked up ideas with the graphics and video Lauren had sent her. "I wasn't sure whether you'd have a budget, but if you do, I'd spend it here." She outlined the best bang for their buck and then all the free options.

"This is incredible, Chelsea," Lauren breathed. "You really know your stuff."

Chelsea shrugged. "I've been doing this for years."

"Do you work for a fancy Sydney firm?" Lauren teased. "Have you met lots of famous people?"

She hesitated, debating what to say. Lauren had always been her confidant when they were younger. Besides, who would she tell? "Did you hear about the recent Aria Simpson scandal?"

Lauren nodded. "What an insensitive thing to say!"

"I worked on the Tours Australia project with her. Her comment got me fired, so I'm not working anywhere at the moment."

Lauren's mouth dropped open. "Why did they fire you?"

"Because the client needed someone to blame, and I was the obvious choice." She closed her eyes. "I begged Aria to apologise, but she refused."

"So what are you doing now?"

"Attracting people to Honeybrook." Chelsea smiled. "Going through Aunt Maggie's things and figuring out what I'm doing next with my life."

Alex delivered their meals. "Enjoy, ladies." He smiled, as he not so subtly tried to see what was on the printout.

Lauren gathered the papers together. "Thanks, Alex."

Chelsea glanced at her plate as he left. A dry schnitzel with a small pot of gravy to pour over it, overcooked chips and a tiny serving of salad which consisted of lettuce, a couple of cherry tomatoes and some grated carrot. "You said this was the only restaurant in town?"

Lauren laughed. "Not the gourmet food you're used to?"

"No." She wasn't a snob, but, "It's not the type of food which will attract people to the area." And that was the problem. Even if she got people to the fair, there needed to be something that would keep people coming back regularly. "Why else do people come to Honeybrook?"

"The lake attracts people for picnics, but they rarely stop in town." She tapped her finger on the table.

"What about a bakery, or antique shops, or a children's playground?"

"The bakery is nothing special, and I heard talk the family who own it are considering moving to Perth. The antique shop is more of a junk shop and aside from the lolly shop, there's nothing special."

"Any wineries in the area?"

"There's one, but people head to the Swan Valley if they're going on a day trip."

"So we need to inform people our winery is better." She made a note.

"*Our* winery?" Lauren asked with a grin.

Chelsea shrugged, not wanting to think about her wording. "You know what I mean. Do they have a stall at the fair?"

"I'll have to check."

"It might be worth giving them a stall if they don't," Chelsea said. But still there wasn't much to keep people returning. "Anything else?"

"There's nowhere really for people to stay," Lauren added. "The pub has a couple of rooms upstairs and there's an old motel down the road tradies and road workers stay at, but that's it now Lilydale is closed. We don't even have a caravan park and the campsite by the lake was vandalised recently." She shrugged. "Aunt Maggie hosted weddings on a semi-regular basis and they attracted day-trippers or weekenders."

Chelsea sat back in her chair. "I had no idea Lilydale was so important to the town."

"It was enough to keep Honeybrook on the edges of the map, but it wasn't our saving grace."

But it was a way to save Lilydale and perhaps help the town. If she brought Lilydale back to its former glory and added workshops and weddings, it might help. She had the promotional skills to come up with a great campaign, especially if she played into the rejuvenation of her aunt's dream.

"Chelsea?"

She blinked and glanced at Lauren.

"Where did you just go?"

Nerves teased her stomach. Why was she even considering this? It wasn't the way to a stable income. Still, she couldn't stop the words coming from her mouth. "Maybe I can bring Lilydale back," she said. "Restore it and expand on what Aunt Maggie was doing."

"Stay here?" Lauren asked.

She hesitated. "I don't know." It was such a huge risk.

But the idea of making Lilydale her forever home appealed.

"You know what you should do?" Lauren drew out her phone. "Get this guy in. He takes overgrown gardens and clears them, recording the process on social media. He's got so many followers." She showed Chelsea a video of a man in high-vis clothing, hacking back lawns and overgrown trees until they were tidy. He had several million followers and each post had hundreds of comments on it.

"He's perfect!" Chelsea found his contact details, saw he was based in Perth, and added it to her to-do list. She could create videos documenting restoring Lilydale, and create a channel on social media. She added Kylie, the woman who reworked the Tours Australia ad in record time, to her list of people to contact tomorrow. She'd give Chelsea some tips on how to do it.

"I can see your mind is running away with itself." Lauren laughed.

Chelsea typed a couple more ideas as she smiled a little sheepishly. "Sorry. Almost done." She put down her phone.

"You don't need to apologise if you think it will help bring this place back to life. Tell me if there's anything I can do to help."

"I will." She turned her attention to her friend. "So, what have you been up to for the past ten years?"

Lauren chuckled. "Now that's a story which will take a while."

****

Chelsea hadn't got home until late last night. Not that Ethan was keeping tabs on her, he was just attuned to noises, especially at night, and the sound of the car engine woke him from where he slept in his swag in the barn. He'd listened to the car door shut and then waited until he heard the telltale thud of her shutting the front door before he'd settled down again.

It wasn't any of his business what Chelsea did, but he couldn't help wanting to make sure she was safe.

The shower he'd had yesterday had been pure bliss, and it felt significant that she'd given him a key to the house, but perhaps he was making too much of it.

They hadn't talked about anything important. His reasons for leaving her were still valid today.

Mila and Dobby were making it work. And if he went into business with Dobby, it might be a different story.

Which reminded him he wanted to ask Chelsea about the land, especially the farmland behind the garden. If Dobby bought Lilydale, he'd take care of it.

He shouldn't get ahead of himself. Today he'd talk to Chelsea about her plans. He dressed for another day of gardening and ate breakfast, debating whether he should go down the road and buy himself a proper coffee. Perhaps Chelsea would be nice enough to make him one.

Ethan wandered outside, glancing towards the house. The blinds were up in Chelsea's bedroom, which meant she was awake. The blinds up had become their sign he could climb the tree outside her window and sneak into her bedroom to steal a few more hours together when they were younger.

Such good memories.

Often they would lie side-by-side on her single bed and talk about their pasts and what they wanted for the future. She was the only one he'd ever told about his different foster families and his mother. Like her, his father had never been part of his life. His mother had succumbed to drugs and had mental illness as a result. She'd been in no state to take care of him, even if she'd wanted to. Which she hadn't.

All that was in the past. It was far more important to focus on the present and the future.

As he moved towards the house, a black Porsche pulled into the driveway. Johann was back. It was still pretty early for a visit. Ethan hesitated. Maybe he should wait until the property developer left before he went over.

Johann's face was red, his fury clear in his scowl and clenched fists as he stormed up the steps and pounded on the front door.

Ethan tensed and strode closer in case Chelsea needed his help.

By the time he arrived, she'd already opened the door and Ethan stopped out of sight at the corner of the house to listen to the conversation. He clenched his hands to push down the urge to play saviour. It wasn't his place to butt in, but it was a struggle not to rush to Chelsea's side and take over, show Johann she wasn't alone.

"Who the hell do you think you are?" Johann growled.

Ethan shifted back to look through the living room window to the front door. Chelsea stood with one hand on the door handle. Her reply was calm. "I could ask you the same question."

"Do you know what you've done?" Johann yelled, his

voice shaking with rage. "You've cost me millions."

Chelsea smiled. "I can't see how, Mr Mueller. I haven't had any business with you."

"Your mother refused my proposal."

"Did she tell you why?"

Ethan didn't like her sweet tone. It would inflame Johann's anger. Every instinct in his body screamed for him to protect her, but it wasn't his place yet. They were merely talking.

"She said she wouldn't deal with a man like me. I can only imagine you gave her an unfavourable impression of me."

"I did," she agreed. "Would you like to know why?"

"Because you got precious about me being in your garden."

"That didn't endear you to me," she agreed, "but that's not the reason." She paused, and Ethan had to give her credit. The way she made Johann work for the information was perfect.

"What was?" Johann asked between gritted teeth.

"I spoke to Darren yesterday."

A slight widening of his eyes. Yeah, he was guilty.

Chelsea continued, "Do you want to know what he said?"

Johann took a step back. "I don't know who you're talking about."

"Liar." The word shot out like a bullet, the calm replaced with anger as she pointed her finger at Johann. "You paid Darren fifty thousand dollars almost a year ago to let the garden die. Your greed destroyed my aunt's life's work."

The pain in her voice made Ethan ache to hold her, to take away any hurt.

"Don't be foolish. No one is going to want this place

now."

"*I* want this place," Chelsea replied. "My mother and I have agreed we will never sell to you, or any company you're affiliated with."

Johann stepped forward, and Ethan tensed. Johann's next words enhanced the threat of his body. "You don't know who you're playing with."

Chelsea's hand tightened around the door handle and Ethan moved to the corner of the house, ready to spring into action. "I can assure you, this is no game, Mr Mueller."

"You have to sell Lilydale to me," Johann said, a little desperation in his tone.

"I don't," Chelsea replied. "You can't make me."

"You obviously don't know who I work for." Desperation morphed into fear.

Definitely trouble. Ethan had heard enough. He stepped onto the porch and strode forward. "Morning, Chelsea."

Johann glared at him but stepped backwards.

"Ethan." Her face was a little pale, as if shaken by the encounter.

He moved so he stood between Chelsea and Johann and smiled at the man. "Sorry, I don't think we've met. I'm Ethan." He held out a hand.

Johann glanced at it, before shaking. "Johann Mueller."

"He was just leaving," Chelsea said.

"Right. Nice meeting you." Ethan stared at the man, then flicked his eyes to the black car and back to Johann.

Johann scowled. "I'll be in touch, Miss McGinnis."

"Don't bother. I have nothing to say to you."

Johann growled as he stalked down the steps to his car. Ethan waited until he drove away before he turned to Chelsea. "The man is dangerous."

Chelsea frowned. "He's a businessman. He can't force Mum to sign over the property." She stepped back to let him into the house, her hand trembling.

"There are many ways he can force her." His voice was grim and Chelsea looked at him with her eyebrows raised in question. "You've cost him a lot. He's not taking that kindly, particularly if his bosses aren't happy." Ethan would find out who they were, because there had been real fear in Johann's voice.

Annoyance flashed in her eyes and then she pressed her lips together. "I'll keep that in mind." She said nothing else as she entered the kitchen. "I was making coffee. Do you want one?"

Ethan smiled, hoping to lessen the tension. "Yes, please. I was hoping you'd offer."

That earned him a quick smile, but it was enough to make him feel warm inside. He blinked. That wasn't the goal here. Sure, he wanted to be friendly, but the increase in his heartbeat wasn't required. He couldn't afford to feel things for her again.

His eyes dipped to her left hand, which was bare. No rings.

He shouldn't be happy about that.

Her laptop was on the kitchen table, as was a tablet and her phone. "Have you been working?"

She hesitated and then nodded.

It shouldn't hurt that she didn't want to share with him. "What do you do?"

"I'm in marketing." She waved her hand. "Though at my last job I was a jack of all trades, creating campaigns, managing people, doing publicity as required."

She had always put a positive spin on everything. "I bet you're good at it."

Chelsea frowned as she frothed his milk. "Apparently

not good enough." She poured his coffee, and they sat at the kitchen table.

"What do you mean?"

"I was fired from my last job because I couldn't control what an asset said on social media." Perhaps his confusion showed because she said, "Did you see the recent controversy about what Aria Simpson said on social media?"

"Who?"

Her laughter rang through the kitchen and curled around his heart. "Thank you. It's good to remember not everyone is obsessed with who is hot right now."

He shrugged, not at all self-conscious. "I don't have any social media accounts."

Her eyes widened. "That explains why I never found you."

"You looked for me?" The little hitch in his heart needed to stop.

She nodded, her cheeks turning red. "After I finished university. I wanted to see how you were doing, but I couldn't find anything."

He had no words. She'd looked him up even after he'd hurt her. "Where are you working now?"

"I'm between jobs. The controversy with Aria Simpson happened last week."

She'd come to Lilydale to escape. It would have made seeing the garden even more traumatic. "I'm sorry."

Chelsea pursed her lips. "I'm not. Not anymore." She sipped her coffee, a slight furrow on her forehead telling him she was debating whether she should confide in him.

"Why?" he prodded.

"Because it brought me home."

He waited, knowing she had more to say. She opened her mouth and then took a sip of her coffee rather than speaking.

It hurt more than he wanted to admit, but she'd always been slow to trust others with her feelings. He needed to let her work up to it. "How was your dinner with Lauren?"

A smile. "Great. It was so much fun catching up with her." She glanced at her laptop. "I'm helping her promote the Honeybrook Fair. You'll have noticed how many shops are closed in town."

He nodded.

"Lauren said the town is dying. They need to bring people back. Lilydale used to attract many people." A smile tugged on her lips.

All at once he knew. "You're going to restore Lilydale."

Her eyes widened, and she nodded. "I went through Aunt Maggie's accounts last night. She made a decent income from the property. If I can restore the gardens, refresh the cabins, and spend time on advertising, I should be able to attract people to town."

"Will you be staying to run the place?" Something akin to hope blossomed in his chest.

"I haven't decided yet," she admitted. "I still need to call Mum and run it past her. She'll need to agree to it, as it's her property."

That reminded him of his call with Dobby. "Is there still the acreage at the back?"

"What acreage?"

"Aunt Maggie once mentioned she had farmland adjoining the property. Her fiancé was a farmer, and he was going to manage the farm while she did the garden."

"I never knew." Chelsea pulled out her phone. "Let me call Mum now. The kids will be at school."

"Kids?" Whose kids?

"My half-brother and sister."

Relief filled him. Not Chelsea's. "How old are they?"

"Ten and eight." She held up a hand to stop him from talking and said, "Hey, Mum."

Ethan shifted back in his seat as she spoke to her mother and glanced around the kitchen. Nothing had changed in here. Perhaps Maggie hadn't been inclined to modernise, or maybe she hadn't had the money. Though from what he knew about her, he suspected the real reason was because this was what she'd chosen with her fiancé and she hadn't wanted to change a thing.

He listened as Chelsea explained her plan to her mother and then asked about the extra land. Her mouth dropped open. "How much?" She nodded. "I had no idea." A pause. "Oh, I can't ask you to do that." Her expression crumpled and tears pricked in her eyes.

Ethan clenched his hands. What had Sabine said to upset Chelsea? He waited, and she sniffed and said, "Thank you, Mum. It means the world to me."

His fists relaxed. They were happy tears, not sad tears. Still, he impatiently waited until she hung up and took a couple of breaths to calm herself. He raised his eyebrows in question.

"She's going to transfer the property into my name." Chelsea swallowed. "She's giving me Lilydale."

He reached out and squeezed her hand, knowing what it meant to her. "That's great."

"She wants me to have the security she never had." She shook her head as if she couldn't believe it. "The property has to be worth a lot. There are sixty-five hectares of land behind Lilydale's gardens."

A decent size. "I have a friend who's considering getting out of the army," Ethan said. "If you think of selling some of the land, he might be interested."

"Does he want to become a farmer?"

Ethan chuckled at the thought of Dobby as a farmer.

"No. He wants to go into security and needs land to set up a training ground."

"For security?"

"Hostage extraction, bodyguard work and the like."

She pursed her lips. "I haven't thought that far ahead, but he could call me and we can discuss."

He liked that she wasn't dismissing the possibility out of hand. "What's your action plan?"

She hesitated. "Are you really interested?"

"I've got a month of leave to fill. I want to know what work I'll be doing."

Chelsea stared at him. "Why do you want to spend your free time helping me?"

It was a good question and one he didn't want to investigate in any detail, but he wasn't ready to leave Chelsea or Lilydale. "Aunt Maggie was one of the few people who showed me any kindness when I was a kid. I'd like to repay her."

"She wouldn't expect any repayment."

"I know." He shrugged. "Seeing the mess the garden is in after all the hours I worked on it… I can't leave it like this."

Chapter 10

Chelsea studied Ethan. While an extra pair of hands would be useful, she hadn't examined how she felt about him being back in her life. The attraction was still there. He'd grown into a very handsome man and sitting next to him at the table, she had an almost electrified awareness of him. He didn't seem to feel the same, his glances friendly and open, but nothing more. Though he was the one who had broken up with her.

That in itself should have her shoving him out the door. "What about your injury?"

"It's fine."

She hesitated. She could arrange it so they didn't even see each other in the sixteen- acre garden if she wanted.

The thought gave her peace. Lilydale had a special place in both of their hearts. This was a simple business arrangement.

"All right. I'd appreciate all the help I can get." She pulled her laptop towards her, waking it out of sleep mode. "I spent last night working out the priorities in my plan to bring people back to town." She turned the computer so he could view the screen and he shuffled closer, his warm arm brushing hers. Her skin tingled, and she pulled her arm away.

An email notification dinged and her heart jumped. "Let me check this." Chelsea clicked on the email from the lawnmower man Lauren had suggested. She'd emailed him as soon as she'd arrived home last night with photos of the garden, and a request for a quote. She'd outlined the problem and what equipment she had.

His response was short. *I'm up for a challenge. Had a cancellation for Friday so could come then.* His number followed the message.

"Yes!" She called him, and within five minutes she'd received his quote and arranged for him to come down Thursday night so he could start early Friday.

When she hung up, Ethan asked, "What was that about?"

"Barry's going to do the paths and grass." Chelsea showed him the videos on social media. "I'm starting some social media profiles for Lilydale to record the restoration." It was one of the first things on her to-do list. "He's going to stay in a cabin, so the first step is making sure at least one is habitable. The outside needs a good clean, and I'm hoping the inside will be the same and nothing needs fixing."

He nodded. "Then what?"

"By the weekend Barry will have done the grass and we can get stuck into the garden. Pruning everything will make an immediate difference, as will weeding and planting fresh annuals." She could see the end result so clearly in her mind. "I'm hoping the bulbs will still be there if we clear out the weeds from those garden beds." She showed him her list. "I need to find an engineer to examine the bridge and other structures around the garden, and someone to figure out why the harbour lake is dry." Maybe it was something as simple as a broken pump.

"The order of the garden beds is so you can open parts of the garden earlier than others?" Ethan asked.

She smiled, not surprised he'd noticed. "Yes. I did the list from memory, so I'll go out today and confirm I haven't missed anything."

"The Japanese garden could be done there." He pointed. "If we close the path that leads further into the garden. And if the Bali gazebo is safe, a few pillows would make it a nice place to read or chill."

His eyes met hers. Did he remember the times they'd spent reading together in the gazebo? The occasional brushes of their fingers, the excitement of sharing a good bit in their books?

She shifted a little further away. "I'll check the tin Aunt Maggie had for gold coin donations is still secure."

He looked back to the screen, but every nerve on her skin thrummed with awareness. She had to get him on board with the plan and then get as far away from him as possible.

By the time they'd gone through and revised the plan adding some of Ethan's ideas, her stomach was grumbling. "Do you want something to eat?" She went into the kitchen, cursing her innate manners. She wasn't supposed to be extending her time with him. "I've just got cereal."

"That would be great." His easy smile made her insides flutter.

Damn it. She turned to get what she needed out of the cupboard. If she was like this just from sitting next to him, what would she be like when he showered every day in the house?

She frowned. That was a point. She could hardly ask

him to do all this work and let him sleep in a swag in the barn. "If you're going to stay, take a cottage." And that way he wouldn't need to come near the house.

"Thanks. I'll pay you rent."

"Don't be silly." She waved a hand. "You'll be more than paying for board with the work you do." Which gave her an idea. If she got enough followers, maybe she could offer opportunities for people to stay for free in return for a few hours of their help in the garden. There were lots of projects on social media which captured people's attention and made them want to help. She wrote another item on her list to investigate it later.

She placed the bowls, cereal and milk on the table, and Ethan helped himself.

It was time she got over this stupid attraction to him. Perhaps knowing what he'd been up to for the past ten years would help. "Is the friend who's thinking about getting out of the army with Special Forces as well?"

He looked surprised by the question. "Yeah. My team leader."

"Does that mean you'll get a new one?"

"Yeah." He frowned.

"I know little about the military," Chelsea admitted. "Does the team leader go on missions?" She cringed, not sure if mission was the right terminology.

"Yeah."

"Do you have a good team?"

"The best," he replied without hesitation. "They're my brothers."

Chelsea's heart swelled in her chest. He'd found a family. It would mean so much to him. Perhaps the army *had* been a better choice than staying with her. He had multiple people he could now turn to. "That's good. I'm glad."

He tilted his head. "You really are, aren't you?"

She frowned. "Of course. You always wanted a family who cared for you."

"I thought you'd be angrier at me."

She pressed her lips together. He wanted to talk about it now? "It was a shock to see you again," she admitted. "And I was devastated when you chose the army over me, but we were young." She shrugged as if her entire world hadn't ended back then. "We're both different people now. There's no point holding on to the anger. I'm pleased you're happy." It was the truth. There was a confident, settled side to him he hadn't had when they were younger.

"Thanks, Chels. The army did help me."

She acknowledged the hurt that she hadn't been able to help him and let it slide away.

"What about you?" Ethan asked. "You've got new siblings since we saw each other last."

"They're hardly new," she said. "I was at university staying on campus when they were born. They're great, but I didn't have time to go home very often and Ezra never warmed to me. I don't think he likes the reminder Mum had another life before him." She'd been happy for her mother. Ezra doted on her and she hadn't had to work. She'd enjoyed being able to stay home and watch her new babies grow.

"It must have been rough, feeling like you weren't welcomed." His voice was low, and understanding shone in his eyes.

Of course he would understand. He'd lived with so many foster families over the years. "Mum always welcomed me, and the kids were pleased to see me. I was happy Mum found someone who loved her so much." She shrugged. "I was so used to moving from rental to rental every couple of years that it wasn't a big deal."

Chelsea glanced around the house. She'd spent every school holiday here, because her mum couldn't afford childcare. In winter she'd explored the house with its dusty attic and myriad boxes and cases. She and Aunt Maggie would play cards, or checkers, or bake something to keep them warm. Lilydale had been her real home. She couldn't remember why she hadn't made the time to visit Aunt Maggie more regularly.

Sadness slid through her, so she stood and collected their dishes, pushing away the memories. "I'm going to review the garden against my plan. Do you want to come?"

"Sure." That easy agreement again. As a teenager his agreement had been quick, as if not wanting to give someone a reason to be unhappy with him. He hadn't trusted they wouldn't turn on him and kick him out.

She picked up her tablet and went outside. On the way over to the cabins, she made notes about what needed to be done to garden beds or plants.

The cabin gutters needed cleaning before they had guests, and the garden beds outside needed weeding, but aside from that, and maybe a quick pressure wash of the outside, the cabins looked good. She unlocked the door to the first cabin and then screwed up her nose as a waft of mustiness enveloped her.

The light switch clicked as she turned it on and she scanned the main room; a cosy couch for two, a kitchen nook and a table that looked out over the garden. The walls were a pale cream and the kitchen cabinets were of a yellowing pine. Not modern, but still in good condition. She opened the window to let in some fresh air and then checked the bathroom and bedroom.

The smoky looking tiles were from the nineties, which was when the cabins had been built, but it would cost too much to replace them. It would have to go on a later to-do list, after Lilydale started making money again.

She turned on the tap, letting the water flow to flush the pipes while she checked the shower and toilet. The shower head had spray coming out at every angle due to a calcium build up so she added options for a cleaner or a replacement to her list.

"It looks pretty good," Ethan said. "Just a clean and airing."

Chelsea nodded in agreement. "I'll clean it today ready for the lawnmower man."

She opened the rest of the windows and made a note to buy some tea and coffee supplies for the kitchen and a couple of candles or air fresheners to rid the rooms of the mustiness.

Then they went to the other two cottages, which were larger, made for families. They were in a similar condition and would be ready for renting as soon as the garden had been tamed. She'd take new photos and design a website. Aunt Maggie had only ever advertised through the council's site, which listed accommodation.

As they made their way through the garden, Ethan made suggestions. "We're out of fire season, so we should be able to have a bonfire with all the plant material we cut down."

"Yeah." She remembered sitting around a large bonfire, toasting marshmallows when she was younger. It had been a nice reward for all their hard work.

"I can service the equipment when I do Elsie," Ethan said as they reached the larger shed. It held a four-wheel motorbike, ride-on lawnmower, and other edging and trimming equipment. "Engines might be gummed up from sitting for so long."

"Thanks." Engines were not her forte.

They both moved to leave the shed and bumped into

each other. Ethan held her arms to steady her as she stumbled, his hands firm. She glanced up at him. "Sorry."

He stared at her, gaze intense, and her breath caught in her throat. It was the same expression he'd had before he'd kissed her for the first time. Her heart rejoiced, but her head shouted no. She stepped away. He'd broken her heart once. She wasn't letting him do it a second time. They could be friends, but nothing more.

She cleared her throat. "Let's continue." She hurried further into the garden.

***

Ethan stared after Chelsea as he willed his heart rate to slow. Holding her in his arms felt so right, but he couldn't let himself get feelings for her again. He'd be back in the army at the end of the month and heading off to whichever hotspot he was needed in.

All she'd ever wanted was a stable storybook family, with a partner who was always there for her. He couldn't guarantee that. He wasn't someone she could rely on every day. He'd never been able to offer her the stability she craved.

Mila's voice in his head scolded him, telling him he shouldn't decide for Chelsea. But he was too late. Chelsea didn't want him now.

He rubbed his chest.

The urge to kiss her had been almost overwhelming. Her competence and organised brain were such a turn on. She'd made copious notes as they'd reviewed the garden and had a way of prioritising the tasks. He wouldn't be surprised if by the end of the day she had a complete project plan with day-by-day tasks to tick off.

She would have done well in the army.

And the moment back in the house, when she'd told

him she was happy for him, made him remember how selfless and giving she was.

Then she'd dismissed what they'd had as a product of their youth and he'd had the crazy urge to argue with her and tell her it hadn't been, that he still cared for her.

Luckily he had a lot of training in how to keep his mouth shut.

It had hurt a lot more than he wanted it to.

But he only had himself to blame.

With a sigh, he hurried to catch up with the woman who still held a piece of his heart.

By the time they were done, it was mid-morning. He joined her in the kitchen and she put on the kettle, then took a packet of ANZAC biscuits from the cupboard. With an apologetic glance, she put them on the table. "They're not as good as Aunt Maggie's."

"Nothing is as good as Aunt Maggie's." He smiled. "But thanks."

"I'm hoping to find her recipe book somewhere. She taught me how to make a lot of her biscuits, but I don't remember all of them."

Another memory hit him of walking into the kitchen when Chelsea was baking. She'd worn a frilly apron and had flour on her face, and all over the bench. She might have been making scones. Aunt Maggie had been out on an errand and he'd been tackling the bougainvillea by the gate and was hot, sweaty and frustrated.

Chelsea had smiled at him and told him the scones would be out in a minute and to wash up. It had been such a homely vision, unlike anything he'd ever experienced. Overcome with emotion, he'd pushed her against the bench and kissed her senseless.

He'd wanted her, wanted the family they could build

together.

Until he realised he couldn't join the army and give Chelsea everything she wanted. He couldn't let her settle for less because of him.

Shaking from the emotion of the memory, he moved to look out the window. How could he still feel so strongly after over a decade?

"Are you all right?" Chelsea asked.

He closed his eyes against the rush of warmth her gentle words gave him. "Fine." He had to say something that would appease her. "Just thinking about Aunt Maggie's biscuits," he lied and turned to face her.

She smiled. "They were pretty amazing." She slid into a chair. "Do you think it's foolish of me to restore the garden?"

The uncertainty in her voice surprised him. "No, I don't. It's what she would have wanted and what's right."

"It's a huge undertaking."

"It is." He sat on the chair opposite her. "But I have no doubt we can do it." We. The word had such a nice comfort to it. A collaboration, a commitment. Maybe he needed to be committed. He was here for a month, until his superiors were happy he was healed. He needed to remember that.

"Thanks, Ethan." She reached out and squeezed his hand. "I needed to hear that."

Her fingers were warm from holding her mug, and they were soft, delicate. The hands of someone who had done no physical work for a while. But he knew she could do it, had seen firsthand how hard she worked when it was required.

The urge to turn his hand up and hold hers was strong, so instead he pulled away. He cleared his throat. "So the next step is cleaning the cabins?"

She nodded. "Aunt Maggie still has cleaning products in the laundry, so I didn't need to buy anything."

They had two days before the lawnmower man would be here to tame the grass and then they could tackle the gardens, but there were plenty of buildings which needed sprucing up.

Ethan got to his feet. "Shall we get started?"

He needed some distance from this amazing woman.

***

They'd been cleaning the first cabin for several hours when Chelsea's phone rang. Glad for a break, she pulled it out and then grinned as she saw the caller's name. "Hey, Kylie."

"One minute it's Aria-shaped panic stations and the next minute you've moved across the country and have sixteen acres of land?" The incredulity in her colleague's tone made Chelsea smile.

"Yeah, it was unexpected for me too." She explained what had happened and how she wanted to record the restoration of Lilydale. Aside from video editing, Kylie was a documentary film maker and knew how to make the topic she was filming into a story.

"The trick is taking a lot of footage," Kylie told her. "The more you have, the better the story you can tell when you edit it together. You also need to decide what story you want to tell."

Chelsea put the phone on speaker and took notes as she spoke.

"Do you have a decent video camera?" Kylie asked.

"Aunt Maggie bought one a couple of years ago, but I don't know how great it is."

"If you're using it for internet promotion, it should be fine." She sighed. "I kind of wish I could come over and film it myself, but I'm in the middle of a project."

"I wish you could too." This was right up Kylie's alley. Though she'd done a lot of marketing work to pay the bills, the documentaries she filmed were all related to the way big companies thought they were above the law. "If you get a chance, you're always welcome to visit. There's plenty of room in the house for guests."

She hadn't spent a lot of time with Kylie, but she enjoyed working with her, and had always figured they would be friends if they could ever make their schedules work together.

"Thanks. I might need a break after I finish filming this documentary."

Chelsea didn't ask her what it was, knowing Kylie didn't like to share what she was working on. She hung up and a minute later, Ethan came out from where he was cleaning the bathroom. "Your friend gave you some good tips."

"She's a documentary maker." It was almost lunch time. "I might go find the video camera. I should record some footage of us cleaning."

Ethan hesitated. "I can do the filming." He shrugged. "I can't be all over the internet."

It took a second for Chelsea to understand why. "Because you're Special Forces?"

He nodded.

That made sense. "Then you might need to be chief cameraman." Or she would buy a tripod and set it up to film her working.

"Happy to be."

They wandered back to the house to clean up. Funny how she hadn't even needed to mention they should take a lunch break. He seemed to know instinctively.

Remembered routines of their summer together.

Her heart clenched. Being with him felt incredibly right

and natural.

She had to remember he had walked away. His gaze didn't hold the desire she thought it did. He'd moved on in his life and didn't need her in it.

Anything else she imagined was wishful thinking.

After they washed up, she went to the linen cupboard to search for the video camera while Ethan got out the makings for sandwiches. The camera was on the top shelf and she couldn't quite reach it. She jumped and inched it towards herself. She jumped again, but it was still out of reach.

"Let me." Ethan appeared next to her and reached over her, trapping her between his hard, warm body and the door as he pulled the video camera bag down from the top shelf.

She inhaled deeply as every sense in her body woke up and celebrated. She clenched her hands to stop herself from sliding them around his waist and pulling him closer.

He paused, camera in one hand, his body still pressed against hers, his eyes on her. Awareness flashed over his face. Slowly he lowered his head.

He was going to kiss her.

No, she couldn't do this. A kiss would kick start her heart and it had no business getting excited here.

It was hard enough keeping the rest of her body under control.

She ducked under his arm and strode back to the kitchen, breathing hard.

Chapter 11

Ethan's heart pounded as he let Chelsea escape to the kitchen while he stood frozen with the video camera in his hand.

What the hell was he thinking?

He'd almost kissed Chelsea, and that would have been a big mistake.

Huge.

He wasn't getting involved with her.

But his body hated him right now. It screamed that the mistake he'd made was *not* kissing her. And a large part of his mind was on its side.

Ethan exhaled quietly, letting his heart rate return to normal. He didn't want to face Chelsea, but he could hardly stay here forever.

He returned to the kitchen where Chelsea was pacing from the kitchen table to the sink and back again. Her whole posture stiffened further when he entered the room and she glanced at him, turmoil on her face and then away again.

Shit. He'd put that expression there. He placed the

video camera on the table and opened his mouth to apologise when Chelsea said, "What was that?" She waved her hand towards the laundry. "Why were you going to kiss me?"

Ethan didn't have a good answer. He rubbed the back of his head. "Sorry, Chels. I guess it was kind of habit. You felt good pressed against me, and…" And what? He desperately wanted to feel her lips against his again. He couldn't say that.

If anything her expression became more devastated. She stopped pacing. "Was that all it ever was for you?" Her voice was soft. "Just physical?"

"No!" How could she even ask that? What they'd had was the most important relationship of his life.

"What was it then?" she demanded.

"You were my everything." The words came out before he considered the consequences.

Her face screwed up in confusion. "Then why did you leave me?"

There it was. All the hurt from the past written on her face. She wasn't as dismissive of their time together as she'd pretended to be.

Still he hesitated. If he told her the truth, she might hate him. He'd never been good enough for her, but she'd been too young to realise it.

The unworthiness stabbed him in the chest and scrabbled to take control of his senses. He stepped back, battling the strength of it, feeling almost as if he was back in the tsunami again, helpless to control it.

He sucked in a breath as he fought not to show the turmoil rushing through him.

Chelsea shook her head. "Never mind." She turned around and the panic intensified.

He could practically hear Mila challenging him to be

vulnerable.

"Because you deserved so much better than me."

She turned back, frowning. "What?"

"The army was my only choice after I turned eighteen. I couldn't afford any other career path because I had no money for food, accommodation, or transport." His foster parents had already told him he had to move out on the day he turned eighteen.

Chelsea nodded. "I know. We discussed it. I supported your choice."

"But you didn't know the reality. All you wanted was a stable family, a partner who was always there for you. I couldn't give you that. I'd be deployed for months at a time and you would be left on your own, having to do everything yourself, just like your mother had to."

Incredulity crossed her face. "What I wanted was you. I could have handled months on my own as long as I knew you were coming back to me."

He shook his head. "But I might not have. I always had my sights set on Special Forces. Any one of my missions could have been my last. I almost died in the damn tsunami." He gestured to his hips. "You would have been left alone. I loved you too much to put you through that."

And the decision had tormented him for years.

Anger flashed in her eyes and she straightened, stalking towards him. "You *did* put me through that. I mourned you, Ethan. I questioned my own worth. I thought myself unloveable by any man. It took me years to work up the courage to go on a date. I was alone." She poked him in the chest. "You did that to me by leaving with no explanation."

Horror filled him. "No, it wasn't meant to be like that."

She threw her hands up in disbelief. "What the hell did you expect? We'd been planning a life together and suddenly you were leaving and didn't want to stay in touch. What was I supposed to take from it? I was eighteen, in love, and I had been rejected by every man in my life, including you."

Oh shit. She was right. What a stupid kid he'd been. Chelsea had told him she was the result of her mother's affair with a married man. The man had never acknowledged Chelsea's existence. Then she'd been excited about getting to know Ezra, but he hadn't been interested in a father-daughter relationship with her. And there Ethan was, adding to her list of shit-for-brains men in her life.

Agony ripped through him and he reached to pull her into his arms, but she stepped away, moving to put the table between them.

He rubbed his chest, her rejection wounding him almost as much as the tsunami had.

Was the fear of it why he really walked away all those years ago?

"I'm so sorry, Chels. I didn't think." No, he'd used excuses to protect himself from the inevitable rejection he'd expected. If he'd been strong enough to think it through rationally, or brave enough to discuss his fears with her, they would have worked things out. God, what an idiot he'd been.

He took a cautious step forward. "I never wanted to hurt you. I only wanted what was best for you. It killed me to walk away. You were the first person I'd ever loved."

"I can't believe what I'm hearing." She strode away from the kitchen into the living area and Ethan followed. "You threw away everything we had together without even having the decency to discuss it with me? *You* got to decide what was best for me?"

He stared at her helplessly. In hindsight he saw what a

terrible decision it was. "I was a kid who'd never loved before, Chels. I wanted to save you from a life of disappointment." He sighed. "I'm so sorry."

Chelsea stopped pacing and took three deep breaths. Then she shook herself, as if shaking away her agitation. When she looked at him, she was calm, as if a mask had slotted over her face. She gave an embarrassed smile. "I don't know why I'm so worked up. All this happened more than a decade ago." She waved her hand. "Water under the bridge. Thank you for explaining. Obviously it was still weighing on me." A short, humourless laugh. "Why don't you go back to the cottage and I'll finish cleaning up and join you in a minute?"

She brushed past him on her way back to the kitchen and he grabbed hold of her arm. "Wait."

She looked at him with her forest green eyes, and he saw his world.

Nothing had changed in his circumstances, but he couldn't let her go a second time. Not without trying.

"What, Ethan?"

He swallowed. "Maybe you got so worked up because you're feeling the same emotions as me."

She raised an eyebrow. "Which are?"

Yeah, he deserved to be the one who laid it all on the line first this time around. "Attraction, longing, the excruciating ache of wondering what we would have been like if I hadn't been such a dumb-ass."

Her lips quirked up for a second.

"Maybe it's being back in Lilydale together, but I've thought about you so often over the years. Leaving you is my one regret."

She shifted, moving ever so slightly closer to him.

Keep talking. Somehow he'd gone from not wanting to get involved to not wanting her to leave in a blink of an eye. "We were good together, Chels. We had a connection and understood each other in a way I've never felt with anyone else." He paused. "I think the connection is still there."

Chelsea pursed her lips, thinking things through. "We're different people now." It wasn't an argument, simply a statement of fact.

He nodded. "Hopefully a little wiser along with the older."

"We live in different states."

Ethan raised his eyebrows. "Are you planning to return to Sydney when Lilydale is done?"

She shrugged. "Restoring Lilydale might fail."

He almost laughed. "With the two of us working on it, we can make anything succeed." It sounded trite, but he believed it. They both had the passion and drive to restore Lilydale and after seeing Chelsea's lists, and project plan, if she couldn't do it, then no one could.

"When did you become the optimistic one?" she asked.

"When I met you." Chelsea had made him believe he could do anything.

She shook her head and shifted away a little, taking three small breaths.

"If I could do things differently, I would," he said, desperate for her not to shut him out.

Chelsea searched his gaze and then placed a tentative hand on his chest. "I'm scared, Ethan. I'm not sure I can handle being hurt like that again."

"I can't walk away again. Not without trying to make things right." He covered her hand with his own. "I can't promise there won't be times when we both get hurt, but I promise not to make big decisions about us without talking to you first."

She closed her eyes and Ethan held his breath, waiting

for her to decide.

Finally she opened them. "If you tried, I'd fight back this time."

Elation filled him as she leaned closer and pressed her lips against his.

The kiss was soft, hesitant at first as they explored each other's mouths, relearning their taste. He slid his arms around her waist and pulled her closer, needing to touch her, feel her warmth under his hands.

This was coming home.

She moaned and the sound sent a shot of lust straight to his groin, but before he could deepen the kiss, she stepped back. She tasted her lips and smiled. "If we keep that up, we won't get any work done."

His heart raced and hope filled him, but with it came a serving of fear. He pushed it down. "What work?"

Her laugh made him grin.

"Come on." She took his hand and led him towards the door. "If seduction is your way of distracting me, it won't work." She glanced over her shoulder. "Today." With a quick grin, she pulled him out of the house.

And in that moment, Ethan knew he had never stopped loving Chelsea McGinnis.

***

Chelsea's heart raced as she let go of Ethan's hand to open the next cabin to clean. Was she making a huge mistake letting Ethan into her heart again? She hadn't been able to resist his earnestness or his gentle touch.

She wanted to believe he was telling the truth. It made sense when she thought about the people they had been. His fear of rejection and her insistence on saying what a great home they would build together.

Perhaps neither of them had been emotionally ready for

the commitment it would take or the hard conversations they might need to have.

She could acknowledge how vulnerable she felt at the time, and how she might have doubted what Ethan was up to during the time he was away.

Her father had cheated on his wife and he'd used work as an excuse to spend time with her mother.

Chelsea sighed, trying to rein in her emotions. Though the kiss had heated her body and made her feel at home all at once, it was just a kiss. There was so much more to a relationship.

Only time would tell if they'd changed too much to make it work.

He had loved her.

Part of her was angry for the despair she'd gone through, but perhaps it had made her stronger. She was damned sure she would question any decisions going forward and not be so meek about it.

"Same deal in here?" Ethan asked. "A good airing and cleaning?"

She brought her attention back to the room and nodded. "These are the family cabins, so if I can take photos when we're done and throw up a quick website, we might get some interest from people who come down for the fair."

"Great idea."

Chelsea put on her favourite playlist and the music added cheer to what was already a good vibe. She caught Ethan mouthing the words to the songs and smiled.

He'd never liked to sing aloud because he couldn't hold a tune, but he knew all the words.

Some things didn't change.

It took only a couple of hours to clean the cabin and they moved to the next one.

As they worked, she mentally reviewed her next priority. She wanted to make sure she had a couple of social media accounts ready to go when Barry arrived. Then all they needed to do was tidy the outside and the cottages would be ready for guests.

Perhaps she'd give a restoration discount and offer a return customer discount as well. And if the social media accounts took off, she could add a page where people could donate to the restoration.

Ethan chuckled and she glanced up.

"What new idea did you just have?"

She flushed. "Just thinking about social media and bookings."

"That brain of yours is such a turn-on, Chels."

Her whole body flushed. "Don't tease."

"Trust me, I'm not teasing."

She didn't have a response. The few men she'd dated in the past said she over thought things and didn't like her lack of spontaneity. But it was hard to be spontaneous when you grew up counting every cent.

She finished cleaning the kitchen and glanced around the space. "Aunt Maggie will have linen somewhere." She hadn't found it in the rooms she'd been through, but maybe it was in the linen cupboard in the house.

"Will you make up all the beds?" Ethan asked.

"Not yet. I'll just do the cabin Barry is staying in." She'd figure out what was best as she had more guests.

Together they left the cabin and she locked it. The day had been productive. They'd cleaned the cabins inside and outside and she'd taken photos to add to her social media and website.

"What's next?" Ethan asked.

"I need to work on the marketing, so you can take a break." She was a little concerned about his limp, which had become more pronounced as the day had worn on.

"I'm good for another couple of hours," he said. "It feels great to be doing something again."

He winced as he took an awkward step.

Chelsea raised her eyebrows. "You don't look like you're good for another couple of hours."

"Nothing a couple of painkillers won't fix."

She recognised that expression. That was his stubborn, going-to-do-what-he-wanted-to-show-he-could look. "What have the doctors told you?"

He scowled. "The fracture is healed, but I'm only allowed light exercise for another month."

"Did you need crutches?"

"I had a walking frame and then a cane." He didn't glance at her.

"Did you bring your cane with you?"

He grimaced. "It's in my car."

She placed a hand on his arm. "I know you hate being injured, but pushing through it won't make it heal any faster."

"What if it never heals properly?"

She heard the fear in his voice. "Then you make the required adjustments to your life. You might not be deployed, but surely there are other roles you could go into."

"I need to protect my team." There was genuine pain in his words.

She squeezed his hand. "Tell me about them."

They climbed the stairs at the back of the house and entered through the laundry. "Dobby's my team leader. He recently got engaged. He met Mila on the mission where I got hit by the tsunami. I've never seen him happier." He grinned. "Mila's great. She called me every day when we got back to Australia and I was in hospital." He glanced at his feet. "I call her Angel because she was the one who found me in the jungle. I thought I'd died and she'd come to fetch my soul."

Chelsea ignored the flash of jealousy and focused on the important aspect. "You almost died?"

"The wave swallowed me whole and then flung me all over the place before it spat me out. I think I lost consciousness once, but I remember grabbing onto a branch which might have been what slowed me enough to escape the wave's pull back to the ocean."

Her stomach clenched at how close he'd come to dying. She brushed his shoulder to comfort herself he was still here. "You're all right now."

"Yeah. I just need to convince command I am."

She kissed his cheek and then put on the kettle and placed the packet of biscuits on the table even though it was late afternoon. She really had to find Aunt Maggie's recipe books. "I'd like to meet Mila. I'm glad you had someone to help you."

"We kept each other company while we were waiting for the team to get back." He lowered himself gingerly into a chair. "She and Dobby were talking about visiting on the weekend, if you're all right with it."

Nerves fluttered in her stomach, but she said, "Sure. That sounds nice." What would they think of her?

Ethan continued talking. "Radar doesn't suffer fools, and is happiest when we're on a mission or training."

"Radar?"

"His real name is Noah. We use nicknames on missions."

His team. That's right. "He likes action?"

Ethan paused. "He gets bored easily. Heath is the joker of the team. He sees the good in everything and everyone. He's a real protector, particularly of women and children."

Ethan smiled. "Then there's Rhys, who looks like a preppy rich kid, but he can be ruthless when he needs to be."

She imagined they could all be ruthless when required.

"Finally there's Mitch. He missed the tsunami mission because he was injured."

"What's he like?"

"He's the best of us all. Seriously good at everything, it's crazy." There was only admiration in his tone, no jealousy.

"You trust them." It wasn't a question.

"We've got each other's backs always."

Chelsea was glad he had them in his life. She poured their drinks and then sat at the table with a sigh. "I'm getting more exercise than I'm used to."

"So what about you?" Ethan asked. "Tell me about your friends."

She sipped her tea, wishing he hadn't asked. "You know Lauren, and I still keep in touch with my friend Libby from primary school."

"What about your friends in Sydney?"

What could she say? "I've been pretty busy with work." She'd tried to keep in touch with her friends from university, but she'd been the one to organise get-togethers and eventually she decided if they wanted to stay in touch, they would call her. They never did.

Ethan frowned. "What about on weekends?"

"I've worked most weekends for the past couple of months, and before that... I read a lot of books." It sounded sad when she said it out loud.

"Chelsea, surely you see people outside of work."

She nodded, not liking the incredulity on his face. "I visit Mum and the kids a couple of times a month." She sipped her tea, trying to think of a change of subject. "Do you still play football?"

He shook his head. "Not so fast, Chels. Why don't you have any friends?"

Why did he have to be so direct with his questions? She took her mug to the sink.

"Chelsea?"

The quiet, gentle way he asked made tears burn in her eyes. She swallowed. "It's not through choice. I'm just not someone who people want to hang out with." She couldn't look at him. Instead she opened a few of the top cupboards looking for Aunt Maggie's recipe books. She didn't hear him get up or walk closer, but she definitely felt his warm hands on her arms as he gently stopped her from reaching for the next cupboard and turned her around.

"Who told you that?" Though the question was quiet, there was a hardness in his eyes.

"No one. But when you're the one always making arrangements and no one calls you, you have to wonder whether they're busy, or if it's you." She shrugged. "My track record with people wanting to stay in my life is pretty dismal." And didn't that make her sound pathetic?

"Christ, Chelsea. I'm sorry for ever making you feel unwanted." Ethan rubbed her arms.

"You weren't the first." She took hold of his hands to stop him from soothing her like she was a child. "I'm reconnecting with Lauren, and when I spoke with Libby recently, she mentioned they were considering a trip back to Australia soon." Which reminded her she should tell Libby she was back in Western Australia for the foreseeable future. "I'm happy in my own company."

He nodded though he didn't seem convinced.

She smiled. "I need to get some social media done before Barry gets here. Why don't you see if the hammock will still hold your weight?"

He chuckled. "Maybe I will. Can I help you with any of

the internet stuff?"

"Are you any good with website design?"

"No, but my friend Noah is a technology whiz."

It was nice of him to offer. "It will be quicker if I do it myself." She kissed him and then shooed him towards the door. "Now, I need to work."

He gave her a salute. "Call me if you need me."

She watched him leave, her heart swelling at his easy offer.

She smiled.

Wasn't it nice she could call him now?

Chapter 12

Ethan headed for the peppermint grove, but when he reached the hammock, he couldn't stop, his brain too busy to relax. Instead he took the path through the public garden, walking slowly, trying to figure out why the sweetest woman he knew didn't have any friends.

He'd destroyed her confidence, and that was unforgivable. The fact she was even willing to give him a second chance spoke volumes to the kind-hearted person she was. Or maybe she still loved him.

No, he wouldn't get ahead of himself.

She could simply be lonely and wasn't that a fucking travesty? She should be surrounded by a solid group of friends who would drop everything to help her, like he had with his teammates.

Instead she had two childhood friends who she hadn't seen in years.

Not good enough.

He needed to prove to her she was important, worthy. He would ensure Lilydale Cottage was restored to its former glory even if he had to do all the work himself.

He spotted some flattened grass away from the path and frowned. They hadn't been over there this morning, and it hadn't been flat yesterday.

Ethan's eyes followed the trail to the north of the property where the road ran along one side. Someone had come onto the property overnight.

His muscles tensed as he scanned the trail in the other direction leading further into the garden. No one was in sight. He snapped a few photos with his phone and slowly followed the trail, searching for any evidence; a footprint, a cigarette butt, a torn bit of clothing.

He almost tripped on a sprinkler hidden under the grass and it moved easily under his foot. Ethan examined it. Definitely broken. Snapped off at the base, which would have taken more force than just tripping on it.

The path continued and stopped near the kitchen window of the house. His stomach clenched as he spotted Chelsea working at the table inside.

Whoever had come into the garden would have seen her last night.

Was it Darren, annoyed by Ethan's demand he pay back the money? Or had it been Johann wanting to keep an eye on what Chelsea was up to?

Either way, Ethan didn't like it. He'd make sure Chelsea pulled the blinds at night and he would monitor the situation tonight.

Uneasy and with his pelvis really aching now, he took Chelsea's advice and lay on the hammock.

While he lay there, he considered the garden from a defensive point of view. Where would he situate cameras to keep watch?

It was impossible to narrow down the access points because the garden butted up against bushland and the farmland, and anyone could enter from all along the fence line.

So it was a matter of considering the target.

If they wanted to spy on Chelsea, that narrowed the paths they would take around the buildings.

A camera on the barn, a cabin and the gazebo would give a good view of people coming and going.

Honeybrook didn't have an electronics store, but Pinjarra wasn't far away and he might be able to pick up a couple there.

It was too late to head there today and if he wasn't quick, he'd not make it to the grocery store to get ingredients for dinner.

He gingerly got out of the hammock.

It was time he showed Chelsea how important she was.

When he arrived back, Chelsea was still sitting at the kitchen table in front of her laptop, her fingers racing across the keyboard. She glanced up, with a moment of confusion before she recognised him. She smiled and pushed a stray bit of hair out of her eyes.

"Don't mind me. I'm going to make dinner, if it won't disturb you."

Surprise flitted across her face. "You don't have to."

"I want to." He placed the groceries on the kitchen bench and then brushed a kiss against her forehead. "I hope you still like cottage pie."

Surprise crossed her face. "It's my favourite."

"Great. Can I pour you a glass of wine?" He held up two bottles. "Red or white?"

Chelsea shook her head as if she couldn't quite believe it. "White, please."

Not good enough. She deserved to be taken care of. She should expect it. He found two wine glasses and poured the drinks. When he placed hers on the table next to her, he glanced at her screen. On it was a Lilydale restoration website showing before and after photos, but in this case, the after photos were what Darren had done to it. He skimmed the text, which told the story. Emotive and heart-felt. "That's amazing, Chels."

"It's not live yet. I need to tweak a few more things. I want to find more before photos. I had some on my phone, but I haven't gone through Aunt Maggie's laptop."

"I might have some." He grabbed his phone from his pocket and flicked through, finding some he'd taken a couple of years ago when he'd last visited Lilydale. "What's your number? I'll text them to you."

She gave it to him and he sent them.

"Do you want a hand with dinner?" she asked.

"No. I've got this. You do what you want."

She sipped her wine. "All right. I'll see if I can get this finished before dinner." By the time he returned to the kitchen, she was back at work, typing fast on her laptop, her focus on the task at hand.

Ethan smiled, loving her concentration, and got to work to provide her sustenance.

When the pie was in the oven, Ethan moved into the living room to do his rehabilitation exercises. The extra time on his feet the past two days had aggravated the ache in his pelvis. Not that he'd admit to it.

But since he'd been here, his drive to return to the army had lessened.

Suddenly he had a new focus. And she was working at the table only a few metres away.

He'd call Dobby later and ask if he was still interested in coming down this weekend. Maybe they could chat about his plans to open a security firm.

When the oven timer rang, he set the table around

Chelsea. "How's it going?"

She typed a few more things and then pressed a button with a flourish. "Done. It's live."

"That was quick. I'd love to see it." He took the pie from the oven and placed it on a pot holder on the table.

"I'll show you after dinner. That smells fantastic. Where did you learn to cook?"

"The army." He topped up her wine and added a salad to the table, while she put her laptop on the kitchen bench.

As Ethan sat, he was struck with how comfortable this felt, how right, as if he and Chelsea had been sitting down to dinner together for years.

It felt similar to sitting down to eat with his teammates—like family. He exhaled as a bolt of yearning hit him.

He hadn't wanted something so much since he was a kid. He couldn't stuff this up.

"Apart from the website, what else do you want to get done tonight?" He passed Chelsea the salad.

"I've created social media accounts on all the main platforms and I want to schedule a bunch of posts so they have content. I'm hoping when Barry comes, he'll link to them and get them in front of all his followers."

Ethan pursed his lips. "Barry the lawnmower man has a lot of followers?"

"Millions." Chelsea grinned at his disbelief. "It's quite satisfying watching him turn an overgrown mess of a garden into one that is neat and tidy."

There was something for everyone on the internet. "So what do you hope to achieve by getting a lot of followers?"

"People love a good restoration story and if they follow the journey, they'll feel a sense of ownership over it. So hopefully, when they consider where to go on holiday, they'll think about Lilydale. If it gets popular enough, I might offer workcations where they stay for free in return for helping in the garden."

He shook his head. "People do that?"

"Yeah. And when it's finished, they'll want to get married here, or have events here, because it will feel like home."

Chelsea lit up with enthusiasm as she spoke. Ethan had to hand it to her. She sold it well. Her optimism was surprising considering the way people had let her down in the past, but he loved her glow. "Let me know how I can help." Perhaps if she achieved her vision, she'd stay here.

He could get out of the army, start a business with Dobby, and live in Honeybrook with her.

"I might need you to do more filming for me."

It took a second for Ethan to come out of his fantasy. "Sure."

He'd do anything to help. Anything to make her his again.

After dinner, he cleaned the kitchen while she finished work on the social media platforms. He found the website online, and it looked incredible, with a simple reservation system for the cottages and plenty of photos of the accommodation and the garden in all its states. There was even a button to donate to the restoration. By the time he finished reading it, he wanted to support Lilydale and Chelsea's work—and he already was. She had a gift of inspiring and enticing people.

Chelsea closed her laptop with a sigh. "I'm done for the day."

It was almost eight o'clock. "Do you usually work this late?"

She nodded. "When I'm in the middle of a project, I do. There're never enough hours in the day."

He moved over to her and slid his hands onto her shoulders, giving them a light massage. Her groan made him hard.

He ignored it and continued to massage the knots in her shoulders. "Chelsea, your muscles are tight. When did you last relax?"

She leaned back into the massage. "Um, what month is it?"

"April."

"I did a Christmas in July thing with mum last year."

Ten months ago. No wonder she was so tense. "You should take better care of yourself."

"Pot, meet kettle."

He snorted. "I know my limits." It had become his mantra since the accident.

"So do I."

He continued to massage gently, and she became limp in the chair.

Finally she sat up. "You're going to put me to sleep if you keep that up."

"I'd carry you to bed and tuck you in."

She stiffened at his words.

Perhaps it was too intimate. He had to be patient. She was still getting used to the idea he had always loved her. He removed his hands and helped her to stand. "Why don't you take a shower?"

She nodded. "Go get your things. You can stay in Mum's old room rather than the barn."

"Thanks." He kept his elation to himself. Sure, she wasn't inviting him into her bed, but the fact she trusted him enough to sleep inside the house meant a lot. He waited for her to go upstairs and then returned to the barn. He packed his gear, putting his camping equipment back in the four-wheel drive and then slinging his pack with clothes onto his back. He locked the car and then examined the latch on the barn. It might be worth getting a lock while Johann was still around.

Before heading inside, he did a loop of the house and nearby garden, making sure no one was around. All the blinds were down inside the house with only a little light slipping out at the edges, but it was impossible to see inside.

As he returned to the house and locked the door behind him, he heard the shower turn off. Before heading upstairs, he checked the rest of the doors and windows were secure and then met Chelsea on the landing.

The hair around her face was damp with the rest of it tucked into a bun and she wore a cute cotton pyjama T-shirt and shorts set with a sloth on the front. He clenched his hands to stop himself from reaching for her.

"Through there." She pointed to her mother's bedroom. "I'll fetch some sheets." She trotted down the stairs, her bun swinging from side to side.

He smiled and went into the bedroom. He hadn't been in here before. Upstairs had been off-limits when he was a teenager and Aunt Maggie didn't know about the times he'd snuck into Chelsea's room at night.

He'd never been so glad she was hard of hearing and took her hearing aids out when she slept.

Chelsea had already been through the room. The dresser was dusted and clear of any knick-knacks and the double bed had been stripped of linen. A worn red rug was underneath the bed, so the person could step onto the soft carpet when they woke, rather than the wooden floorboards.

The wooden desk under the large window was also clear and dusted. Ethan walked over to peer out at the night. This room faced the public garden side, and he lowered the blind so anyone walking down the street couldn't see in.

"Here you go." Chelsea walked in and dumped the sheets on the dresser. "I think I found the full set." She pulled out a pale blue bottom sheet and found the corners.

He moved to the other side of the bed and together they fitted it and then she threw the top sheet on. When it was lined up neatly, she went to tuck it under.

"Woah." Ethan held out a hand.

"What's wrong?"

"Who taught you to make a bed?"

She screwed up her face. "I taught myself."

He shook his head. "You tuck it in like that and it will never stay tucked." The army had drilled into him how to make a bed correctly. He went around her side and hip-bumped her out of the way, showing her how to do the proper corners.

She grinned and raised her eyebrows. "I stand corrected."

Her cheeky grin loosened the restraint he held, and she gasped as he dragged her into his arms. "Are you giving me lip, soldier?"

She licked her lips, her eyes wide. "I wouldn't dare."

As much as he wanted to plunder her mouth, he relaxed his hold so she could escape if she wanted to and brushed a stray hair behind her ear. "Just for the record," he murmured. "You can give me lip, any time you want." He rubbed his thumb over her lips. "Can I kiss you?"

She took a second before she nodded.

Slowly, ever so slowly, he lowered his mouth to hers, seeing her eyelids flutter shut just as their mouths met. Soft, luscious lips tasting of mint. She must have brushed her teeth when she'd showered.

His tongue teased, and she opened for him, and they

explored each other unhurriedly.

She was everything he remembered and more. Every taste and touch sent throbbing desire through his body, imprinting on him.

Chelsea was the only one he needed.

She was the only one he wanted.

Her moan held a hint of desperation and he deepened the kiss, dragging her closer, fitting her soft body into his.

He could happily spend his entire night like this. He ran a hand down her back, over her perfectly curved buttock, and she moaned, but broke the kiss.

"Ethan... I can't. Not yet."

It took all his willpower to relax his hold and let her step away. "Too soon?"

She nodded.

He exhaled. He would give her all the time she needed, as long as she didn't walk away. "Then how about I teach you to make a bed?"

Her laugh gave him a different type of rush, one straight to his joy centre, and he grinned as he showed her what to do.

***

Chelsea woke to the sound of magpies chortling outside her window. She smiled and stretched, rolling over to look outside. A black and white bird sat on the balcony railing calling its good morning to the world. A dusky light filtered into her room telling her it wasn't long past sunrise. She snuggled deeper underneath the patchwork quilt that had been on her bed for as long as she could remember and for the first time in a long time, she felt... content. She was home in Lilydale, had a project she was excited about, a new relationship with Ethan to consider.

Everything felt right.

Their kiss last night had awoken a desire in her she'd long since thought had died, but the amount of passion scared her.

That much passion could lead to heartbreak as well.

Though lying in bed the night before, she'd decided perhaps it was better to be loved and left than never to be loved at all.

She would bet Ethan was a much better lover now than their awkward teenage moments together.

Perhaps she could give her body what it wanted.

Something to think about later, when she'd achieved her list of tasks for the day.

They'd made such great progress getting the cabins ready for guests, and while she would eventually like to update the furniture and renovate the kitchens and bathrooms, they were adequate for now.

Barry was arriving this evening and by tomorrow night, she'd be able to walk along the paths without fearing she'd tread on a snake, and she'd be able to see exactly what she was working with.

She stretched again and got up, making the bed with a smile as she did the corners as Ethan had taught her, and then quietly opened her bedroom door. Ethan was sleeping across the hall and she didn't want to wake him. His pelvis had been aching so badly last night he'd taken a painkiller to numb it. She'd make sure he didn't overdo it today—though she wasn't sure how she would stop him. Maybe there was something he could do while sitting down.

As she walked down the stairs, visions of her straddling his lap, kissing him, filled her head. She'd been so tempted to invite him into her bed last night, but her heart refused to rush things.

"Morning."

Chelsea let out a soft shriek as Ethan's greeting surprised her out of her thoughts. Her face flushed as she took him in, standing in her kitchen wearing a tight-fitting T-shirt and knee-length shorts. He held up a mug. "Coffee?"

"Yes, please." She placed a hand on her chest to calm her heart rate, but the vision of him standing in her kitchen at this time of the morning only inspired thoughts that increased it.

"I hope I didn't wake you."

She shook her head as she sat on a stool. "No, that prize went to the magpie outside my window." She smiled. "How's your pelvis?"

He glanced at her with a smirk, but said, "Not as sore today. Those tablets are pretty strong. I didn't wake once all night."

"I'm glad." She took the coffee he handed her.

"What's the plan today?"

"I want to check the road to the cottages, make sure there are no potholes which need filling, and check the gate is in good condition. If it's too difficult to open, I'll need to fix it."

"I came in that way," Ethan answered. "The gate squeaks and is stiff. Could probably do with a coat of rust inhibitor, some lubrication and then paint."

Of course. She'd forgotten his car was still parked in the barn. Chelsea unplugged her phone from where it had been charging, added the items to her list, and then flicked to the new social media channels she'd set up. A few interactions and comments, but not many. She'd finish scheduling the rest of the posts today and add some videos as well.

"I need to buy a few things for the cottages, so I'll buy paint then." Her finances weren't endless, but if Darren paid back the money her mother had given him like Ethan had asked him to, she would have sufficient funds.

And if he didn't, it just meant she had to get the cottages profitable quickly. "I want to buy a few annuals for the garden beds in front of the cottages as well, to bring some colour to them."

"I can weed them while you're gone."

Chelsea hesitated. "Should you rest today?"

Ethan glared at her. "Don't you treat me like an invalid."

She touched his arm. "I'm concerned. You were hurting last night, and you always had to prove yourself."

He squeezed her hand. "I'm fine, Chels. I'll sit on the grass while I weed."

Though she would still worry, he knew his body best. "All right." She finished her coffee. "Before I forget, I'm going to take the linen out and make the bed for Barry."

"Let me. I've seen the way you make them." He winked.

"You can help." She grabbed the linen from the cupboard and departed out the laundry door.

As she approached the cottages, the smell of manure tickled her nose. She frowned. There weren't any farms nearby and there was no breeze. She pushed past a hedge and her footsteps faltered. Ethan bumped into her and steadied them both, but she hardly noticed as she stared at the mess of the small cottage.

Both front windows had been smashed and chunks of manure were stuck to the wall.

She moved forward, but Ethan stepped in front of her. "Let me check it out."

The hardness of his tone and his alertness halted her automatic retort. Instead she said, "Do you think they're still here?"

He shook his head, but still he moved cautiously forward, scanning the surroundings.

He peered through the window, swore and turned back to her. "Call the police to report this. I'm going to check the others." He moved down the path to the other cottages while Chelsea approached the building, taking stock of what needed to be fixed. The manure was dry but shouldn't be difficult to wash off. The windows needed fixing. She peered through as Ethan had done and spotted an open bag of manure on the floor. The table next to the window was also covered in flecks of dung.

Damn.

She called the police and followed Ethan. More dung covered these cabin walls, but the windows remained intact.

She screwed up her nose as the smell reached her.

Charming.

Someone answered the phone, and she reported the incident and was told officers would be there soon.

Ethan's face was a thundercloud. "Someone's been watching us."

Chelsea frowned. "What makes you say that?"

"You can't see the cottages from the road. No one could know we spent yesterday cleaning them."

Chills ran along her arms. "I launched the website and social media last night."

He looked at her. "What are the odds someone random saw them and decided on a whim to come and undo all the work we just did?"

He was right. "You think Johann did this?"

He nodded. "Or Darren. They're the only two who would care what we're doing here."

She scanned the garden. There were plenty of places a person could hide and watch them. She rubbed her arms.

"The police are on their way."

The cottages covered in dung wouldn't be hard to clean, and Barry could stay in one of them rather than in the single cottage which had been damaged. It wouldn't cause a big delay. "It looks more like a temper tantrum."

"But someone must have carried the dung in."

She shook her head. "There were bags in the gardening shed."

Together they walked over to the shed, where the door was wide open. Sure enough, the bags of manure were missing, but nothing else had been touched.

"I'll buy a padlock when I go shopping today."

"Buy one for the barn, too."

The sound of a car had them both walking back towards the street. A police car pulled into the driveway and the man who stepped out was around their age, with black hair and a slim frame, and looked vaguely familiar. His lips broke out in a grin. "Ethan! Chelsea! What are you both doing back?"

Ethan stiffened for a second next to her and then relaxed. "Josh. Who in their right mind gave you a gun?"

He grinned. "Probably the same guy who let you into the army."

They slapped each other's backs in a man hug.

Chelsea smiled and stepped forward to hug Josh, who had been Ethan's only friend in the town. "It's good to see you." They'd spent many an afternoon at the lake together with Lauren, though Josh and Lauren had always only been friends.

"I heard what Darren did." Josh glanced around the garden. "I should have known you wouldn't let the garden go to seed, but I was busy with… other things." He frowned briefly and his next smile seemed a little forced. "When did you two get back together?"

Chelsea glanced at Ethan, not certain what to say.

"It's a new thing," Ethan said.

She gestured for Josh to follow her. "I'll show you the damage."

Josh took a kit out of the car and followed her back to the cottages. He scowled and took a couple of photos. "Could be bored kids. Did you hear anything last night?"

"Nothing," Chelsea said.

"I took a couple of painkillers and was out of it," Ethan said. "Timing is pretty coincidental to be kids. They've had a year to vandalise the property when no one was here. Why wait until Chelsea is back?"

"You've got a suspect?"

Chelsea hesitated. "There's a property developer who wanted to buy Lilydale, and I refused to sell. He was pretty angry."

"And I told Darren he had to pay back the money Chelsea's mother paid him for maintaining the garden," Ethan added. "He might be upset enough to do this."

Josh took out the fingerprint kit and dusted different areas around the door. Chelsea handed Josh the keys as he turned back to them.

He grinned. "Thanks. You were always a couple of steps in front of us."

Chelsea smiled. She'd been the organiser of the group, making sure they had food, drinks and sun cream for their outings. Those days were some of her best memories.

Before Josh stepped inside, he said, "I'll be a while here. I'll come and find you when I'm done."

"All right. I'll go take more video for online," she told Ethan.

He nodded, but made no move to join her. "I'll stay and catch up with Josh."

She frowned. More likely to discuss the incident, but

she had too much to do to worry about him being all protector right now.

She wouldn't let whoever it was halt her plan.

Not now she had a purpose.

With a wave, she went back to work.

Chapter 13

Ethan waited until Chelsea was out of earshot before he followed Josh into the cottage. It was good to see his friend again. If he'd realised Josh was part of the local police, he might have been nervous, but Josh's greeting had put him at ease. He'd always been easy-going and non-judgemental.

"Don't mess up my crime scene." Josh held up a hand to stop Ethan from entering any further.

"Any prints?"

"Some, but they're probably Chelsea's." He glanced over. "What's got you worried?"

"The property developer, Johann Mueller. He's got a mean vibe and he seemed afraid of his bosses." Ethan should have already investigated Johann's company, but he'd been distracted by spending time with Chelsea again.

"I'll look into it."

Some tension in Ethan's muscles dissipated. He was expecting to have to justify his thoughts, but perhaps their history together had Josh accepting his opinion.

"You still in the army?"

Ethan nodded and then paused. "On medical leave."

Josh stood and surveyed the cottage before turning his attention back to Ethan. "What happened?"

"Broke my pelvis."

Josh winced as he packed up his things. "That's got to hurt."

"Yeah."

"What brought you back here?" Josh walked outside.

"I came to visit Aunt Maggie."

Josh winced. "You didn't know? Shit, mate. If I'd known you still kept in touch with her, I would have tracked you down and told you."

"Not your fault. I didn't keep in touch."

The man shrugged. "You had your reasons. Honeybrook wasn't exactly kind to you."

That wasn't entirely true. "I had to make a clean break." But he had never forgotten what Aunt Maggie had done for him.

They walked through the hedges, and Ethan spotted Chelsea taking video footage with her phone over in the public area of the garden. Her hair was loose for the first time, flowing past her shoulders. She wore a shirt with kind of frilly sleeves and a navy-blue skirt and was smiling and gesturing while she spoke.

She looked happy and comfortable.

"Chelsea looks as if she's done well for herself," Josh commented.

Ethan nodded. "She's some kind of media publicity person now. She's working with Lauren to promote the Honeybrook Fair and she's recording the restoration of Lilydale on social media in the hopes of bringing more people to the area."

"I hope she succeeds. Honeybrook needs a break."

Ethan frowned. "Why is it so bad?"

Josh shrugged. "Not enough jobs. None of our generation stayed and stores can't make a profit. There are some farmers who are still doing well, but few people come through town now the new highway gets you down south faster, and fewer stop."

Ethan hadn't cared for the town, but if Chelsea was to be successful, it needed to bounce back. "Those campgrounds still open around the lake?"

"Yeah, but they're not in good condition. Someone trashed the toilets out there and the council doesn't have the funds to repair them."

"Shame." They'd spent some fun weekends camping by the lake. Usually it was when his foster parents thought he was working at Aunt Maggie's.

Chelsea spotted them and waved, walking towards them with a smile.

Damn. He'd missed her smile, the way it lit up her face and made him feel about ten-feet tall, because she was genuinely happy to see him.

Josh laughed and shoulder bumped him. "Glad to see some things haven't changed. You still get that goofy look on your face when you see Chelsea."

Ethan didn't deny it. "She always was the best thing to happen to me."

"Thanks, mate."

Ethan grinned. "But you were my first real friend." He sobered. "Sorry I didn't keep in touch."

"Don't sweat it."

They fell silent as Chelsea approached. "You two look like you're up to no good."

"I was just telling Ethan how good it is to see you both," Josh said as they followed her back towards the house.

"Did you find anything?"

"Got some prints, but they might be yours. Can you come to the station later so I can check?"

"Sure. I need to do some shopping, so I'll drop by then. Can I get you a coffee?"

Josh eyed her coffee maker draining on the sink as he got out his notebook. "If it's proper coffee, you can." After she laughed, he said, "Tell me more about the property developer."

While Chelsea told Josh about Johann, Ethan made his friend a coffee and then told him about his interaction with Darren.

When they were done, Josh said, "I have to be honest with you. Unless the prints aren't yours, there's nothing tying either of them to the vandalism. However I want you to keep me informed about any further interactions with them."

Chelsea nodded. "Can I clean the cottages now?"

"Yeah. I'm done with them." He finished his coffee. "Thanks. Hopefully I'll see you around town." There was a slight wistfulness about Josh's tone.

Ethan hadn't thought about his friend much over the years, because so many of his memories of Josh were tied up with Chelsea, but it sounded as if Josh needed someone to talk to.

Ethan clapped him on the shoulder. "We should go for a beer."

"That would be great." A smile and a flash of relief.

Yeah, he would definitely make time for his old friend. His childhood was long behind him now and there was nothing he needed to hide from. He'd made something of himself.

When the police car drove away, he turned to Chelsea. "Should we clean the cabins?"

She chuckled. "Absolutely."

He took her hand, and they got back to work.

***

It was almost dark when Barry arrived from Perth. Chelsea opened the newly oiled gate and directed the middle-aged man, who was still wearing his high-vis work gear, to the barn where he could lock his car up for the night. He whistled as she took him to the freshly cleaned cottage. "This place must have been amazing when it was in its prime."

Chelsea nodded. "It was. That's why I want to restore it. My great aunt would have hated to see it like this."

Barry dumped his bag inside the cottage and ran his hand through his thick dark hair. "Why don't you take me for a tour before it gets dark? That way I can plan my shots tonight and figure out where to start."

"Sure." She pointed out the different pathways through the garden and the areas that had been lawn.

"Any sprinklers?"

"Probably, but I don't know where or if they're still working. If you break any, we'll fix them."

He took notes as he went, asking a few questions as Chelsea showed him where the garden beds had been.

When they were done, she asked, "How long do you think it will take?"

He pursed his lips. "If there aren't too many tangled surprises amongst the tall grass, it should only take a day to uncover the paths." He shrugged. "Then maybe another day to hack back the lawn. I've got a colleague heading down tomorrow to help out."

She shook her head, amazed so much could be done in such a short time. The weeds and long grass felt insurmountable. "I can't tell you how much I appreciate you coming at short notice."

He grinned. "I like a good challenge and my followers love the more difficult gardens. They'll love this."

Chelsea smiled. "I'd like to share your videos on my social media. I've only just created accounts for Lilydale, but I have a few followers."

"Of course. I'm happy to cross-promote."

"Thank you." They returned to his cottage. "There aren't many places to get dinner in Honeybrook," she said. "You're welcome to join us at the house. We're making pizzas."

Barry smiled. "Thanks. I'll freshen up and be over in half an hour?"

"Sure." Chelsea returned to the house where Ethan had already chopped toppings for the pizzas. He looked up as she walked in. "How did it go?"

Seeing him in her kitchen preparing food for them both sent her heart soaring. "Great. Barry thinks it will take him only a day or two to do everything."

He raised his eyebrows. "Impressive. Is he coming for dinner?"

"Yeah, he's cleaning up." She appreciated that Ethan hadn't felt the need to join her when she greeted the man and took him around the garden. She poured them both a glass of wine and her phone rang.

"Hey, Lauren."

"Hey. I heard Josh visited you today. I wanted to make sure it was a social visit and there was nothing wrong."

Chelsea didn't bother asking who she'd heard it from. "As lovely as it was to see him again, it wasn't social. Someone vandalised the cottages we'd just finished cleaning."

Lauren gasped. "That's awful. Do you need help with anything?"

"No. It didn't take long to clean up, and I managed to

sweet talk the glass fitter in Pinjarra to come out and replace the broken glass."

"Do you know who did it?"

"No." She changed the subject, not wanting to talk about her suspicions of Johann and Darren. "Were you able to authorise me to your social media?"

"Yeah. That was the other reason I called. But I feel bad about this, Chelsea. We can't pay you for your work."

"I'm happy to do it."

"If you're sure. I'll email it to you now, but if you don't get time, that's fine."

Chelsea glanced out the window as Barry walked towards the house. "I've got to go. The lawnmower guy you suggested is here for dinner."

"Did he agree to do Lilydale?"

"Yeah. He's starting tomorrow."

"I'll have to drop by after work to check it out."

"See you then." She hung up and went to let Barry in. She made the introductions and left Barry and Ethan to make the pizzas while she reviewed the links Lauren had sent her.

They used scheduling software so she could upload all the posts at once and they'd be posted on different days. Chelsea sorted the posts into groups. By the time she was done, Ethan was setting the table around her again.

She flushed. "Sorry. Lauren sent me some things for the campaign." She turned to Barry, who had a beer in his hand. "I'm doing some work for the local council to promote the annual fair. It hasn't been doing well over the past few years."

"I remember the Honeybrook Fair," he said. "My parents used to bring us down for the day. It was always fun."

"It's at the end of the month if you want to relive the

nostalgia," Chelsea told him.

He nodded. "I might. The kids would love it and with it being the end of the school holidays, they'll be bored with all the usual things."

She hadn't considered the school holidays. She made a note to check the start date. "I could give you a discount on the family cabin if you want to make a weekend of it."

Barry laughed. "You don't need my help with promotion. You're a born sweet-talker, but I'll take you up on the offer. Book me in."

Chelsea grinned as a thrill passed through her at having her first paying customer. She entered his details in the booking system and sent him an email confirmation with payment details and then packed up her laptop as the pizzas came out of the oven and they sat down to chat about the plan of action for tomorrow.

By the time Barry left for the night, she was more confident in her ability to make Lilydale work.

Ethan had already cleaned the kitchen and was locking the back door as she closed the front door behind Barry.

It was comforting to have someone help her check the house was secure.

Everything about Ethan felt comforting and right.

He came back into the room and his gaze centred on her—direct, encompassing, like she was his entire world.

She hadn't felt like that since they were together as teenagers.

And therein lay the problem.

As much as she wanted to run into his arms and forget about all the heartache he'd caused her, she couldn't. It would be foolish not to go into this expecting some sort of heartbreak. They didn't even live in the same state.

But she longed to have him hold her in his arms again and kiss her senseless.

She'd dreamed of waking up in his arms for more than a decade.

Could she give herself the physical aspect while protecting her emotional self?

"You're doing a lot of thinking over there." Ethan stayed at the base of the stairs, his hand on the banister.

She nodded.

"Chels, I'm not expecting anything from you. I know I hurt you and it will take time to trust me again—if you trust me at all. I'll take whatever you're willing to give me."

Of course she trusted him. She trusted him in all things, except maybe her heart. But there was no reason she couldn't enjoy his friendship and his body until her heart had time to be convinced.

Heart pounding, she walked towards him and slipped her hand into his. Without words, they climbed the stairs together and in the corridor outside their bedrooms they paused.

Ethan watched her patiently, waiting.

Letting her decide their future this time.

With a gentle tug, she pulled him into her bedroom. It had always been Ethan for her.

Chapter 14

Chelsea turned to Ethan and slid her hands up his chest to circle the back of his neck. His hands slid gently around her waist, his eyes searching hers.

She smiled at him. "I trust you, Ethan. I want to see if we've both improved at this since we were younger."

His chuckle sent a shot of heat through her. "I can guarantee I've improved from the nervous, fumbling teenager I was back then."

She raised her eyebrows. "Prove it."

"With pleasure." His lips touched hers, firm and persuasive, teasing, tempting her to open for him. She willingly did, tasting him, a taste as familiar to her as the coffee she drank every morning. They'd spent hours making out as teenagers and fumbling with clothes, hormones ready, but not sure what to do.

This kiss had none of the messy fumbling, but all the desire as she rose to her toes and met kiss for passionate kiss.

She ran her hands through his short hair as his fingers brushed her waist at the spot her shirt met her waistband, teasing them both.

"More." She tried to pull away so she could remove her shirt, but Ethan wouldn't let her go.

"Give me a second, Chels. I'm struggling between wanting to devour you in seconds and savouring you for hours." He kissed slowly down her neck. "I've dreamed about making love to you in so many ways for years. I want to do them all at once and I don't want to stuff up this first time we're together again."

His confession tamped some of the urgency zinging through her body but only ramped up her desire for him. She arched her neck to give him better access and groaned as his tongue tickled her sensitive skin. "I vote for all the ways. We've got all night."

He groaned and captured her lips again, drawing her closer, and shifting them back towards the bed. She slid her hands up his back, feeling his warm, hard muscles under her fingertips. So much harder than the lean teen he had been, and infinitely more so than the few other men she'd been with over the years.

Every inch of him was a warrior.

The back of her legs hit the bed, and he held her steady so she didn't fall. His fingers deftly undid the buttons of her shirt until it gaped open. He pushed it off her shoulders and she let go of him long enough to let it fall away.

His hands cupped her breasts, thumbs rubbing her already peaked nipples through her sensible cotton bra. Fire raced through her, heating her core as he dipped his head to take one nipple into his mouth.

She moaned, feeling his hardness pressed against her.

"You're beautiful, Chelsea." He unclasped her bra and then his fingers and mouth were against her flesh.

Holy mother. Her whole body felt as if it was about to

combust. She rubbed against him as her hands struggled to lift his shirt.

He drew back for only long enough to strip off his top before gathering her into his arms. He started to lower them to the bed and paused, a laugh escaping him.

Chelsea blinked. "What?"

Before she could process, he picked her up, and she wrapped her legs around his waist.

"Our first time might have been in that single bed, but we can do better this time around."

She chuckled. Of course. She hadn't even processed that in her desire for him. He carried her across the hall to his room and she used the opportunity to nibble on his neck and rub her aching parts against his.

His breath panted as he lowered her onto the double bed. "You're killing me, Chels." He made quick work of undoing her skirt, and it fell to the floor.

She lay on the bed in her underpants as he stepped out of the rest of his clothing.

Wow. Ethan had filled out in all the right places. Her eyes scanned his body, noting scars which hadn't been there before. She'd ask him about them later, but right now, she wanted his body against hers.

She held up her arms to bring him in and he grinned, climbing onto the bed, but staying down by her crotch. His fingers brushed her dampness, and she arched her hips, needing more.

"I've dreamt about your taste." He dipped a finger underneath the hem of her underpants. "Wondered whether it was as incredible as I remember." He brushed her clitoris and then went lower, sliding between her wetness.

Chelsea gasped. "More."

He nodded. "There's so much more I'm going to do

with you." He brought his finger to his mouth and sucked, his eyes closing as he savoured her taste.

Chelsea hadn't thought she could be more aroused, but she was wrong.

He groaned and opened his eyes. "You taste better than I remembered." In an instant, he slid her panties down and threw them on the floor. Then he settled between her legs and licked her long and slowly.

Shots of pleasure filled her, and she moaned. "Please."

He licked her again, and then again, taking his time as the desire built inside her. She needed him, wanted to feel him inside of her. "Please," she begged, unable to form more words.

He slid two fingers inside her and she tried to arch off the bed, but he pinned her to it, slowly licking and thrusting his fingers at the same pace as the sweet agony of pleasure increased. "More."

"You'll get more," he murmured, the vibrations of his voice adding to the sensations. "But first I need you to come for me, honey." He thrust and licked her again, and she was caught in his thrall. Another lick and thrust. "Come for me."

She was helpless to refuse his demand. The wave of pleasure peaked, and she cried out as her orgasm swept through her body, over and over again as he touched her.

She gasped, her breaths nothing but pants as she climaxed and came down.

Ethan withdrew his fingers and licked his lips. "Better than all my fantasies." He slid up her body, kissing her as he went, and drew her into his arms. His grin was playful. "Better than the last time we did this?"

Chelsea didn't have the energy to laugh. "Are you done?"

His grin turned wicked. "Not even close." His next kiss

was demanding, drawing more from her and she clung to him as the heat built again.

"I ache for you, Chelsea."

"Then take what you want."

He groaned as he shifted, grabbed a condom out of the pocket of his pants, and slid it on. He covered her with his body again, holding himself just above her. "Are you sure?"

"Yes. Please. I need all of you."

He slid into her, filling her, and she arched into him. The feel of his weight against her, his body inside her was exquisite. She raised her hips, encouraging him to move.

"Give me a minute, honey. I'm savouring the moment. I never thought I'd be here again and you feel so much better than I remember."

His words filled her with another kind of pleasure, the type which fed the centre of her mind and heart.

Then he moved, slowly at first, drawing out each stroke. He kissed her chest, her neck and finally her lips, and the depth of his passion soothed her. She met him kiss for kiss, thrust for thrust, as the tempo increased.

He lifted her hips so the angle rubbed against all her pleasure receptors and her climax built. "Yes."

"Come for me again, honey."

His order, followed by a deep thrust, tipped her over the edge and her orgasm exploded from her. He groaned as his climax followed, pleasure covering his face.

When they were done, he collapsed next to her on the bed, pulling her close.

Chelsea smiled at his heavy breathing, glad she wasn't the only one overcome. She kissed the base of his neck. "I'd say we've both improved a little."

His choked laugh sent love careening through her body, and she grinned.

***

The scent of wood smoke tickled Ethan's nose, and he woke. It took him a second to realise he was in the spare bedroom and he held Chelsea in his arms. He smiled, snuggling in as the smell hit him again. He frowned. Definitely smoke.

At this time of year it shouldn't be a bush fire, but the bush did border them on two sides. He slipped out of bed and padded naked to the window, pulling the blind aside to look out.

Bright orange flames greeted him, moving across the overgrown grass. Fuck. "Chelsea!" He dragged on his pants and slapped on a light to find his shirt.

"What?" She bolted upright in bed, blinking, her eyes blurry with sleep.

"The garden's on fire. I need you to call the fire brigade." He slid on his shoes as she nodded and threw back the sheets, grabbing her phone and glancing towards the window. She reached for her shirt.

"Fire brigade first," he ordered. "Then come and grab a hose."

He thundered down the stairs, struggling for a moment to unlock the back door, and then raced around the corner of the house to where the garden hose was kept.

It wasn't there.

He swore, frantically looking around. He'd used it two days ago to water some of the garden beds he'd weeded, and there was no reason for Chelsea to have moved it.

The smoke was thicker here and heat already radiated from the flames.

But there was another hose closer to the fire, on the corner of the main house garden and the public area. He plunged through the tall grasses and found it in place. Quickly he turned the tap and to his relief, water poured out. He directed the spray on the grass in front of him, wetting it down as he moved towards the high, out of control flames.

Mother nature out of control.

Just like the tsunami.

His feet locked and his chest tightened as he struggled to move forward towards the danger.

There was no way to control the fire.

He was at its mercy.

A shout broke through the haze of panic. He turned his head.

Barry ran towards him. He'd forgotten about the lawnmower man.

"Where's the ride-on mower?" Barry shouted.

The question shocked him out of his fear. If they could cut a fire break, it would slow the flames. The volunteer fire-fighters would take at least half an hour to get here. He thrust the hose at Barry. "I'll get it."

And start the sprinklers. No telling what condition they were in, but they might work.

He headed for the barn first, ignoring the relief filling him that he was running away from danger. He was helping here as well. As he ran he spotted Chelsea dragging another hose from the other side of the house.

Shit. He couldn't let her close to the flames. He had to move fast. Get between her and the danger.

He pushed himself harder.

This was no accidental fire. They'd done nothing on that side of the garden today and as far as he knew, there was nothing over there that would spontaneously combust.

He should have kept watch again instead of falling asleep in Chelsea's arms.

He unlocked the barn's combination lock and ran to the reticulation panel. The first five stations were on the public side of the garden and he switched on the station between the fire and the house. It would then cycle to the station closest to the house.

He took two seconds to relock the barn in case the arsonist was still around, then headed for the garden shed.

He swung both doors wide, relieved he'd serviced the equipment already. The mower started first go, and he drove it down the path, through the gap in the hedges and towards the flames.

It might have been years since he'd last mowed the lawn at Lilydale, but the shape of the garden was imprinted in his memory. He lowered the blades and cut a straight swathe through the long grass, the flames racing closer. Across the garden, several trees were engulfed, including a couple of eucalyptus.

He hoped they didn't explode.

But at least some sprinklers had come on, spreading water across the garden.

Ethan steered as close as he dared to the front of the flames, coughing at the smoke, keeping his face turned away from the flames, and then did another pass, and another, each one giving Barry and Chelsea a layer of protection.

Finally he heard the wail of the fire engine as he finished cutting the grass he could reach. Barry had found a shovel from somewhere and was digging a trench through the freshly mowed grass, so there was no fuel for the fire and Chelsea was fighting to keep the flames from the house.

The engine parked close to the house and within minutes was connected, and a deluge of water was drenching the flames.

Ethan parked the mower out of the way and ran back to Chelsea. Tears welled in her eyes, but it could have been because of the smoke, or because the garden was burning.

Already the fire-fighters had doused the leading edge where it had been creeping along the trench they had cut, stopping it from getting any closer to the house.

However the Japanese pagoda was engulfed in flames and he couldn't see how close the fire had got to the Sydney Harbour Bridge replica.

"The fire-fighters have this side." He took the hose from her hands. "We can check the other side."

Chelsea nodded and he turned off the hose, coiling it, and together they moved back to the hose he'd originally been using. Further around the garden, Barry was still digging a trench to stop the blaze from spreading to the north.

Every instinct in Ethan screamed at him to get Chelsea out of there. "Come on, you can wait on the road by the fire truck." He grabbed her arm, but she shook it loose.

"I'm not leaving."

Again his chest tightened and his hands shook, but he recognised her determination. Where was the safest place for her? Ethan pointed towards Barry. "Fine. Drag the hose over there." He turned it on and helped her pull the hose through the remaining long grass to the other edge of the fire. "Have you got it?"

She nodded again.

He didn't like her silence. He gave her a quick hug. "It will be all right, Chelsea. We'll stop it."

Her exhale was shaky, but she glanced at him. "I know."

Good. "I'll get another shovel and help Barry." He jogged back to the garden shed, his eyes adjusting to the darkness after the glow of the fire. It was impossible to spot anyone who might be watching their efforts.

When it grew light, he'd call Josh and ask if he'd had

any luck with the fingerprints or discovering whether Darren or Johann had alibis.

And then he'd invite Dobby and his team down for the weekend. They would set up watch to make sure nothing happened tomorrow night.

The doors of the shed were still wide open, and he grabbed a shovel and hoe and returned to the fire. From the north side, he spotted the fast attack vehicle on the western boundary, spraying the flames, stopping them from spreading across the road to neighbouring houses.

People had come out of their houses to watch the spectacle. Some had found tools of their own and had joined Barry digging the trench, while others had garden hoses that stretched just far enough across the road to wet down the vegetation that hadn't burnt yet.

Ethan was thankful it was a still night. The smoke hung around, but at least the fire wasn't being fed by the wind.

He dug until the anxiety faded, his muscles burned and the break reached the road before he stopped. The flames were lower now, not as intense, and the glow on the horizon was the sun waking.

No trees or structures burned, and the grass was blackened and smoking, with just patches still alight. The fire-fighters had the blaze under control. He moved back to the house, searching for Chelsea. Barry stood back against the hedge watching the final flames being doused, and Chelsea was talking to a firefighter who was about their age. He joined her and slipped a hand around her waist. She leaned into him.

"Zach found the source of ignition," Chelsea said. "There's accelerant. It was deliberately lit."

Though he'd guessed that was the case, anger rushed into him. "Have you called the police?"

Zach nodded, removing his helmet and wiping the

sweat from his forehead. "Josh will be here soon. I was telling Chelsea we should be done in about half an hour. I'll leave a team here to monitor for an hour or so, in case something flares up."

"Can I get your men something to drink or eat?" Chelsea asked.

Zach smiled. "We're all good. Always bring plenty of water with us. Why don't you go inside and rest, and I'll let Josh know where you are when he arrives?"

Chelsea looked dead on her feet. "Good idea," Ethan said.

He led her back to the house, stopping to speak to Barry. "Thanks for your help. Why don't you clean up and then come get some coffee at the house?"

"Coffee sounds amazing. Then we can see if there's anything left for me to work with."

They turned back to the blackened mess of the garden. There were undamaged patches but it still wasn't bright enough to see everything.

"Come on." Ethan nudged Chelsea and they returned to the house. They both smelled of smoke. "Shower first."

Chelsea moved where he led her, her gaze dim. "You OK, Chels?"

She shook her head. "Do you think Johann or Darren did this?"

"Unless you've got any other enemies we don't know about, I think there's a good chance it was one or both of them."

"Why would anyone be so greedy?"

It wasn't a question he could answer, so he directed her into the bathroom and helped her out of the T-shirt and pants she'd thrown on with no underwear. His body responded, but he ignored it as he turned on the water to the right temperature.

He undressed and then pulled her in with him, lathering her with soap and massaging her shoulders. "We'll find who did this, Chelsea."

"What are they going to try next?"

"I don't know." But he appreciated the fact she realised they wouldn't stop. "I'll invite my team down to help me keep an eye on things."

"I can't ask them to give up their weekend."

"You're not asking, I am. They'll be more than happy to help." He poured shampoo into her hair and lathered it, taking the time to massage her scalp before letting her rinse while he washed his own. Then he added the conditioner to her hair to soak in and turned her to face him. "I've got this, Chelsea. I won't let them destroy Lilydale." He kissed her.

"I'm scared," she said. "If you hadn't woken, the house might have caught fire."

He was well aware of that, but he kept his words light. "Special forces, remember? We sleep light."

A ghost of a smile flickered across her lips and he kissed them. "Soak for as long as you need, Chelsea. I'll make coffee and wait for Josh."

She grabbed his hand before he could leave the shower. "Thank you, Ethan."

He kissed her hand, keeping his anger from his face. "You're welcome. I'll see you downstairs."

He dressed in his room, letting the fury at what could have happened flow through him, and picked up his phone. Dobby answered on the first ring. "What's wrong?"

"I need your help."

"Where and when?"

Ethan smiled. Whoever was terrorising Lilydale was in for a big surprise.

Chapter 15

Chelsea trudged down the stairs, her body heavy, head foggy. The shower had helped, but the stench of smoke was embedded in her nostrils and she only needed to glance outside to see the blackened remains of the garden.

Maybe it was a blessing in disguise. Perhaps the fire had killed the weeds and left her with garden beds ready for planting.

A fresh start.

Over the smell of smoke came another aroma, that of freshly made coffee, and warmth infused her as she spotted Ethan in the kitchen making coffee. Josh was already seated at the table dressed in his police uniform, drinking his first cup, and Barry was also there.

This wasn't what he'd signed up for. "Thank you for your help, Barry."

He glanced up. "No problem. It's such a shame so much of the garden burned."

"I won't hold it against you if you would prefer to head straight back to Perth this morning."

He straightened. "Are you kidding? It's more of a

challenge now. Ethan tells me this isn't the first thing to go wrong. If I can highlight the issue, whoever is doing it might think twice."

Chelsea felt a little of the tension dissipate. "Thank you." She could do with the exposure for her Lilydale social media profiles.

Ethan handed her a mug of coffee and kissed her cheek. "Feeling any better?"

"A little." She sat at the table and smiled at Josh. "Sorry for getting you out of bed so early."

He grinned. "You provide the best coffee in town, so I'm not complaining."

Chelsea pursed her lips. "Isn't there a coffee shop?"

"The bakery sells coffee, but it's terrible."

She pulled out her phone and made a note to investigate having a coffee van come to the garden once a week when it was ready to open to the public.

Ethan sat next to her. "At the rate you're going, this is going to be a never-ending project."

She sighed. "If it ever gets off the ground." They needed to catch who was doing this.

"Did you get any hits from the prints?" Ethan asked Josh.

"They matched Chelsea." He gave an apologetic look. "Tell me what happened last night. Barry, why don't you start?"

"Something woke me," he said. "At first I thought it was a possum on the roof, but I saw a shadow go past the window."

Ethan leaned forward. "Did you get a look?"

Barry shook his head. "By the time I pulled the curtain aside, whoever it was had gone. Then I noticed a flickering light in the garden. I realised it was flames, so I dressed and ran outside. That's when I noticed you looking for the hose."

Ethan nodded. "It wasn't where it was supposed to be. Chelsea, did you move the one by the house?"

"No."

So whoever had lit the fire had made sure they wouldn't have easy access to a way of putting it out. Luckily because of the size of the garden, there were multiple taps and hoses.

Josh turned to her. "When did you wake?"

She gestured to Ethan. "He woke me." Her face flushed as she remembered what they'd done last night.

"The smell of smoke woke me about four thirty," Ethan said. "I peered out the window and saw the flames, told Chelsea to call the fire brigade and raced out there to fight the fire."

"Did you see anyone?"

"No."

Josh made some notes. "I'm going to look around and talk to the arson investigator. I'll ask you to all stay in here until I've searched for footprints and any other evidence."

Chelsea nodded. "Of course. Can I offer you breakfast before you go?"

He got to his feet. "The coffee's enough for now."

She walked him to the door and watched as he greeted a female officer who had arrived on the scene.

"It will take a couple of hours for the burnt ground to be cool enough for me to work there, so I'll start near the cabins when Josh gives the all-clear," Barry said.

"Thank you." She sat back at the table as Ethan took eggs out of the fridge.

"Bacon and eggs for breakfast?"

"OK," she replied, though she wasn't hungry.

Someone was determined to destroy Lilydale and her chance at a new life.

She had to figure out how to stop them.

***

It was a couple of hours before Josh returned to the house. Chelsea lit candles to counteract the stench of smoke and spent the time scheduling posts for both the Honeybrook Fair and for Lilydale, as well as contacting media outlets to promote the fair, while Ethan chatted to Barry.

"The fire was started by petrol." Josh sighed. "Any traces of the person have been burned away by the fire." He looked weary.

"What about by the cottages?" Ethan asked.

"Not a lot there either. Some squashed grass, but not enough to get a footprint from."

Chelsea smiled. "Thanks for trying."

After he left, and Barry went to get ready, she turned to Ethan. "Why would someone light the fire on the north-west side of the property and then head east, away from the roads?" It had been bothering her all morning.

He smiled. "Do you think the lake trail is still there?"

"It might be. Aunt Maggie liked her evening walks by the lake." With it only a twenty-minute walk away, she and Ethan had sometimes slipped away from the garden to swim there with Josh and Lauren.

"I'll check it out while you and Barry do your social media thing."

She frowned. "Will you be safe? Maybe you should wait for your friends to arrive."

He stood and pulled her to her feet, brushing a kiss against her lips with such tenderness she almost forgot what she'd asked him. "I love that you're concerned, but I'll be fine. The culprit is long gone and I'll be careful."

She couldn't erase the thought of someone hiding behind a bush ready to attack, though she knew it was highly unlikely. "Take your phone with you," she ordered. "And tell me if you find anything." She didn't want to lose him so soon after he was back in her life.

"Of course." He kissed her again. "You go slay your videos. You look gorgeous."

She smiled and ran a hand down the colourful summer dress she'd picked up from the op shop when she'd last gone into town. So much more casual than her usual business attire and it made her feel lighter, more relaxed. More like the Chelsea she could be whenever she was at Lilydale, not the Chelsea trying hard to please everyone.

He strode across the garden towards the cabin and out of view and Chelsea picked up her video camera and phone. She'd made a list of the videos she wanted to take, including some showing the damage from the fire and talking about the vandalism. It was doubtful it would stop Johann if he was responsible, but it felt good to be talking about it.

Chelsea spent the first few hours taking videos and helping Barry, moving the camera when it needed to be moved, carting the clippings to the compost heap, and bringing him drinks and food. They'd agreed he would be the one to do the before and after video reveals of the garden, but she could take photos of the progress.

He worked fast. Far faster than she'd expected, but all she'd had to do was show him which way the paths went and he ripped through it with his whipper-snipper and edger. His colleague, a guy who wasn't far out of his teenaged years, rode the lawnmower, taking several passes to get the grass low enough. By mid-day, all the paths on the private and cabins side of the garden were clear, and the lawn had been mowed. It wasn't pretty with the grass yellow and bare in patches, but it was far more accessible and the garden beds had been redefined.

He'd revealed the bones Chelsea was working with.

When Ethan returned, they were filming, so he pointed towards the house. She nodded. There wasn't much he could do with cameras all around.

As Barry packed up his things, Chelsea said, "Let's break for lunch."

"Sounds great."

Ethan was in the house putting the final touches on a platter of sandwiches.

Her steps slowed. How incredibly thoughtful. She hadn't asked him to prepare lunch. It warmed her heart. She kissed him and asked, "Did you find anything?"

"The lake trail is still there. I told Josh."

Hope filled her. "Good. Maybe he can find a clue at the lake."

Ethan nodded, but his sceptical expression told her that he doubted it.

Something had to lead back to whoever was doing this. She wouldn't let them win.

After lunch they moved to the burnt public side of the garden. The smell of smoke lingered, and Chelsea braced herself as she walked through the hedge.

Blackened grass everywhere. Her chest tightened and she swallowed hard. It would regrow. Fire was a trigger for a lot of native plants to bloom. This might all be a great blessing.

She almost convinced herself. She took the main path, pointing details out to Barry. The Japanese pagoda was a smouldering mess, but the fire had stopped short of the native garden. The area around the dry harbour lake had all been burnt, but the metal structure of the Sydney Harbour Bridge replica remained intact.

Cupid was covered in blackened ash, but the pruned

rose bushes looked intact.

The peppermint grove with the hammock underneath had avoided damage.

It could have been so much worse. Some of the tension lifted from her. Most of the damage had been to the lawn, and the overgrown garden beds they would have had to weed anyway. She smiled. Johann would be annoyed.

"Might be good to keep an eye out when I get started," Barry said. "Just in case there are any embers underneath that I uncover by mowing or blowing."

"I'll do that," Chelsea said. "You get your things, and I'll film the video footage I need before you start."

Ethan stepped back under a peppermint to watch while she did her pieces to camera. She did half a dozen, taking in different parts of the garden, wanting to make sure she had something suitable.

"I'm done."

Barry and his colleague carried the equipment through the hedges, and two four-wheel drives pulled into her driveway, one black and one white. She shaded her eyes as five very fit men got out, each scanning the area as if by habit. The last person to get out was a short woman who wrapped her arm around a stocky man with a well-trimmed beard who was slightly shorter than the others. Ethan pushed away from the tree with a grin.

"They're early."

His teammates. A bundle of nerves swept over her. These were the men who meant the most to Ethan.

What if they didn't like her, or think she was good enough for him? No one except Ethan and her mother had ever thought she was good enough.

She brushed a stray hair behind her ear.

Ethan held a hand out to her. "Come on. I'll introduce you."

"Ah, why don't you show them to the cabins and I'll join you later?"

He frowned. "What's wrong?"

She waved a hand. "I should take more shots. I don't want to get in the way of your reunion."

Ethan stepped closer, pulling her into his arms. "Why are you nervous?"

Honesty. That's what she'd wanted from Ethan and so she had to give him the same. "They're your brothers, Ethan. They may not like me."

"They will love you, because I love you. They'll be thrilled we're back together."

She stepped back. He'd said the 'L' word.

How could he drop it so casually into the conversation? This wasn't the right time. She hadn't figured out everything yet. She couldn't rush this. Not this time.

There was too much at stake.

But she had to say something. She grabbed onto the other part of his statement. "They know about me?"

"Yeah." He smiled, not seeming at all concerned she hadn't said the words back. "We know everything about each other. It's part of our bond." He brushed a kiss on her forehead. "Mila's here too, and you said you wanted to meet her."

The woman who had saved him after the tsunami. Yeah, Chelsea wanted to thank her.

She let out a deep breath. "All right. Lead the way."

***

The group was gathered by the fence line, surveying the damage with varying levels of displeasure on their faces.

Formidable was the word that came to Chelsea's mind.

As she and Ethan walked out from under the shade of the peppermints, the group turned as one to watch them.

Ethan raised a hand in greeting and Mila waved back, but the men gave various versions of a nod.

Mila was petite with her long, brown hair tied back in a ponytail. She wore jeans, a casual T-shirt and sneakers.

The man with his arm around Mila's waist had to be Dobby, and the blond with the preppy look must be Rhys, but she couldn't pick the others from Ethan's descriptions of them.

As they approached the group, Ethan let go of her hand and hugged Dobby. "Thanks for coming."

"Looks like you need a hand."

Ethan nodded. "This is Chelsea."

Dobby grinned, turning his severe expression into one of friendliness. "It's great to meet you finally. I'm Dobby. This is Mila."

Before Chelsea could respond, the tall blond man stepped forward with a smile. "Ethan failed to convey how beautiful you are."

Ethan backhanded him playfully. "This lothario is Rhys, the sweet talker of the group."

Chelsea smiled. "What did he say?"

"A few things." A man of Middle Eastern descent stepped up. "I'm Heath, and these other two are Noah—" The tall man with long, dark hair tucked into a man bun and a bushy beard raised his hand— "and Connor. He's our dog-whisperer." Shortblond hair, lankier than the others, with an easy smile.

"Mitch had a family thing," Dobby said, and the rest of the men scowled.

Chelsea glanced at Ethan, but he didn't explain the issue. "Nice to meet you all. Why don't you come inside?" She led them towards the house and Mila fell into step beside her.

"I don't want to sound weird, but I'm so thrilled to

meet you. Ethan spoke of you a lot during his rehabilitation and I feel like I know you already. I'm glad you got back in touch."

This woman had saved Ethan's life. "I'm glad he was around to reconnect. Thank you for saving him."

Mila waved her hand. "I didn't really. I just found him after the tsunami receded and showed the team where he was. They carried him to safety before the next wave hit."

Chills ran through Chelsea. "It was that bad?"

Mila nodded. "It's not a day I like to remember."

Chelsea squeezed her hand and then led them into the house via the front door. She switched on the kettle. "Tea or coffee?"

"The usual?" Ethan asked.

Nods all around.

"Two espressos, two white teas, a black tea and two flat whites." Ethan grinned. "I'll help."

"No, I've got this," Chelsea told him. "You fill them in on what's been happening." She could handle making a few hot drinks. She placed the last biscuit packet on the table and then searched the remaining cupboards until she found Aunt Maggie's recipe book. She clutched it to her chest. This afternoon she'd bake and have decent biscuits in the house.

She made the drinks as Ethan told them about Darren and Johann, the vandalism and the fire. "There's a trail behind the property I want to check out in more detail."

"Any security cameras?" Noah asked.

"None. Crime rate is pretty low in Honeybrook," Ethan answered.

"You want us to set up a watch tonight?" Heath asked.

"Yeah, but I don't want to scare him off either if he's watching."

Rhys nodded. "We can make a show of leaving after

dinner."

Chelsea brought the espressos to the table, and Ethan pointed to Rhys and Noah.

"We'll do a full survey to make sure all points are covered," Dobby said.

Chelsea made the tea, fascinated by the way the men understood what each other meant without needing further clarification. She glanced at Mila, who looked equally interested.

By the time the drinks were made, the men seemed to have agreed on a plan, but she wasn't sure what it was. She glanced at Mila. "Did you understand any of that?"

Mila laughed. "Not much. I'm sure they'll fill us in." She gave Dobby a look, but it was Ethan who answered.

"You're going to show them through the garden and put them to work, while Dobby and I scope the trail behind the house," he said. "Then we'll need to go to the shops and buy food to feed this lot for dinner."

"I can't ask you all to work in the garden." These were soldiers who were here to catch the culprit, not pull up weeds.

Rhys shrugged. "We were planning to come and help before the attacks. This place meant a lot to Ethan as a kid."

And that was apparently all the reason they needed. She could understand why Ethan considered these men as brothers. "I appreciate it, though you might regret the offer when you see my list."

"Can't be anything worse than what we've done in the past," Heath said.

Her mind ticked over about where would be the best. "We'll have to wait until Barry is done in the public garden." At Connor's frown, she said, "He's filming himself and I don't want to risk him catching you on camera."

Connor smiled. "It's not a problem for me. I'm not special forces. I just tag along sometimes."

Dobby grinned. "You rescue one dog on a mission, and Connor's your friend for life."

There was a story she'd like to hear one day.

"I noticed one of your structures burned," Connor continued. "I'm an engineer as well, so I could check it out for you."

Chelsea nodded her thanks, too overwhelmed to speak. She'd been wondering how much it would cost her to get someone to review all the structures in the garden and make sure they were still sound. She swallowed hard. "That would be great."

Ethan gathered up the cups, and the men got to their feet, making the area feel crowded but safe.

So many people willing to help. Aunt Maggie would have been thrilled.

Chelsea led the way out of the house. "Let's put you to work."

Chapter 16

Ethan grinned as Chelsea made quick work of assigning his teammates tasks. He loved the way they accepted her lead, even Noah, who had a few issues working with others. As they split into groups, he rubbed his chest. Never in his wildest dreams did he imagine returning to Lilydale and having so many people supporting him.

"She'd make a good drill sergeant," Dobby commented as they slipped away from the others and headed for the lake trail.

Ethan nodded. "Her brain is incredible. You should see the plan she has for this place and it keeps growing. It's going to be insane by the time she's done."

"You two back together?" Dobby asked.

Wasn't that a good question? "Maybe. Kind of. I hurt her pretty badly, but she's giving me a second chance, and I can't stuff it up."

"Looks like you're doing a pretty good job so far. Having us help has to earn you a few Brownie points."

"I appreciate it."

"Don't sweat it."

They hiked up the trail, which wound through the bush behind Lilydale. "Was this the farmland area?" Dobby asked.

"I don't know where Aunt Maggie's land goes," Ethan admitted. "I've been meaning to look it up. Chelsea didn't realise there were more than the sixteen acres of garden."

"It's less than eighty minutes from here to the CBD," Dobby said. "Ninety to the barracks."

"Yeah."

"Bit of a long commute."

Ethan understood what he was saying. "I've been thinking about it. Wanted to ask you how far along you were in your plans for a security firm."

"Got a business plan. Scoping out some potential clients." He gestured to the bush. "Thinking about training."

"Would you be willing to employ a busted special ops soldier?"

"You know I would, but is that what you want? Don't you want to be involved with this business Chelsea's building?"

An excellent question. "I want to help her set it up, but the event planning, hospitality, publicity thing isn't for me. I don't like people enough and would miss the action."

"I could do with a partner. I'll email you the business plan. You can tell me if there are things I've missed."

And just like that, he had a new option. Gratitude filled him. "Thanks, mate."

The trail came out at Honeybrook Lake. About twenty metres from the edge of the bush was a car park where two cars were parked. An older woman was walking a fluffy white dog, and a father was pushing two kids on swings at the nearby playground.

"Your arsonist could have parked here and walked to

the house." Dobby checked his watch. "Would have taken about twenty minutes, maybe thirty, if he wasn't very fit."

Ethan nodded. "A long way to carry a couple of jerry cans." He scanned the light poles, but none had security cameras mounted.

"Maybe he stashed them closer earlier in the day."

It would be a big risk. Someone could have seen him. He pursed his lips. Maybe Josh could ask at the local petrol station whether anyone had filled up some jerry cans recently.

He pulled out his phone and called his friend.

Josh chuckled when Ethan had explained his thoughts. "Already done."

"And?" Ethan asked.

"And it's police business and we're following some leads."

Frustration filled him. "Come on, Josh."

"Not a chance. You'll want to take matters into your own hands. I've already had several calls about two four-wheel drives full of suspicious-looking men arriving at Lilydale Cottage."

Ethan glanced at Dobby and grinned. "Just my teammates helping in the garden for the day."

Josh snorted. "Right. Don't do anything that will require me to arrest you."

"I can promise you we'd leave no trace."

"Not comforting," Josh said. "Talk to you later."

Ethan hung up.

"You seem pretty friendly with the police here," Dobby said.

"I went to school with Josh. He's a friend."

"He won't get in our way?"

Ethan considered it. "Probably not as long as we do nothing too overt."

They returned to the garden where his team had already made a difference. Noah was poisoning the remaining weeds growing around and through the paths, Rhys had the hedge trimmer and was pruning every bush and hedge in sight, Mila was weeding one of the garden beds, and Heath was clearing the leaf litter off the garden shed roof.

Chelsea and Connor were nowhere to be seen. Ethan ignored the flicker of concern. They'd be in the public garden where Barry was working. He headed in that direction.

"What do you want me to do?" Dobby asked.

Though the grass was cut, it was yellow and sparse. What it needed was a good watering, and he had no idea whether the sprinklers in this area still worked. "I'll get you on sprinkler duty with me after I've seen Chelsea. In the meantime, why don't you help Mila weed?"

Dobby nodded and with a grin went to see his fiancée.

Rhys had already done the hedge around the house's private garden, and there was no need to brush past branches to get from one area to another. Ethan stopped to check where Barry and his cameras were before he continued into the garden, circumnavigating the reading gazebo to stay out of the shot.

Barry and his colleague had done an amazing job on the paths, which were all visible and clear of dirt and debris, and what was left of the lawn was short. He'd even edged the garden beds, so it was clear where they started and the lawns ended.

Ethan found Chelsea standing with Connor, examining the Sydney Harbour Bridge.

"It's good quality metal," Connor said. "No rust and the footings are solid. All it needs is a clean and maybe a coat of paint."

"That's great news," Chelsea said. "I was reluctant to

walk on it without getting it reviewed."

"Smart," Connor said. "I've seen things that look solid and yet fall apart at the slightest pressure."

Ethan slid his arms around Chelsea's waist, needing to touch her after so long apart. "Shall we try it?"

Together they walked out to the middle of the bridge and peered over the edge. Barry had run the mower over the remaining burnt grass along the harbour lake basin and uncovered the base of the fountain, which used to shoot water into the air when the lake was full.

"I don't know how long it's been empty," Chelsea said. "I've been meaning to ask Lauren or Josh."

"If the clay is still good, it should hold water again," Connor told her. "You'll want to check any drainage pipes and pumps though."

Ethan tapped his fingers on the railing of the bridge. "It's been pretty dry the past couple of winters. Maybe the annual rainfall hasn't been enough to keep it full."

Chelsea drew out her phone and added a couple of notes. Ethan grinned. He loved her organised nature.

"Is there anything else you need me to review?" Connor asked.

"No. Thank you."

"Any time. I'll go ask what the others need me to do."

Ethan waited until he was gone before he turned to Chelsea and kissed her. "How are you feeling?"

She smiled. "Amazed. I can't believe the transformation Barry did or that your team is willing to help. I'm so glad you have them, Ethan."

So was he. He'd finally found the brothers he'd desperately wanted for years. The wail of the blower stopped, bringing some quiet to the garden. He couldn't see Barry from here.

"Shall we see if he's finished?"

Chelsea held his hand, and they crossed the bridge and wandered down the path to where Barry was packing up his camera.

"The garden looks amazing!"

Barry grinned. "Well the fire made it a little easier. Not such thick grass to get through. I should have some good video. I'll email you when it goes up."

"Thank you so much." She hugged the man and the three of them gathered his things and walked him and his colleague back to his car and trailer.

"Make sure you shower before you go. Can I get you something to eat or drink?"

Barry shook his head. "Nah. I need to get home to the family this evening. I'll freshen up and then hit the road. I'll have the videos up by Monday."

"All right. Then I'll see you on the Honeybrook Fair weekend."

He grinned. "Sounds good to me."

After he left, Ethan said, "I'm going to run to the shops and get food for dinner. Do you need anything?"

"Yes. I wanted to get ingredients for some of Aunt Maggie's biscuits."

Ethan grinned. "I'll buy. I haven't had a Father's Favourite in years."

They walked back to the house to find Heath climbing down from the roof after cleaning the gutters.

"All in place?" Ethan asked.

"Yeah. Feed looks good."

Chelsea frowned. "What feed?"

Perhaps he should have mentioned it to Chelsea before going ahead. "Heath's set up surveillance on the buildings so we can record anyone who comes into the garden tonight."

"Oh."

"It's temporary," Heath assured her. "We'll take it down when we catch whoever's doing this. Same as any mission."

She raised her eyebrows. "Am I your mission?"

He grinned. "Well, kind of. Saving Lilydale, protecting you, and helping Hawk here."

She glanced at Ethan.

"Nickname."

"From the actor?"

He grinned, pleased she'd picked it. "It was Dobby's idea."

They headed inside. "Thank you for cleaning the gutters, Heath." Chelsea got out her phone and crossed something off her list.

"My pleasure. What's next?"

She hesitated as she entered the kitchen and pulled out a bottle of cold water, handing it to Heath.

Ethan could practically hear her doubts about whether she could ask Heath to do more. "They came here to work, Chels."

Heath nodded.

She took three deep breaths as she blinked back the tears and straightened with a smile. "Then I guess we need to mulch the branches Rhys is chopping down. We can mulch the garden beds Mila and Dobby are working on to keep the weeds at bay until I plant something new."

Heath grinned. "I get to have all the fun. Is the mulcher in the gardening shed?"

"Yeah." Ethan watched him leave. "The other guys are going to be jealous."

Chelsea laughed and then her expression turned serious as she hugged him. "Thank you for bringing them here."

"They offered as soon as they heard what happened," Ethan told her. He enjoyed the feel of her body tucked into his before she stepped back.

"I'm not used to having so much support."

His heart broke for her. "Then you'll need to get used to it. You've got all of us now."

Though doubt still showed on her face, she nodded. "Thank you."

"Any time." He hated that she had any doubts, but it was his fault. It would take her time to trust again. He kissed her gently. "Better give me the shopping list before the shops shut. We'll have a riot on our hands if we don't feed them."

That earned him a smile as she grabbed a notepad from Aunt Maggie's desk and jotted down ingredients. "I'll get you some money. My purse is upstairs."

"No, I'm good. I've got this." He wouldn't have her paying. He kissed her again to stop her protest. "See you when I get back."

Then he left before she could argue further.

He'd show her she deserved to be cared for.

***

Later that afternoon, Chelsea glanced up from where she was weeding by the house as an unfamiliar green hatchback pulled into her driveway. She stood, stretching the aches out of her stiff muscles, and then waved and grinned as Lauren got out.

Lauren gazed wide-eyed at the burnt garden as Chelsea walked over. "What happened?"

It was surprising Lauren hadn't heard about the fire. "Someone set the garden alight last night."

Lauren swore. "This was arson? Why didn't you call me?"

Chelsea blinked at the question. It had never occurred to her to call Lauren.

Lauren hugged her. "Are you all right?"

"Yeah. It looks worse than it is." She'd never had a friend she could call when something went wrong, but it felt nice that Lauren might become that friend. "Come inside and I'll tell you about it."

As they walked up the front steps, Lauren murmured, "Are you aware you have several extremely hot men working in your garden?"

Chelsea grinned as she noticed Rhys and Noah nearby, keeping their eyes on her. She waved to them to let them know everything was fine. "They're Ethan's friends."

Lauren walked into the house and then fanned herself. "Sign me up for helping tomorrow if they're still going to be here."

"They will be, but you don't need to help." It was getting late and probably about time they called it a day.

"Remember what I said about the lack of our generation in town? I never meet anyone."

Chelsea chuckled. "All right." She held up a bottle of white wine, and Lauren nodded. "Why don't you stay for dinner and you can meet them?"

"I'd love to, but unfortunately I can't stay long." She leaned against the bench. "So what happened?"

"Let me just tell them they can finish." Chelsea went outside and spotted Ethan by the barn where he'd been testing the sprinklers. "Drinks time."

He nodded. "Be in soon."

Chelsea returned and sank onto the sofa next to Lauren, her feet and muscles aching from trying to match Ethan and his friends' pace. She sipped her wine and told Lauren about the fire and their suspicions.

Lauren frowned. "I wasn't going to say anything, because I thought I might be imagining it." She pressed her lips together as the team came inside and Mila flopped onto the sofa across from them.

"Ugh. I thought my fitness had improved this year."

Dobby bent down and brushed a kiss on her lips. "Your fitness is plenty good enough for me."

She blushed and swatted him away, taking a long drink from her water bottle.

Chelsea made the introductions as the living room filled with people.

Ethan grinned at Lauren. "So good to see you again."

"Likewise. You've all been busy."

Chelsea nodded. "I really appreciate your help."

Mila grinned. "It looks good, doesn't it? All you need is some good rain to get the grass to spring back and some flowers in the beds and you won't know the cottage side had been neglected."

"Yeah." Rain was forecast for early next week. She turned back to Lauren. "What were you going to say before they came in?"

"It's possibly nothing."

Ethan moved closer, his gaze laser sharp on Lauren. "What do you know?"

Lauren leaned back. "Geez, Ethan. Tone it down."

The entire room had gone silent and everyone was watching them. Chelsea shifted in her seat, suddenly aware of how lethal all these men were. She squeezed Lauren's knee and whispered, "Ignore them."

"Impossible." Lauren coughed. "And now I'm wondering what they might do if I tell you."

Ethan made a hand gesture to the team. "Food's in the fridge." As one, the men stopped staring and moved to prepare dinner, but every one of them was still listening.

Chelsea let out a breath.

Ethan squeezed her shoulder. "Sorry, Lauren. I didn't mean to be so aggressive."

Lauren sipped her wine and, despite her bravado, Chelsea noticed a slight tremor in her hand.

"They're a lot when they get into protective mode, aren't they?" Mila said with a smile.

"I'll say." Lauren sighed. "I caught up with Leyton yesterday."

It took Chelsea a moment to remember Leyton was the planning person at the council. "What happened?"

"I asked him if he knew anything about the retirement village planned for Lilydale. He said it was a rumour and when I told him that was good because you were back in town, he grew kind of pale. He made an excuse to leave and hurried away."

"He knows something," Ethan said.

Lauren nodded. "That's what I thought, so I followed him to his office and heard him mention the name Johann, but then someone spoke to me and I missed the conversation."

Interesting. It made sense Leyton would be involved because the zoning on the property would need to be changed for the units.

"Sounds like we're paying Leyton a visit," Ethan said.

"No, you aren't," Lauren said. "I'll tell Josh and he can deal with it."

"Are you worried about me or Leyton?" Ethan asked.

"Leyton." She stared at him as if daring Ethan to deny it.

Ethan chuckled. "He's got nothing to worry about if he's done nothing wrong."

"Hence why I'm worried." Lauren sipped her wine, her bravado back now the rest of the team were busy preparing dinner.

"Thanks for telling us." Ethan went outside with Noah to light the barbecue while Rhys and Connor chopped vegetables in the kitchen as if they hadn't spent the past few hours working hard in the garden.

Dobby brought over a glass of wine for Mila. "You ladies sit there and enjoy. We've got dinner sorted."

Chelsea waited until he was busy in the kitchen getting more drinks before she asked, "Are they always like this?"

"You mean, do they always cook and take care of others?" Mila said. At Chelsea's nod, she smiled, "Always. It took a bit of getting used to. They have their own rhythm after working together for so long."

"Do you ever feel you're intruding?"

"Never. As soon as they realised Dobby and I were together, they accepted me." She smiled. "It helped that I found Ethan."

Chelsea lowered her voice. "Are you allowed to tell us about it?" She glanced at Lauren. "Ethan was caught in the tsunami last year."

Her eyes widened.

"I'm not sworn to secrecy like these guys, but I know what I should and shouldn't say." Mila sipped her wine. "My mother is a major-general in the army."

Interesting. "What can you tell us?"

"I was volunteering on an island in Indonesia late last year when the big earthquake struck. I ran into this lot. They were looking for something and I pointed them in the right direction. Then the tsunami struck. I was caught up in it and so was Ethan when he was separated from his team." She shuddered, taking another sip of wine. "I clung to a tree to stop being dragged back into the ocean and then searched for Ethan. He was badly injured."

"It must have been terrifying." Chelsea squeezed her hand. "He was lucky you found him."

"He helped me. I knew the team would be back for him, so I flagged them down, we found a stretcher and moved him out of harm's way."

"And then you were extracted?"

"Eventually."

There was more to the story than Mila could tell her. Chelsea tamped down the urge to ask for details. Being with Ethan she would have to get used to not knowing things. She might not even know which country he was in.

"Is it hard?" she asked. "Not knowing what Dobby is doing and where he's going?"

"It is," she admitted. "But I take comfort in knowing he's got all these amazing men around him who will do all they can to protect each other."

She could see why. They'd come here to help her because Lilydale had meant something to Ethan. That was a genuine family.

Not long afterwards, Ethan and Noah brought the meat inside. Lauren stood. "I'd better go. I might be able to get away tomorrow afternoon to help."

Chelsea hugged her. "Call me. We might have had enough by then."

Lauren waved goodbye to the others and Chelsea walked her to the door. "Thanks for telling me about Leyton."

Lauren shrugged. "If he's behind this, then he deserves what he gets. I'll call Josh when I get home."

Chelsea waited until she drove away and then closed the door. She smiled at all the people who sat shoulder to shoulder at the table. Aunt Maggie would have liked to have seen her kitchen full.

"Here's the plan," Dobby said when they were eating. "Mila will stay in the house with Chelsea and Connor. The rest of us will make a show of leaving after dinner. It will be dark, so if anyone is watching, they won't see who's who."

Chelsea frowned. "And what are you going to do?"

"We'll park the cars and double back, taking up the positions we identified today to watch for trouble."

"Whoever is doing this would be stupid to come back now," Chelsea said. Surely the fact they stopped the fire from destroying the house would be enough to dissuade them.

"Or desperate," Rhys pointed out.

"I called Josh this afternoon," Ethan said. "Johann was in Perth, and Darren can't be tied to it as yet. Now we have this Leyton in the mix."

Maybe Darren would be stupid enough to return, particularly if Johann was still paying him to cause trouble.

"I dropped by Darren's when I went to the shops to ask if he'd got the money together that he owes Sabine," Ethan continued. "He said he'd have it by Monday."

"How did he seem?" Chelsea asked.

"Annoyed, but not anxious."

Interesting. Wouldn't most people be anxious about having to find almost fifty grand within a week?

"What are Chelsea, Connor, and I supposed to do?" Mila asked.

"Stay here where it's safe," Dobby said. "Watch a movie. Go to bed. There's no point staying awake all night."

Chelsea frowned. "If it's safe here, why is Connor staying?"

"Backup and comms," Ethan said.

"I hate the idea you're out protecting me while I sleep comfortably in my bed." Sure, they were trained for this kind of thing, but it still felt wrong.

"Truth is, these two are rather protective of you two." Rhys gestured to Dobby and Ethan and then herself and Mila. "If it's Darren like we think it is, he won't stand a chance against us, but Connor is just in case."

"Plan B." Mila raised her eyebrows at Dobby.

He grinned. "Exactly."

"And if Connor is here with you, Dobby and I can focus on the job without worrying about you," Ethan added. "He'll monitor the cameras and tell us if there's any movement."

He made a good point. "All right."

Conversation turned to what needed to be done tomorrow in the garden.

"Won't you be too tired after staying up all night?" Chelsea asked.

Dobby grinned and Mila said, "They don't need to sleep." She rolled her eyes. "It's a special forces and egotistical man thing."

All the men made sounds of protest, as if they were wounded.

A smile hovered on her lips as Chelsea retrieved her list of notes. "In that case, I'd like to get the garden beds around the cottages replanted before we get too many guests, so they feel more welcoming, and we need to finish fixing the sprinklers."

"Where's the nearest nursery?" Heath asked.

"Pinjarra, which is about twenty minutes away."

"You and Mila can pick out plants tomorrow while we work on the sprinklers," Ethan said.

It felt as if she was leaving all the hard work to them.

"I'm game." Mila grinned. "I could do with a break from weeding."

Chelsea smiled. "All right." She checked her list. "Then it's more pruning and weeding in the public garden and taping off the Japanese garden, so no one gets hurt." It had been one of the draw cards to the garden, so she'd have to get it fixed soon. "If I can replant some of the garden beds there and figure out why the harbour lake is dry and fix it, that should bring people back to the garden. It was always a gold coin donation for entry, but it might help." Plus the rain next week would help green up the lawn.

"I can check the lake," Noah said, looking at Ethan. "I did some work building dams before the army."

"That'd be great."

Chelsea frowned. Noah had said little and hadn't been overly friendly. She wasn't sure what she'd done to offend him. Maybe she'd ask Mila after the others left.

By the time they finished dinner, everyone had volunteered for jobs the next day. Connor started on the dishes, and the other men headed for the door.

Chelsea stopped Ethan before he left. "Be careful." She hugged him a little too tightly, not wanting to let go.

"Always. If you hear or see anything you think is off, you tell Connor and he'll investigate or get in touch with us." He tapped his ear. "Now come out and act as if you're waving friends goodbye." He made sure the porch light was off and opened the door.

Chelsea followed them down to their cars. "Thank you so much for your help today," she called out.

"No worries. We can come back next weekend if you need more help," Dobby called back.

She swallowed her smile as they got into the two cars and she waved them off.

As their taillights disappeared around the corner, she walked back to the lights of the house. Someone had shut the curtains in the living room and kitchen, letting only a little light peek out around the edges. The steps creaked as she climbed them and let herself back into the house, shutting and locking the door behind her.

Mila was waiting at the kitchen table and as the door

closed, Connor came out of the laundry.

"Time to party?" Mila joked.

Chelsea couldn't shake her worry for Ethan. She spotted Aunt Maggie's recipe book on the kitchen bench. "Feel up for some baking?"

Connor grinned. "I volunteer to be chief taste tester."

She laughed as Mila nodded. "Let's get started."

Chapter 17

Stepping into the darkness dressed in his night fatigues was like coming home to Ethan. He smiled, readiness zinging in his veins as Rhys switched off the engine and all sound faded away. He'd found a gate into Aunt Maggie's farm property earlier in the day and they parked both vehicles inside near the neighbouring bush where they wouldn't be spotted by anyone who might drive by.

They checked the comms as they moved back to the garden. He hadn't asked Dobby where he'd got the equipment from, but it was top quality.

Before they reached the lake trail, they separated; Rhys, Noah and Dobby heading right to come at the garden from the eastern side, and he and Heath coming from the south.

Maybe he was being paranoid expecting the garden to be hit again tonight. The fire had done significant damage, but it still hadn't stopped Chelsea from going ahead with her plans to renovate and Ethan suspected that would be enough to irritate Johann.

And now they had both Darren and Leyton as potential

suspects.

He kept scanning the area, moving quietly, listening for anything out of place, or any sounds of a motor vehicle. They were far enough from the main highway that any cars were a faint rumble.

The wire fence marking the start of the garden came into view and Ethan let Heath climb through first before following. It felt strange not to have a rifle in his hand, but he had a knife at his belt.

Heath split off, heading for a spot close to the gate where he could monitor both the road and the back of the garden.

Ethan continued to a tree between the cottages and the main house. Connor would monitor the security cameras Heath had set up and would notify them if they caught any movement.

He climbed up onto the lowest branch of the liquidambar, his pelvis twinging as he did so. Taking a second to shift, he climbed to the next branch. From here he could see the house, kitchen garden, cottages and over the hedge into the public garden.

He settled in to wait.

***

Chelsea found she didn't like waiting, so the distraction of cooking Aunt Maggie's favourite biscuits was welcome. Connor had set a laptop on the table monitoring the security camera feed while she and Mila cooked up a storm.

By ten o'clock, they'd made almond bread, Father's Favourites and melting moments, and were waiting for the banana bread to come out of the oven. The entire kitchen smelled like Chelsea remembered from her childhood; sweet and delicious.

A pang of loss swept over her.

Mila yawned. "When this one's done, I'm going to bed."

"There's no reason for you to wait up," Chelsea told her. "I can take it out. I'll show you to your room." She'd made up Aunt Maggie's bed earlier in the evening when Dobby had gone through the plan.

"All right. Wake me if anything happens."

Chelsea took her upstairs, made sure she had a fresh towel, and showed her where the bathroom was before returning to the kitchen.

"Any movement?" she asked Connor.

"A couple of cats and a possum." Connor stretched.

"Can I get you a drink?"

"Coffee would be great."

She made herself a coffee too. She wouldn't sleep knowing Ethan was out there waiting for someone to attack.

As she placed their mugs on the table, the timer rang and she removed the banana bread from the oven and left it on the sink to cool.

Then she set up Aunt Maggie's ancient laptop on the table.

"Are you going to work all night?" Connor asked.

"Maybe."

"Ethan and the guys know what they're doing."

She nodded. "I know. Have you worked with them much?"

"On occasion."

"And you're a dog handler?"

"That's my primary role."

"Do you enjoy it?"

"Beats working with people." A frown crossed his face and then disappeared.

Chelsea smiled. "I understand."

Connor gestured to her laptop. "What are you doing?"

"Going through Aunt Maggie's laptop to make certain there's nothing important on there. It might have useful information about the way she ran Lilydale Cottage."

"So you're staying here?"

She bit her lip. "Maybe. Possibly. I haven't decided yet."

"I get that. It's difficult making decisions about your life when you were on one path and are suddenly thrown onto another."

Had something happened to him? She hesitated. It was a personal question to ask someone she barely knew. Instead she nodded and logged in, bracing herself for the mass of folders spread across the desktop. Aunt Maggie had always said she liked her folders where she could find them, but the lack of organisation was like an out of tune string on a guitar for Chelsea.

She scanned the titles: garden, house, bills, Chelsea.

With a frown, she clicked on the folder with her name. She leaned back in her chair as a folder full of screenshots of her work opened. She flicked through them, recognising clients she'd worked with in the past and the graphics she'd done for them.

Her chest squeezed. Aunt Maggie had kept them all. A sob broke out before she could stop it, and Connor glanced up.

"Are you all right?"

She nodded as tears blurred her vision.

"Chelsea, what's wrong?" The gentle, but slightly panicked tone to his voice made her swallow hard.

She waved her hand at the computer and exhaled. "A folder. Me."

Connor's face showed his understanding, and he

squeezed her hand. "I'm sorry."

She smiled drawing comfort from his touch. She exhaled again, dabbed at her eyes, and cleared her throat. "Aunt Maggie kept copies of all my work. I didn't know she followed what I'd been doing."

"It sounds like she was an incredible woman."

"She was." Chelsea drew back her hand so he could concentrate on his surveillance. She closed the folder and clicked through the rest of the folders, one by one. There were a few things which might be useful; invoices of where she got supplies, a list of people who had stayed in the cottages and some photos of the garden Chelsea could use in her promotion.

Finally she opened Aunt Maggie's email account. As far as Chelsea knew, Aunt Maggie had used it for logging into websites when she shopped online and little else. They'd set up an auto-responder after the funeral to tell senders Aunt Maggie had died and to contact Sabine for anything.

The inbox was full of spam and junk mail, which Chelsea reviewed before unsubscribing from newsletters or deleting. There were a few enquiries about accommodation which Chelsea kept. She could contact them later and tell them Lilydale Cottage had reopened.

Finally when she was done, she went to click on the Trash folder to empty it, but she clicked the Sent folder instead. With a sigh, she was about to click the correct folder when a name jumped out at her.

Johann Mueller.

Chelsea's heart raced as she clicked on the email. Aunt Maggie was refusing to sell Lilydale Cottage to him and, from the tone, she was annoyed.

Aunt Maggie was always polite.

Chelsea read the email from Johann, which was below it. He outlined all the positives and offered Aunt Maggie a unit of her own in the complex.

That wouldn't have gone down well. Aunt Maggie was fiercely independent and liked her space. Living so close to someone in a unit would have driven her mad.

Chelsea kept scrolling through a long email trail which had started a couple of months before Aunt Maggie had died. Around the time Johann's firm was working on the sports complex.

Give Johann his due. He was persistent.

But one thing bothered Chelsea. She glanced at Connor. "If you wanted to buy Lilydale, why would you wait for a year before approaching the new owners, particularly if you'd been in discussions with the previous owner?"

Connor didn't look up from the screen. "Maybe circumstances changed, and you were focusing on a different project," he suggested. "Or because you wanted to distance yourself from the negotiation."

"There was no need to distance himself from the negotiation if he had done nothing wrong."

Connor's gaze flashed to hers. "How did Aunt Maggie die?"

"She fell off a ladder." Horror filled Chelsea. She shook away the thought it might not have been an accident, unable to contemplate someone going to such desperate lengths to obtain a property.

But the vandalism and fire suggested perhaps Johann was.

Before she could suggest it, Connor straightened, his gaze sharp on the screen in front of him.

"Target at section two carrying a jerry can."

Chelsea's heart pounded as she pushed back her chair and raced around the table to watch his screen, her horror replaced by fear for Ethan. Connor pointed to one frame and a moment later a male figure wearing a dark hoodie passed by carrying a jerry can.

"Target at section three."

The man was the same size and frame as Darren, but Chelsea couldn't see his face. "Should I call the police?"

Connor shook his head. "We don't want to scare him away. He has to do something more than trespass."

"So we have to wait."

Connor nodded. "We wait."

***

At Connor's call, Ethan breathed a sigh of relief. This would be over soon. At the second call, he dropped from the tree branch to the ground. Whoever it was, was headed this way.

Rhys and Noah would fall in behind the intruder, cutting off his escape route, and Ethan would follow when he passed.

The man had a jerry can.

Anger simmered in Ethan's stomach. The garden's destruction hadn't been enough. If he was a betting man, he'd bet a structure would be the next target.

He hoped it wasn't the house.

At the crunch of footsteps Ethan slowed his breathing, ready to act at a moment's notice. The man walked past, not even in a crouch, but brazenly as if he had every right to be there. Though Ethan couldn't see his face, he had the same build as Darren. He waited until the man went down the path towards the barn before following. He spotted Rhys's tall frame in the shadows and Rhys gestured he'd go down the far side of the barn.

Ethan nodded and continued following the intruder.

A low curse had Ethan shifting back against the oleander hedge. It was followed by a mutter and the rattle of the padlock on the barn door.

Did he think they would make it easy for him?

A moment later the smell of fuel drifted towards Ethan. Time to move.

He slipped around the corner, spotted the man pouring the fuel along the wall of the barn and tackled him to the ground, planting his face into the dirt and pulling his arms behind him. The muffled cries soothed Ethan's soul, but not the ache in his pelvis from the move. "Target neutralised." It was almost too easy.

The rest of his team shifted out of the shadows, Noah standing up the jerry can, Dobby telling Connor to call the police, and Rhys standing guard in front of the barn. Heath shone his torch on the man's face as Ethan tied his hands together and hauled him to his knees.

Forty years old, greying hair, scowling face.

Not Darren.

"I'm guessing you're Leyton." A widening of the man's eyes told Ethan he was right.

"Let go of me," Leyton bellowed.

"Not going to happen," Ethan told him pleasantly.

"We'll watch the petrol," Noah said. "In case he's got help lurking around."

Good idea. Darren could still be involved, plus Josh would want to capture the evidence before they neutralised it. He dragged the man to the front porch with Heath and Dobby accompanying him.

"Police called. Chelsea wants to come outside," Connor said in his ear.

"Let us do a sweep first."

Heath and Dobby disappeared into the shadows to check the rest of the garden. At one time, Aunt Maggie had lights in different areas, so it lit up at night, but Ethan had tested them yesterday and none of them were working.

Something else to fix.

"What are you going to do with me?" Leyton demanded.

Ethan dropped his voice, murmuring in the man's ear. "If it were up to me, I'd make you disappear. Will anyone miss you?"

"It wasn't my idea." The bluster was replaced by fear.

Ethan smiled. "I didn't see anyone with a gun to your head as you walked through the garden carrying the jerry can."

"He might as well have. He has evidence I lit the fire last night."

"Who has?"

"Johann. He said if I didn't finish the job, he'd turn me in to the police."

Ethan grunted. "Well it seems to have backfired, because you're going to gaol anyway. Was Johann bribing you to approve his development?"

Leyton pressed his lips together.

"Bribery and arson. I'm guessing you'll be in prison for a long time."

Leyton swore as headlights turned onto the road and the police car pulled into the driveway. Josh and a female police officer got out of the car.

Josh shook his head. "Leyton, what are you doing here?"

"This guy kidnapped me, took me from my bed and brought me here. He's trying to pin the fire on me," Leyton shouted.

Ethan barked a laugh. "We've got surveillance of him coming into the garden. He poured petrol over the barn wall, but we stopped him from lighting the match. Noah has the jerry can. And before you arrived, he admitted to starting the fire yesterday."

"You'd better show me the footage," Josh said. "Julie, can you guard him out here?"

Rhys appeared from around the side of the house. He gave Julie a warm smile. "I'll help."

She smiled back and nodded.

Ethan shook his head at Rhys in amusement.

Julie was probably capable, but Ethan felt better with someone he knew guarding Leyton. He unlocked the front door and let Josh into the house.

His gaze fell on Chelsea, who still wore what she had been wearing when he left. Her eyes were heavy and she should have been in bed hours ago. "Did you wait up?"

She nodded and waved her hands. "I couldn't sleep knowing you were out there, and I had work to do." She smiled at Josh and then took the couple of steps across the room to hug Ethan. "It wasn't Darren?"

He shook his head, holding her in his arms for a moment before letting her go. The fact she'd stayed up for him, and was worried about him, created an unfamiliar feeling in his chest.

Josh cleared his throat. "It was Leyton, the guy from the council planning office. Is that the surveillance?" he asked Connor, who still sat at the table in front of the laptop.

"Yeah." Connor shifted so Josh could look at it. Mila moved next to him, wearing pyjamas and looking as if she'd just woken up.

Ethan held Chelsea's hand as he watched the footage of Leyton sneaking across the garden carrying the jerry can and then pouring it over the barn. Ethan's take down of the man took seconds and Josh let out a whistle. "Remind me not to get on the wrong side of you." He took a card out of his pocket and handed it to Connor. "Can you send me a copy of the footage?"

Connor nodded.

Ethan smiled. "Leyton said Johann had evidence of him lighting yesterday's fire and threatened to turn him in to the police if he didn't light one tonight."

"It's time to question the man himself." Josh glanced at Ethan and Chelsea. "I'm assuming you're coming?"

"Yes," Chelsea answered.

Outside, Josh read Leyton his rights as he arrested him for trespass and attempted arson.

"Johann's gone crazy," Lleyton blustered. "He wants the land, but Chelsea won't sell."

Chelsea stiffened next to him, and Ethan wrapped an arm around her shoulder, while concerned filled him. "How do you know the land is now Chelsea's?"

Lleyton shrugged. "That's what Johann said. He spoke to her dad yesterday."

"Step-dad," Ethan and Chelsea said at the same time.

Josh nodded. "Julie, do you want to gather evidence at the barn while I watch him?"

"Of course." She got the evidence kit out of the car and Rhys showed her the way as Heath and Dobby returned.

"All clear," Dobby reported.

Great. Ethan asked Leyton, "Was the arson his idea?"

Leyton nodded. "Said Chelsea wouldn't want to keep something that had been destroyed."

"Why didn't he do it himself?"

"Said he was too close to it, but no one knew about me."

"Why did you do it?"

Leyton pressed his lips together. "He threatened my family. Turns out his bosses are some kind of organised crime people."

Ethan exchanged a glance with Dobby. "Who exactly?"

"I don't know, but they sent photos of my kids at

school and my wife in town. They're watching us."

"I'll get Noah and do a wider sweep," Heath said and headed towards the barn.

"How did you meet him?" Ethan asked.

"I worked with him on the sports complex development last year. He wanted to know if there was any land in the area for his retirement home. There wasn't, but he drove past Lilydale Cottage one day and asked me to introduce him to Maggie."

Ethan stiffened. "Johann met Maggie?"

Leyton nodded. "But she refused to sell."

"I just discovered emails between them going back before Aunt Maggie died," Chelsea said.

That put a whole new spin on things. He exchanged a glance with Josh.

"What happened next?" Josh asked.

Leyton looked away. "She died, and Johann asked me to change the zoning laws. He was certain Maggie's heirs would sell."

"Then why didn't he ask us until now?" Chelsea asked.

"Ah, I don't know." He shifted in place. "Maybe it was to give time for the garden to die."

The dodgy vibes coming from Leyton were like a siren. "Did you know about his arrangement with Darren?"

Leyton nodded. "Johann asked me to monitor him. Make sure he did nothing in the garden, but it wasn't necessary. Darren knew a good thing when he had it."

"Johann spent a lot of money to get Lilydale," Josh said. "Why?"

"You'll have to ask him."

"What if Aunt Maggie's death wasn't an accident?" Chelsea asked, her voice soft.

The night froze. Every person stiffened at the suggestion, but the blood drained from Leyton's face.

Son of a bitch.

Ethan lunged forward, but Dobby hauled him back. Leyton scrambled away and Josh towered over him. "What do you know?"

"I didn't do it!"

"Who did?" Ethan growled. The urge to torture the answers from Leyton was strong, but Chelsea's soft whimper demolished it and he pulled her into his arms.

"It was an accident."

"Keep talking," Josh suggested.

"We went to visit Maggie. She was on her roof cleaning out the gutters and told us to leave or she'd call the police. Johann kept persisting, trying to persuade her to come down. Eventually she did, and she said she was calling the police." Leyton squeezed his eyes closed. "Johann got mad and shoved the ladder. She fell and hit the ground. Her head hit a rock." His eyes filled with tears. "Johann checked her pulse, but she must have died instantly."

Chelsea shook in Ethan's arms.

Fury and grief warred inside him. "So you just left her there?" Ethan demanded.

"Johann said we'd be arrested for murder. I couldn't go to gaol. It was an accident."

Ethan narrowed his eyes. "Johann pushed a ladder with an old woman on it. What did he think would happen? At best she would have broken bones." He shoved his emotions down so he could focus on the facts.

"It was then that he told me who he worked for. That he could make me disappear, or hurt my family. Please, I didn't want to do it. I liked Aunt Maggie." Tears filled his eyes.

Julie and Rhys returned, but Ethan's attention was all on the snivelling man in front of him. They needed to know more about Johann and the people he worked for.

"I've heard enough," Josh said. "I'll get my colleagues in Perth to bring Johann in for questioning." He helped Leyton into the backseat of the police car and then walked back to Ethan. "I don't want you near Johann."

Ethan said nothing.

"I mean it, Ethan." Josh glanced at Chelsea. "Can you talk sense into him?"

She looked up at Ethan. "Aunt Maggie wouldn't want you getting into trouble for her."

He exhaled and nodded, though part of him wanted to storm Johann's house and demand answers. Chelsea needed him. "Call us when you have more."

Josh and Julie got into the car and drove away.

Chelsea turned to him. "Is Johann likely to be in Honeybrook?"

Ethan shook his head. "He'll want an alibi for tonight. We should be safe for the rest of the night." He glanced at Dobby as he pulled Chelsea inside and Dobby nodded, knowing they needed more information on the enemy. "You need to sleep."

"We both do."

"Yeah." There was no way he was sleeping tonight with the possibility Darren was out there still, but Chelsea wouldn't sleep if she thought he wasn't.

Connor and Mila were in the living room. "I'm beat," he said. "See you guys in the morning."

"'Night. We'll pack up here and hit the hay too," Dobby replied.

Ethan smiled. They wouldn't sleep without a debrief and the mission wouldn't be over until morning.

He climbed the stairs, stripping out of his clothes and leaving them and his boots by the door.

Chelsea slid into his bed without question. "I can't believe Johann killed Aunt Maggie. All for a piece of land."

He pulled her into his arms and kissed her. "He'll pay for it." There might not be any evidence aside from Leyton's statement, but somehow Ethan would ensure he paid.

"She wouldn't have hurt anyone." Tears fell from her eyes and Ethan's heart broke.

"I know. I'm sorry, Chels." He held her as she cried and her body grew heavy. A few minutes later her breathing became even. He held her for a little longer to make sure she was asleep.

It felt so right to have her in his arms that he struggled to pull away. She shifted, turning over, mumbling something, and he waited another moment before he climbed out of bed, gathered his clothes and slipped out of the bedroom.

He dressed in the darkened hallway, carrying his boots and socks downstairs, where only Connor was still monitoring the surveillance.

"Everyone's back out there," Connor reported. "Haven't seen anything on the cameras."

"Good." Hopefully they were being overly cautious. "Tell us if the status changes."

Then he headed outside to climb a tree.

Chapter 18

Chelsea woke to find the bed next to her empty and cold. She blinked to clear the fog from her eyes and brain and checked the time.

Seven o'clock.

Surprise made her sit up. She'd thought she would sleep a lot later.

So what had woken her?

Ethan must have left some time ago if the bed was cold, but she remembered him holding her as she cried.

Memories flooded back. Aunt Maggie's death had been no accident.

The wave of sorrow and anger washed over her. How could someone be so callous and greedy?

Johann needed to be stopped. Would Josh have news by now?

She dressed and brushed her hair, tying it up in a quick bun before heading downstairs. Her kitchen was full of special ops men making bacon and eggs and, more importantly, coffee.

Her gaze met Ethan's and his grin washed some of the

fatigue and sorrow from her.

"Morning, honey." He swept her into a hug and kissed her.

She clung to him, trying to get her brain to function at a reasonable pace. "You're all up early."

"It happens when you don't go to sleep," Noah mumbled. Dobby elbowed him and Chelsea's eyes widened.

"You didn't sleep?" She turned to Ethan. "You came to bed with me."

He nodded a little sheepishly. "I got up after you went to sleep. We weren't sure whether Darren might also appear."

Hurt filled her. He'd been out there risking his life while she'd been safely tucked in bed. "You lied to me."

Ethan pulled her into the laundry where they had more privacy. "Technically I didn't say I was going to sleep," he said, and then immediately held up a hand to ward off her retort. "But yes, I implied it. You needed to rest, and I didn't want you to stay awake worrying about me when I was fairly sure we were being overly cautious."

She frowned, trying to process past the pain in her heart. In her tired state she wanted to cling to her hurt, but a tiny rational part of her brain told her to consider how much more exhausted she'd be if she hadn't slept. And she had a whole day of work planned.

"You decided for me without giving me a choice." She gave him a stern look. "Again." Would this be what their relationship would be like? Ethan always thinking he knew what she needed and taking away her agency?

He winced. "You're right. I didn't think of it like that. I'm sorry."

She sighed, and slumped against the cupboard. Was this a dealbreaker? Not today. She'd deal with it later when her brain could think more rationally. "Don't do it again." She squeezed his hand and then stepped past him into the kitchen. "Who's in charge of coffee?"

Heath raised his hand. "One flat white coming right up."

Chelsea smiled and sank into a chair. "Any news from Josh?"

"Not yet." Ethan set the table around her.

Rhys was piling bacon onto a plate, and Noah had cooked enough scrambled eggs to feed an army. Dobby and Connor were nursing coffees at the table.

"Will you sleep after you've eaten?" Chelsea asked.

"We'll sleep in shifts," Dobby said as he dished up. "An hour or two at a time is all we need."

"Are you expecting trouble?"

"Always," Heath said. "It's when you don't expect it you get caught out."

That made an odd kind of sense.

Dobby gulped down his food and got up. "I'll be back in a couple of hours."

"Make sure you get some actual sleep," Rhys said with a wink.

Chelsea smiled as Dobby headed upstairs to where Mila was still sleeping.

After breakfast Heath shooed her out of the kitchen promising to clean up. Feeling more alert, she said, "I'm going to check the barn."

Ethan stood. "I'll join you."

Chelsea waited until they were outside before she asked, "Are you coming with me because you believe there's still danger?"

"My main reason is to spend time with you alone," Ethan said. "And to apologise again for lying to you." He held her hand as they walked. "And because I won't feel comfortable about having you out of my sight until Johann is caught."

"Do you think he'll escalate?"

"If he's desperate enough. We have Leyton on record accusing him of manslaughter."

Which was enough to make anyone desperate. "Did you have any other problems last night?"

"Other than insects crawling all over me and a possum peeing nearby, no."

Chelsea laughed, warmth filling her. Ethan and his friends had gone to so much trouble for her. "What about the others?"

"It was quiet."

The strong stench of petrol wafted from the barn doors and she screwed up her nose, thankful they had locked the door. If Leyton had got inside, it might have been a different story.

"Do you know what neutralises the petrol?"

"Baking soda or lemon juice might help according to the internet." Ethan grinned at her. "I searched this morning."

Already a step ahead. She continued over to the cottages. She would make sure everyone had linen, but she also wanted to estimate how many plants she needed to buy for the nearby garden beds. "I need to test the sprinklers in this area before I head out." No point planting things if they wouldn't get watered. And if she needed reticulation supplies, she could buy them at the same time.

"Already done," Ethan said. "I fixed everything with supplies Aunt Maggie had." He checked the time. "Josh should call us soon. We can confirm we can clean up and then turn the sprinklers on."

Chelsea turned in a circle, taking in all the work still to be done. "Am I crazy?"

"No more than the average person." He smiled. "You mean about the garden?"

She nodded. "Aunt Maggie struggled to keep up with it when it was in good condition. It's going to take months of work to get it back to any semblance of what it was." Was she truly up for the challenge?

"If it's what you truly want to do, you'll make it work, Chels. I guess you need to ask yourself, do you want to commit the time to it? Do you want to stay?"

The intensity in his gaze made her look away. Those were the questions she had to answer, but there were some variables that needed to become static before she did. And one of those was whether she and Ethan had a future together. Honeybrook was too far from Perth to ask him to commute daily. But did she want to go back to living in a city?

"In an ideal world, what do you want your future to be?" Ethan asked quietly.

She closed her eyes. Her fantasies had always revolved around Lilydale. Bringing her children here to visit Aunt Maggie and play in the gardens. Having a husband who adored her. Living nearby so she could help Aunt Maggie as she got older.

Those fantasies had been obliterated after Ethan had broken up with her and been replaced with having a job which earned enough so she never had to rely on any man.

Now she wasn't ready to let those fantasies back in. "I don't know."

"Can I tell you my new fantasy for the future?" Ethan asked.

She nodded as she wandered over to the nearest garden bed to pull out a stray weed that had been missed.

"It's being with you."

She glanced at him, her heart jumping.

"In whatever form you want. I've spent too much of my life regretting leaving you, and I'm not spending the next decade doing the same."

It was hard to breathe. He couldn't mean it. "You're based in the city. It's too far to drive every day."

He shrugged. "I mentioned Dobby is setting up a security firm. He's put a bunch of plans into motion already, and he'll give me a job."

She frowned. "Where will you work?"

"I can base myself here. I won't need to be in the city all the time and depending on the jobs we get, I might still travel."

Chelsea exhaled. "I wouldn't want you to give up your career for me."

He stepped closer. "I won't lie to you. The army saved me, gave me purpose and a sense of self-worth and the friends I have made…" He gestured towards the house. "They're my family." He took her hand. "But I don't need the army any longer. I'm financially secure, I can get my adrenaline fix working with Dobby, and my apartment wasn't ever a home. But seeing you again and being at Lilydale feels like being home."

The emotions in her chest were too big to put into words. The fear, the joy, the love. "I appreciate knowing that, Ethan."

A flash of disappointment crossed his face, and she reached for him, not wanting him to get the wrong idea. "It's a big decision to make and knowing what you want… that you want me… it makes a huge impact. I just need time to consider things when I'm not overwhelmed by you and your friends, when I'm not being harassed by a property developer, and not overcome by grief going through Aunt Maggie's things." Which was another thing she needed to finish.

She took a breath. "I want you, and I want Lilydale, but just because I want them, doesn't mean I can make it work. I need to plan it out, think it through."

He smiled, pulling her into his arms. "All right. I get that's how your brain works. If you need help planning, or if you need me to take distractions away so you can think, you say the word."

Was it any wonder she loved him?

While she had no doubt he would push if she prevaricated for too long, or if she was stuck in indecision, the fact he understood this was her way of processing things meant everything.

She brushed a kiss against his lips. "Thank you."

Her phone rang and she put it on speaker when she saw Josh's name. "Morning, Josh."

"The good news is we've got enough from Leyton to arrest Johann for his part in what happened to Lilydale," Josh said.

"And the bad news?" Ethan asked.

"Johann wasn't at home when the Perth police went to arrest him. His wife said he left at six to go fishing with friends, but the friends he's supposed to be with are at home. His wife can't get hold of him and said he was anxious when he woke, saying something about missing a phone call."

Ethan grabbed Chelsea's hand and dragged her back towards the house, making her break into a jog just to keep up. Johann could have made it to Honeybrook by now if he'd come straight here after leaving his house, but why would he? Unless Leyton was supposed to call to say he'd done the job.

"Maybe he has a mistress and fishing is the excuse he

gave his wife," Chelsea suggested. It was what her father had done during his affair with her mother.

"Maybe," Josh agreed. "I wanted to give you the heads up just in case."

"We'll keep an eye out for him," Ethan said.

The team looked over as they walked through the front door. It was slightly disconcerting how alert they were all the time. "Thanks Josh."

"There's more," Josh continued. "We looked into Lleyton's claims about the company Johann works for. They are on our radar."

Every person in the room went still. "Tell me more," Ethan barked.

"I shouldn't even be telling you that," Josh retorted. "The most I could get out of my colleagues was to tread very carefully. Johann might be what he seems, a project manager with few scruples, or he might understand exactly what his superiors do and therefore be desperate not to let them down."

Chelsea's skin prickled. It would explain the lengths Johann had gone to to get Lilydale.

"Understood," Ethan said. "Keep us up to date with anything new."

"I'll try." Josh hung up.

Ethan ran a hand through his hair as Heath asked, "What do we know?"

"Johann's in the wind," Ethan replied.

"Last seen?" Rhys asked.

"Leaving his house at six. Supposed to be going fishing, but he's not with his friends."

"What do you need?" Noah asked.

"We'll keep it casual," Ethan said. "Do work in areas we can't be seen from the road, so he doesn't know how many of us there are."

"Is he likely to come here if the police are after him?" Chelsea asked.

"We don't know what he's likely to do," Ethan said. "I don't want you going anywhere alone today. One of us should always be with you, even if you're going inside to use the bathroom."

Concern filled her. "Why would Johann attack me, especially with you all around?"

"He might be desperate and not thinking straight. It might be simply for revenge for messing up his plans. I'm not risking it."

Around him the rest of the men nodded. Mila came down the stairs looking refreshed. Her footsteps slowed. "What happened?"

"They couldn't catch Johann, and his company is associated with organised crime," Chelsea told her.

"Level of danger?" Mila asked Ethan.

"Unknown, but Johann's probably desperate."

Mila nodded. "We'll keep together." She smiled sympathetically at Chelsea. "At least there's plenty to keep us busy."

Chelsea was soothed by her forthright acceptance. Mila knew what these men were capable of and had faith in them. Chelsea knew Ethan wouldn't let anything happen to her. Some of her fear faded. "I guess you're right." She smiled at her new friend. "Can I get you a coffee?"

***

Unease settled around Ethan as they divvied up the tasks for the day. He pulled Chelsea aside. "Why don't you spend the day going through Aunt Maggie's things?"

She glanced at him. "You mean lock myself inside?"

"Yeah."

"Not going to happen. Besides, the next room I need to

go through is Aunt Maggie's and Dobby is sleeping in it."

He opened his mouth and she put her finger over it.

"No, you're not waking him. I'm not hiding away because Johann lied to his wife about where he would be. I haven't done enough work in the garden, and I can't expect you and your friends to work so hard on your days off."

"We're not great at relaxing," Heath joked. "You saved us from a weekend of boredom."

She rolled her eyes. "Nevertheless, I want to do some of the work. I want to look back and know I contributed."

"You'll have plenty of opportunity," Rhys said.

Chelsea just looked at Ethan.

"Fine, but you're working with me, and I've got sprinkler duty."

She screwed up her nose but nodded. "Fine."

They headed outside. Today was overcast and there was still the hint of both smoke and petrol in the air.

Chelsea explained to each soldier what she wanted done. She'd let them choose their task, and they had chosen locations that would give them a good spread throughout the garden to keep watch. Heath was working with Mila to ensure she was safe while Dobby slept.

Ethan didn't think Chelsea had noticed.

Finally they returned to the barn where the reticulation panel was. "There are ten sprinkler stations," Ethan said as he opened the cabinet where all the switches were. He reviewed the dated display which was familiar from his youth. "I haven't done the ones in the public garden yet."

"Do we turn each one on and see what works and what doesn't?"

"Let's go into the garden first and check the sprinklers are clear. Barry would have uncovered most of them, but it's better to identify broken ones before we get everything wet." He picked up the plastic box which contained sprinkler spares. "Shall we?"

A couple of hours later, they had reviewed and tested the sprinkler stations which were in the public area of the garden.

Chelsea yawned. "Morning tea break?"

"Yeah. I noticed you made some things last night."

She grinned. "All your favourites. Plus I figured I'd need a lot to feed your friends."

As they returned to the house, he whistled and yelled, "Smoko!"

Rhys glanced over, acknowledged the call, and gestured to someone Ethan couldn't see. Word would spread.

Chelsea filled the kettle and had made a couple of espressos by the time everyone had washed up and come inside. She handed the espressos to Noah and Rhys and then spread the food options over the table. Ethan grabbed a Father's Favourite, a chocolate ball made from Weet-Bix and condensed milk and covered in coconut. He closed his eyes as the sweet flavour hit his tongue and memories of his teenaged summer came back to him.

Aunt Maggie had fed him well, which he appreciated, because he hadn't been allowed to help himself to food in the pantry at his foster parents' place. Everything had to be approved beforehand, and most of the time he'd been told to wait until dinner.

He reached for another ball and Heath grabbed one. "They must be good if you're already going back for seconds." He bit into it and nodded. "Really good. Chelsea, you want to forget about Ethan and marry me?"

Chelsea laughed and Ethan ignored the small burst of jealousy, though he glared at Heath. "Back off."

Heath grinned and fetched his tea from the kitchen.

When they were all seated around the table, Ethan asked, "Any signs?"

One by one they shook their head. "Pretty quiet," Noah answered.

Perhaps it was a good thing, though he hadn't heard from Josh, which meant the police hadn't tracked down Johann.

He called Josh as Heath told Chelsea, "Most of the garden beds cottage side are ready for plants."

"Chelsea and I can head to the nursery after we've eaten," Mila said. "I can feel some retail therapy coming on."

Chelsea grinned. "That would be fun."

Ethan exchanged a glance with Dobby. Would they be safe?

Josh answered. "Nothing new to report."

"No sign of him here either," Ethan told him. "Did Leyton say anything about needing to call Johann?"

"No, he said he hadn't arranged anything. I've got to run." Josh sounded harried as he hung up.

Ethan repeated the information to the others.

"Maybe he did go fishing," Mila said.

"Or perhaps Darren was supposed to call him," Chelsea said. "Just because he didn't light the fire, doesn't mean he's not still involved."

She was right.

"Maybe it's time to pay Darren another visit," Ethan said.

"Why don't you do that while we go to the nursery?" Chelsea said.

Ethan shook his head. "You're not going anywhere alone."

"Mila's coming with me."

"How about we call Lauren and invite her?" Mila

suggested. "Then there will be three of us. He's not likely to try anything with two witnesses."

Was she right and he was being paranoid? He glanced at Dobby, who gave a subtle shake of his head. Yeah, he was worried about Mila too.

"Invite Lauren if you want, but I'll drive you to the nursery. My car is bigger." He wouldn't leave Chelsea unguarded.

"We'll visit Darren." Rhys grinned.

Noah cracked his knuckles. "It'll be fun."

Ethan chuckled. His friends always had his back. "Thanks. Let's get to it."

"Great!" Mila grinned at Chelsea. "I've never been plant shopping before."

Chapter 19

Chelsea couldn't prevent the stir of nerves in her stomach at the thought of leaving Lilydale to go plant shopping. Should she stay close to home until Johann was caught? Should she visit Darren with the team and demand answers?

She was tired of being targeted.

But she wasn't a warrior. The strong rational side of her brain told her to leave it to the experts.

"Are we calling Lauren?" Mila asked.

Chelsea blinked, pushing aside the nerves. "Sure." It would be great to do something with her two new friends. Chelsea rang Lauren. "Want to come to the nursery and buy plants?"

"You know how to sweet talk a girl." Lauren chuckled. "I'd love to, but something came up this morning. Can I help you plant them later?" There was a hopeful, wistful tone to her question.

When this was over, she would sit down with her friend. Find out what was really going on in her life. "Of course. We'll be back in a couple of hours." She hung up and said to Mila, "She's busy, but she'll come around later."

"Great. I hope Dobby finds a training area near here so we can see each other regularly." Mila linked her arm through Chelsea's. "I haven't met many women since I moved to Perth and I'd love to spend more time together."

"I'd like that." She paused. It was definitely another tick in the column for staying in Honeybrook.

Ethan brought his four-wheel drive out of the barn, and Chelsea climbed into the front seat, Mila sitting behind her. The inside was clean and had the sweet smell of cherry blossoms.

Mila sniffed. "Nice scent."

Ethan's cheeks reddened. "It reminded me of Chelsea."

Chelsea's heart hitched as she glanced at him. "When did you get it?"

He smiled. "When I went grocery shopping the other day. I noticed the car smelled stale."

He'd remembered. She'd had a cherry blossom moisturiser pack during their summer and had used the lotion and lip balm constantly.

It was still her favourite scent.

They drove out of town. Ethan tracked every car driving past, his hands tightening on the wheel when it was a dark-coloured car.

Surely they didn't have to worry about someone coming towards them. If anything, they'd have a tail.

"How long's your list?" Mila asked.

"Long." She grinned. "We'll just buy what we can fit in the back." Which was a pretty decent space, and far bigger than her hire car boot.

"They might offer a delivery service," Ethan said.

Good idea. Perhaps Aunt Maggie had been a regular

customer since this nursery was the closest one to Honeybrook.

Maybe Chelsea should mention her aunt's name.

Ethan pulled up in front of the nursery which had wide gates at the front and an entrance lined with pots overflowing with flowers and greenery. Towering gums shaded the building on the side and as they walked through they were greeted with several different paths to take, all lined with rows and rows of plants.

"This is incredible," Mila said as she took a trolley from nearby.

Chelsea smiled as she took her own trolley, remembering the day Aunt Maggie first brought her here, gave her a trolley and told her she could fill it with whatever plants she wanted for her own garden bed.

It had been thrilling and nerve-wracking, and though Aunt Maggie had given her advice on what plants would suit the soil and the amount of sun the bed received, in the end, Chelsea had been able to buy anything she wanted.

Her first choice had been a banana passionfruit.

With a sad wistfulness she wandered towards the native plants. They would work for the garden beds she wanted to establish with little fuss. Then on to the annuals for those where she needed a pop of colour immediately, and then she spotted the banana passionfruit vine.

Her steps slowed. It wasn't on her list of plants to buy, but the photo of the ripe fruit on the accompanying tag made her mouth water.

Ethan grabbed two and put them in his trolley.

She glanced at him.

"You'll replace them eventually," he said. "Might as well be now."

Her heart ached. He kept doing things to show how well he knew her. It made her love him more.

Mila looked at the plant. "I've never heard of banana passionfruit."

"It's amazing," Chelsea said.

They continued around, buying a couple of hedge plants for areas where the hedge had died, and some sweet-smelling honeysuckle and jasmine for areas where people would sit for extended periods. She'd done her research, making sure she bought plants that flowered at different times of the year, so the garden always had some kind of focal point.

"Are you landscapers?" the cashier asked as she rang up the purchases.

"No." Chelsea smiled. "I'm restoring Lilydale Cottage in Honeybrook."

"Maggie's place?" the cashier asked.

"Yes. She was my great aunt."

"Then you qualify for the same discount as she had."

"Thank you."

Despite the discount, Chelsea's breath left her when the cashier rang up the total and Chelsea handed over her bank card. If more people stayed in her cottages, it would go a long way towards paying for the restoration. She doubted she'd see any money from Darren, despite his promises.

"I need to take some photos of the plants for social media."

Mila and Ethan moved aside so she could take the photos and then record a live video. People commented and liked it, saying they couldn't wait to see the results.

It was all coming together. She hadn't felt this excited about something since… well, she couldn't remember being this excited ever. Not even when she got a new job.

"I'm just going to run to the bathroom," she told Ethan when she was finished filming.

Ethan frowned and scanned the area. "I'll come with you."

"It's not necessary. You can view the whole nursery from here. There's only one entrance."

"There's another at the back," Ethan said.

She hadn't noticed. "Is it open?"

"No."

"If you're worried, I'll go too." Mila smiled. "You can start loading this lot and we'll be home, surrounded by the team in no time."

He scanned the area again. Chelsea kissed him. "I'll be fine. I promise. Johann won't kidnap me in broad daylight." She glanced over his shoulder and frowned. "Is that Darren?"

Ethan spun around, putting himself between her and Mila. She peered around him as Darren walked towards them. What did he want?

Darren stopped a couple of metres away and eyed Ethan warily. "I'd like to speak to Chelsea."

Chelsea shifted so she stood next to Ethan. "What do you want?"

"I can't get the money for you. The bank won't give me anything because I'm not working."

Odd that he would come here. Had Noah and Rhys told him where they were going? It didn't seem likely. "I'll ask my mother what she wants to do about your breach of contract."

"How did you know we were here?" Ethan demanded, his voice low and lethal.

Darren took a step back. "I, ah, followed you."

"No, you didn't," Ethan said. "I watched for tails and no one was behind us."

Darren's face paled, and he looked around, as if searching for an answer.

Ethan stepped forward. "How did you know we were here?" Each word was slow and clear.

"Leyton told me."

"Try again," Ethan growled. "Leyton is in gaol."

Darren swore. "It was Johann, all right. He said I needed to come and talk to you here."

"Why?" Ethan's gaze roamed the area.

"I don't know."

"Where is he?"

"I don't know."

Ethan stepped even closer, and Darren held up his hands in surrender. "Honestly, I don't! He just called and said I had to come here and tell Chelsea I didn't have the money."

"And if you refused to come?" Ethan asked.

Darren pressed his lips together.

"I'd answer him if I were you," Mila said. "He looks pretty mad."

Chelsea grinned and then her bladder reminded her she'd been heading to the bathroom. She scanned the other shoppers. No sign of Johann.

"He'd tell the police about something I did."

"Like vandalise my cottages?" Chelsea asked.

Darren squeezed his eyes closed but said nothing.

She turned to Ethan. "I really need to use the bathroom. Can we continue this conversation in a minute?"

He nodded and clapped Darren on the shoulder. "You're coming with us."

They all walked over to the bathroom, and Ethan rang Josh.

Chelsea left them to it as she ducked into the small stall. What possible motive could Johann have to send Darren here? It could have waited until they got back to Lilydale.

Outside Ethan yelled something she didn't quite hear, and then there were pounding footsteps across the loose gravel. "Ethan?"

No answer. Quickly she finished and dashed out of the bathroom. Across the nursery by the main gate, she spotted Ethan tackling Darren to the ground, Mila right behind them.

Darren must have run for it.

She stepped forward and a movement in her periphery caught her attention. Before she turned, pain exploded in her head.

Then everything went black.

***

It was immensely satisfying to tackle Darren to the ground, even though pain shot up Ethan's body at the jolt. Darren's body cushioned his fall, and Ethan brought Darren's hands behind his back to stop him moving further.

"Get off me!" Darren yelled.

"When the police get here." Ethan glanced up as Mila reached them, gasping for breath.

"What's going on here?" a nursery worker demanded.

"Citizen's arrest," Ethan said. "This man is wanted for vandalism. The police are on their way."

"Could you move him away from the entrance? You're scaring away customers."

Ethan scanned the area to find all eyes were on them. He smiled. "Sure." He tossed his car keys to Mila. "I've got cable ties in the back. Can you grab them?"

He dragged Darren to his feet. What had he hoped to accomplish by running away? The police would have tracked him down at home.

He needed to get back to Chelsea, so she knew it was

safe to come outside. He'd yelled at her to stay put when Darren ran.

A quick glance at the bathroom made him freeze. The door was wide open.

Where was Chelsea?

He scanned the nursery looking for her pink shirt, but there was no one who even vaguely resembled her.

"Here." Mila thrust the cable ties at Ethan and he tied Darren's hands behind his back as he scanned again to make certain he hadn't missed her. "Can you see Chelsea?"

"No."

He dumped Darren to his knees and tied another cable tie around his ankles before grabbing Mila's hand. "This way." No way he'd leave Mila alone. If anything happened to her, Dobby would kill him.

He dragged her towards the bathroom, his heart pounding as he scanned the area, hoping Chelsea was crouching down to examine another plant. As he cleared the office, he spotted the back gate wide open.

There was the unmistakable engine roar of a sports car.

Fuck.

Ethan dropped Mila's hand and sprinted to the gate in time to see the black Porsche turn the corner, heading for the highway.

Johann.

He spun around. "Car!" he yelled to Mila, who jolted and sped back the way they came. He dug his phone out of his pocket and dialled Dobby.

"You need—"

"Johann has Chelsea," Ethan interrupted.

"Mila?"

"Safe." He scanned the highway and spotted the Porsche drive by. "Black Porsche heading south on the highway. En route to car."

"We'll head north now."

Good. He caught up with Mila, who tossed him his car keys. Darren was back on his feet, but Ethan didn't care. The police could deal with him.

Behind him Mila yelled, "We'll be back for the plants."

Ethan leapt into his car and waited only long enough for Mila to jump in before tearing out of the car park.

In the distance, the Porsche rounded a corner and drove out of view. "He's left town, still heading south."

"Roger," Dobby replied through the car speaker. "We've cleared Honeybrook."

Ethan pressed the accelerator to the floor as he shifted through the gears. Next to him, Mila was calling the police.

There wasn't anything they could do. He had to catch up before Johann hurt Chelsea.

Maybe he already had.

He should have let Darren run. It was a rookie mistake. Protect the target always.

Why hadn't Chelsea stayed inside?

Ethan clenched the steering wheel and went around the bend. Up ahead in the distance was the Porsche.

Twenty-five kilometres between here and Honeybrook, and only a few roads where Johann could turn, but he was pulling away. His Porsche had a lot more horsepower than Ethan's four-wheel drive.

The car disappeared around another bend. "Lost eyes," he reported.

"The operator contacted Josh," Mila said. "He's on his way."

Ethan nodded but kept his eyes on the road. Up ahead, a car towed a caravan slowly. He switched lanes to pass it, only to face a truck. He swore, slamming on the brakes, and moved back into his lane.

"Don't you have an accident with Mila in the car,"

Dobby said.

Ethan didn't answer, his heart pounding.

The truck roared past with a loud honk of its horn and Ethan shifted again, but there were several more cars coming towards him.

"Fucking caravans." There had to be an overtaking lane soon.

"Just heading past Coolup," Dobby reported as Ethan finally got past the caravan.

That was the halfway point. "You haven't seen him?"

"No."

Shit. Maybe he'd turned off. "Mila, where are we? Check what roads are between us and Coolup." They'd only been past one road and a couple of farm entrances since he'd lost sight of the Porsche.

"There's one," Heath chimed in over the phone.

So two possible options.

He passed a sign telling him he was five kilometres from Coolup and then spotted the road Heath had mentioned. He pulled over. "Stopping at the road." He pulled out his phone to see where it went. "Any chance Johann reached the town before you did?" He might have turned there and be hiding in the streets until they passed.

"Unlikely. He would have had to pass the same vehicles you struggled to pass," Noah said.

Their black four-wheel drive pulled in behind him and Dobby jumped out, running to the passenger side to check on Mila.

"I know where they are!" Rhys yelled, getting out of the car.

Ethan strode over to him. "Where?"

"Johann's company has a development near here. The road you drove past will take you straight there."

It was their best option.

"Heath, there's a drone in the back," Noah called from behind the wheel. "Get it out."

Dobby and Mila joined them. "Rhys, Heath, go in Ethan's car. Mila will come with us."

Ethan nodded as a plan formed. If they had a drone, they could survey the development and ascertain if Johann was there.

If he wasn't… it wasn't an option Ethan wanted to think about. "Connor, search for alternatives. Anyone got a sat phone?"

They all shook their heads, but Dobby passed him an ear comm they'd used last night. "Let's go."

In moments they were driving at speed towards the turn off. Ethan called Josh, while Heath set up the drone in the back.

"What the hell happened?" Josh demanded.

"Johann took Chelsea at the nursery. We think he's taken her to the development on…" He glanced at Rhys.

"Timbertop Road."

He repeated the information. "Did you get Darren?"

"Yeah, the Pinjarra police picked up an irate Darren from the nursery," Josh said. "We're on our way. Does Johann have any weapons?"

"I don't know."

"Don't go in until we get there. I've contacted our hostage negotiator."

Ethan wasn't waiting. Not with Chelsea in danger. "Can't guarantee that." He turned onto the road and accelerated again.

When Josh didn't reply, he glanced at his phone. No signal. "We've lost mobiles."

"Ear comms are still good," Connor reported.

Good.

"We're two kilometres out," Rhys reported.

"Show me," Heath said as the drone beeped.

Rhys held up the map on his phone.

"Let me launch the drone," Heath ordered.

Though it pained Ethan, he slowed so Heath could set the drone going. "Won't it be faster if we get closer?"

"Noah doesn't scrimp on his toys," Heath said, staring at the control screen. "This thing can cut across the bush and go ninety ks an hour."

Ethan reached an intersection. One way was bitumen and the other gravel. "Which way?"

"Left," Rhys said.

Gravel. The dust could warn Johann they were coming before he heard them.

"I've got eyes," Heath announced. "The black Porsche is at the development. I can't see either Johann or Chelsea though."

Ethan exhaled. It was a start.

"Find somewhere to pull over," Dobby said. "We'll go on foot. Connor and Mila will stay with the cars in case we need them."

And to keep Mila out of harm's way.

Ethan found a spot off the road and pulled in. He strode to his boot and pulled out several camping knives he used for cooking and held them up. "Anyone need a weapon?"

Rhys and Heath shook their head, taking out a multi-tool similar to the one Ethan had in his pocket. He sorted through his things, grabbing more cable ties, a mirror and a few other useful items.

Dobby and Noah joined them and Heath held out the drone display so they all could see. "The units don't have roofs yet and I've scanned them all. The only place Johann and Chelsea can be is in one of the two demountables on site."

"Can you look through the windows?" Ethan asked.

"I can't get the right angle. If I go too low, there's a chance they'll hear the drone."

"Most likely it's the one closest to the car," Noah said.

Ethan nodded. It was also the closest to the gate and the short side facing the entrance had no window. That would benefit them.

"Show me the entrance and exit points," Dobby said.

Heath panned the drone around the demountable. A door and two windows on the side that faced the road, no windows on the opposite short side, and two windows facing the front fence of the compound.

Ethan nodded. "Here's the plan."

Chapter 20

Chelsea's head pounded as she struggled to wake. What had happened?

The roar of an unfamiliar engine added to the pain. Was she in a car? She groaned and forced her eyes open.

"Don't try anything."

Chelsea winced at the barked order as she glanced at the driver.

Johann.

Shit.

Fear shoved the pain out of the way at his angry scowl.

The last thing she remembered was coming out of the bathroom and seeing Ethan tackle Darren to the ground.

Then pain.

Johann must have hit her over the head and somehow got her into his car with no one noticing.

Maybe Darren was simply the distraction.

She glanced in the side mirror but couldn't see a four-wheel drive behind them. They were speeding down the road and she turned her attention forward as a massive timber truck headed straight towards them. She shrieked as

Johann swerved back into the correct lane just in time.

Chelsea's heart raced as she fumbled with her seat belt and clipped it in place. Not that it would help much in a head on collision with a truck.

She took three deep breaths before asking, "What are you doing, Johann?"

"I'm showing you what Lilydale could be."

Confusion made her frown. Did he not realise the police were after him? There was no way for him to salvage this. What did he hope to gain by kidnapping her?

They were going too fast for her to jump out of the car and her head still spun from the blow. She touched the back of it gingerly and winced at the pain.

Had Ethan noticed she was missing yet? He must have and was somewhere behind them or searching for her. Subtly she felt her pockets. Her phone was still there, as was her wallet. If she called him without Johann noticing, he might be able to track her. They were heading south down the highway. How long had she been out? It couldn't have been long, which meant they wouldn't be at Honeybrook yet. Perhaps Ethan's team could stop Johann on the way through.

Johann slowed and made a sharp turn down a side road. Chelsea grabbed the roof to balance herself and winced as the back of her head hit the seat headrest.

Flat farmland was all around them with no houses or cars in sight.

Johann was driving as if someone was after him, but there was no one behind when she checked the side mirror again. Cautiously she slipped her hand into her pocket and drew out her phone far enough to see the screen.

She checked Johann, but his focus was on the road.

"This is all Maggie's fault," Johann declared, making Chelsea jump.

That's right. He'd killed Maggie. Fear and anger filled her in a potent combination. But perhaps she could learn something. She flicked to the recording app on her phone and pressed record. "What is?"

"This whole situation." Johann waved his hand around. "If she'd sold me Lilydale when I first asked her to, none of this would have been necessary."

"You mean you wouldn't have shoved her off a ladder and killed her?" The words shot out before she considered if it was wise to antagonise him.

"That was an accident!" Johann yelled. "I wanted to scare her."

"You wanted to bully a seventy-year-old woman into selling you the property she'd lived in her whole life?"

"She didn't need all the space. She was being selfish."

Chelsea gritted her teeth. "Why not choose somewhere else for your development?"

"Because people want to be close to Perth. It was perfect, and I'd promised my bosses I would get the land. They aren't people you want to disappoint." He braked sharply as they came to a T-junction and then turned left onto a gravel road. He drove a little more slowly, probably worried he'd damage his car.

That was right. Johann's company had ties to organised crime. What would they do to Johann if they realised he hadn't bought Lilydale?

Would they come after her if he failed?

Real fear filled her as her brain cleared enough to realise the full severity of the situation.

Though Johann was driving slower now, Chelsea still wasn't sure whether she'd be able to jump out without breaking something.

What other options did she have?

No weapons, not even a pen on the floor and Chelsea

hadn't brought keys with her. But she could run when they stopped, and perhaps she'd be able to outrun him.

Not far ahead was construction fencing and a gate into a property development. She recognised Johann's company name on the poster.

"This is what Lilydale could be." Johann gestured to the row of bland, cookie-cutter units packed close together along a street. "Homes so the elderly can be independent but still have support if they need it."

Chelsea didn't disagree with the concept. "Why do you need Lilydale if you have this development?"

"We've sold everything. There's more demand than supply with the baby boomers getting older and our surveys show there are a group of customers who want a more rural location." He spoke as if giving a presentation to stakeholders.

Perhaps that was what she was.

Chelsea wasn't certain where they were, but it must be somewhere just south of Pinjarra and towards the coast.

Johann pulled up and grabbed something from the floor. He brandished a butcher's knife towards her and she shrank back against the door, her hand scrabbling to find the door handle.

"I don't want to hurt you." The slight desperation in his gaze made Chelsea freeze.

She swallowed. "What do you want me to do?"

"We're going into that building." He gestured to the nearby demountable.

"Is it the construction office?"

"Yeah."

She glanced at the bush. Should she run for it? It would be hard going through the dense undergrowth, and Johann would catch her in the car if she used the road.

But it was her only hope. Whatever his plan, he

couldn't let her go when he was done. Not if he didn't want to go to gaol.

She got out and dizziness swept over her as she straightened. She clutched the door frame for support as she tried to get her legs to work but it was as if they were jelly.

Frustrated, she closed her eyes until the dizziness faded.

Johann grabbed her arm. "Come on."

Damn. Running had been her only option. Now what was she going to do?

She breathed slowly, concentrating on her steps. Perhaps she could reason with him. "I'm assuming no one works here on the weekend?" She stumbled towards the demountable building, her steps unsteady and nausea making her want to vomit.

"Not at the moment. We might ramp up the project after we're at lockup. Our clients want to move in by Christmas."

Which was still eight months away. It was a pretty impressive schedule if they stuck to it.

He glanced at her. "That's why we need Lilydale as soon as possible." His expression had morphed into salesman mode; an attempt at charm which only came through as insincere.

The change was more frightening than the anger. This spoke more of delusion. Did he really believe she would change her mind after he had kidnapped her? Whatever his plans, her best option was to stall him long enough for Ethan or the police to find her. Or find a weapon and attack when he wasn't expecting it.

But first she needed him to put down that viciously scary knife.

Chelsea's heart raced as she walked into the demountable. "Perhaps I was a little hasty in refusing you.

Lilydale would be perfect for your requirements."

Johann nodded, though he looked a little suspicious.

"Do you have a concept?" Only the one door, but four windows she could escape from. She stopped next to the filtered water stand with plastic cups next to it. "May I have a drink?"

Johann nodded, and placed the knife on a credenza just next to the door.

Chelsea poured a glass, making note of the kitchenette on the other side of the room. She might find a weapon there.

Johann opened a drawer and pulled out several large drawings, placing them on the meeting room table in the middle of the room. Still between her and the door.

Her head pounded with pain and the dizziness was still there. Carefully she wandered over and traced the road on the image. "That's the road which winds around Lilydale?"

"Yes. We'd have one entrance into the community to ensure security and a hundred and fifty units." Suddenly he was smiling at her and in full pleasant salesman mode.

It filled her with unease, but she could play along. At least he wasn't threatening her with the knife.

Residents would live on postage stamp blocks with no garden. Some people might appreciate it, but it would reduce Aunt Maggie's work to nothing, the lush coolness of the garden to brick and concrete, which would raise the ambient temperature. It was already hot in the summer with the sea breeze not cooling this far inland.

Chelsea hated the idea, but she kept her distaste from her face. "Will there be a range of unit sizes?"

"A couple of three bedrooms, but mostly one or two. The oldies don't need the space."

His condescending tone irritated her but she didn't react. A faint familiar whirring noise reached her ears.

She'd heard it on the shoots with Aria. They hadn't had any generators and their technology had consisted of cameras and… drones.

Hope filled her.

"Could you turn on the air-conditioning?" she asked. "It's hot and I'm dizzy." She cleared her throat and waved a hand at her face, trying to make enough noise so he didn't hear the whirring.

"Of course." Johann moved to the remote next to the door and in moments the hum of the air-conditioner blocked out any sound of the drone.

Outside a drone flew from above the units to over the demountable and out of sight.

Was that Ethan?

She hadn't noticed any farmhouses nearby and there was nothing to attract drone enthusiasts unless they wanted an empty space to fly.

"What are you looking at?"

She glanced at Johann. "The units. Are they the same as you've designed for Lilydale?" She moved away from the window.

"Yes. They're very popular."

"Have you got the floor plans?"

"Of course."

He went to another drawer, but was still between her and the door. She sat at a desk across the other side of the room. The window next to her was fixed in place, with no way of opening it.

She took the sheets Johann handed her and slowly perused each one. What other questions could she ask?

"Would you be willing to sacrifice a couple of units to create a village green?"

Johann frowned. "The design has already been approved."

"Oh. It seems so sad for all of Aunt Maggie's garden to disappear," she said. "It was such an important part of my childhood."

He puffed out his chest. "This is not a negotiation, Miss McGinnis." He stormed back to the cabinets, drew out another document, and picked up the knife. "You don't understand. If you don't sign this, I'm dead. They'll kill me and my family." He waved around the knife.

Fear skittered through her and she held up a hand of placation. "Who will?"

Johann hesitated.

This was his vulnerability. "Johann, I don't want to put your family in danger, but I need you to explain what's going on."

Johann thrust the document at her and then stepped back. "I fucked up."

Chelsea glanced down at the paperwork. A contract of sale for Lilydale. She shifted in the seat, ready to defend herself with the wireless keyboard on the desk if necessary. "How?"

"I was so sure Maggie would sell. She was ancient and should have been relieved for me to make her such a generous offer for her land so she could retire in peace."

Chelsea struggled not to show her scorn. She swallowed and said, "Aunt Maggie loved her place."

"I promised my bosses it was in the bag. For the past year I've been pretending the company owns the land. All the designs are done and we've already sold a dozen properties."

He really was in deep.

"I thought your mother would be glad to get rid of it, but no, she had to send you here."

Chelsea shifted a little further away from him. "Do your bosses know what you've done now?"

He shook his head. "They can't. If the authorities find out and bring attention to their legitimate business, I'm dead."

It made sense if the construction company was owned by organised crime.

Johann turned to her, eyes begging. "Please, you have to sign it. You have to save me and my family."

She kept her voice low, sympathetic. "I can't sign it. Lilydale belongs to my mother." Didn't he realise the contract would never stand up in court if he coerced her signature?

"Ezra told me she'd transferred the property to you," Johann growled, raising the knife.

Chelsea shrank back. "She might have. She was going to, but I didn't think it would go through so quickly." Her eyes didn't stray from the knife, but she wanted one question answered. "How is Ezra involved?"

"I met him at a conference. When I discovered his connection with Lilydale, I thought he'd be able to convince your mother to sell."

"Did he say she would?"

Johann shook his head. "Said it wasn't up to him." His disgust was clear.

A sliver of relief filled Chelsea. She would have hated to discover Ezra was more involved. It would have devastated her mother.

"Don't put a date on it. That way if she hasn't signed it over, we can put the correct date on later."

Right. He wouldn't let a little technicality like that stop him. She picked up the contract. "May I read it?"

"No!" he yelled. "You will sign it. You've caused me enough trouble as it is."

Chelsea shrank back as he towered over her, fear making it hard to breathe. She needed space from him.

"Could I have a pen?" She gestured to the one on a desk across the room. "And another glass of water? My head is spinning."

If she spilled water on the contract, he'd have to print another copy.

And maybe give Ethan an opportunity to get to her.

Because she didn't know what Johann would do to her after the contract was signed.

***

Ethan jogged the kilometre from the car to the development with his team and they split into two groups. One would go through the front door, and the other would monitor the back in case Johann somehow fled.

Ethan would like to see him try.

Heath crouched at the corner of the building and gestured for them to move into position. Dobby was watching the bush side, and Ethan was following Rhys and Noah into the building. It galled him not to go in first, but Rhys had argued if he went in last, he'd have the job of securing the hostage, which meant he would get to Chelsea first.

He agreed.

He crept under the nearest window and used his mirror to peer inside. Chelsea sat at a table on the opposite side of the building to him and Johann stood over her, brandishing a knife.

He wished he had a gun. Johann was too close, and no matter how fast they were, Chelsea would be in a vulnerable position if they burst in now.

He needed Johann to be across the room.

What were the chances?

Ethan used hand signals to tell the others what was happening. They ducked past him and took position by the metal steps leading to the door.

Ethan followed them and placed his hand on Rhys's shoulder, who had his on Noah's. He raised the mirror again and spotted Johann moving towards the door.

Chelsea was out of his range.

Ethan slapped Rhys's shoulder. In seconds Noah had booted open the door and charged inside. By the time Ethan entered the room, Noah and Rhys had Johann on his stomach, arms behind his back, the knife on the floor out of his reach.

Chelsea rose to her feet with a gasp and he was across the room in three steps, gathering her into his arms. "Are you all right?" He inhaled her hair, the scent calming him.

She clung to him. "I am now."

She trembled, and Ethan ignored the urge to hit Johann. Chelsea needed him. He stroked Chelsea's back. "You're safe. Did he hurt you?"

She placed a hand on the back of her head. "He hit me on the head to knock me out. It's pretty sore and I'm a little dizzy."

"Let me look. Rhys, get over here. He's our medic."

Dobby replaced Rhys standing over Johann and was telling Connor to bring the cars. Outside, Heath lowered the drone onto the ground.

Rhys smiled at Chelsea. "Glad you're in one piece. What hurts?"

"My head." She turned and the matted blood in her hair made Ethan take a step towards Johann. Dobby shook his head.

Heath walked in as if he was visiting a friend. "I called the police. They'll be here soon."

Chelsea turned her head. "Mila?"

"With Connor. They're on their way." Rhys gently prodded her injury and then examined her eyes. "Doesn't feel as if your skull is fractured. We'll take you to get scanned at the hospital to make sure there's no swelling."

The two four-wheel drives pulled up and Mila and Connor got out. "I'll take her now," Ethan said.

Connor walked in and grinned. "Looks like you didn't need me."

"I heard the drone." Chelsea glanced at Heath, who still had the controller in his hands. "I hoped it was you. I wanted Johann away from me, so I asked for a drink."

"Clever," Noah praised.

"Bitch!" Johann spat.

Chelsea ignored him and gestured to the drawings on the table. "Those are his plans for Lilydale."

Ethan didn't care. He drew her into his arms again. She was safe.

That was all that mattered.

"Let's get you to the hospital."

***

The doctor had finished examining Chelsea before Josh arrived at the hospital to take their statements. It was just as well, because Ethan wasn't letting anyone near Chelsea until she'd been given the all-clear. Her mild concussion meant she had to rest and be woken every couple of hours during the night, but other than that, she was fine.

Ethan had never been so relieved.

"How are you feeling, Chelsea?" Josh asked.

"I'm all right."

They were waiting for her discharge papers so they could go home.

"Johann?" Ethan asked.

"Arrested and charged with a bunch of crimes. He won't see the outside of a prison cell in a while."

Good.

Chelsea pulled out her phone. "I almost forgot. I recorded him talking about Aunt Maggie's death." She played back the recording, and Ethan clenched his hands. He almost wished Johann had been harder to take down.

"Send it to me," Josh said. "Johann's bosses reached out to me, and they want to speak with you. They deny any knowledge of what he did."

"How did they know about it?" Ethan demanded.

"Johann's wife gave my colleague their number. Said someone at work might know where Johann was."

"I don't want them knowing Chelsea's name," Ethan said.

Josh sighed. "They already do. Sounds as if they know all about Lilydale, but Johann had told them he had a signed contract and works were starting next month."

"No wonder Johann was so desperate," Chelsea said. "Did they say what they wanted?"

"To offer condolences and compensation."

Ethan glanced at Chelsea. Compensation would help revive Lilydale, but was it wise to take money from a company associated with organised crime?

"They can call me," Chelsea said.

Ethan opened his mouth to protest and Chelsea interrupted. "They already know who I am, Ethan, and the police know they know. There's no point hiding from it."

She was right, but he didn't like it. He nodded.

Ethan held her hand as Josh asked his questions, and by the time the nurse returned with the discharge papers, Chelsea had also spoken with the CEO of the property development firm.

Ethan felt marginally better knowing Josh had heard the whole conversation and the CEO had known Josh was listening.

Josh smiled. "I'll call you tomorrow with any updates."

She hugged him. "Thanks."

Ethan shook his hand. "Come over for a beer when you're done."

Josh nodded. "If it's not too late."

The guy looked exhausted with dark bags under his eyes. Ethan would make time for him in the next week. But right now, Chelsea was his priority.

He drove her home, and the late afternoon sun reflected off the first-floor windows of Lilydale Cottage.

Chelsea yawned as Ethan opened his door. "We never picked up the plants."

Ethan shook his head. "We can do it tomorrow." He helped her out of the car, hugging her close, unable to get enough of her to reassure himself she was safe.

"I'm exhausted," Chelsea said. "Who knew being kidnapped would be so tiring?"

His gut clenched. He was pleased she could joke about it but, "I keep seeing the empty bathroom and not knowing where you were." The horror and helplessness.

She squeezed him. "You were being a badass with Darren."

Not good enough. He shouldn't have left her unprotected. "I told you to stay inside until I got back."

"And I already told you, I didn't hear you. I was worried you'd been attacked."

Voices outside had him leading Chelsea away from the front steps and around the side of the house. Over in the garden underneath the gazebo were his team, Mila and Lauren.

Chelsea gasped and pointed at the group of plants that had been sorted by type near the cottages.

Ethan grinned. Someone must have stopped by the nursery to get them.

"You remembered the plants," Chelsea said as they

reached the group. "Thank you."

"That was Lauren," Rhys said. "She was unloading her ute when we arrived back."

"Josh called me," Lauren said. "I figured you'd be too busy with questions to go back for them. I watered them but wasn't sure where you wanted them planted."

"The plan will be somewhere on her phone." Heath grinned.

Chelsea tapped her pocket. "That's right, but we all deserve the evening off."

"We helped ourselves," Dobby said, gesturing to the biscuits and drinks on the table.

"I told them you wouldn't mind," Lauren added. "Aunt Maggie always had an open cupboard."

Ethan felt a pang of sorrow as Chelsea nodded with a sad smile. "My house is your house. I appreciate you coming to my rescue so fast."

There was only one chair left, so Ethan pulled Chelsea down on his lap, circling her with his arms. She passed him a Father's Favourite.

So casual. So right.

"Did you learn anything from Josh?" Dobby asked.

"It sounds as if Johann had got himself in a bind," Ethan said when he'd swallowed the treat. "His employer thought he'd bought Lilydale and construction was starting next month. They're willing to pay back the money Darren stole, plus damages if Chelsea agrees to keep their name out of the press."

"Are you going to accept it?" Mila asked.

Chelsea nodded. "I'll never know for sure if they knew about Johann's methods, but I'm hoping Mum will let me keep the money to repair Lilydale and to honour Aunt Maggie's memory."

Ethan loved that she was practical about it. Some might

consider it a bribe, but Chelsea was right. They could do so much with the money and he suspected Sabine would be happy for Chelsea to keep it.

He imagined the garden full of people helping Chelsea achieve her dream.

And he was right by her side.

"What about Darren?" Mila asked.

"He and Leyton have been charged for their part in the whole fiasco and are looking at gaol time," Ethan said. "And Chelsea recorded Johann confessing to killing Aunt Maggie, so he'll be charged with that as well."

Aunt Maggie's goodness and vitality had been cut short. It would be good to pay tribute to her. She deserved so much more than that.

Chelsea curled into him. "I should call my mother."

Sabine would be equally devastated.

"I'll go with you." He wanted to support her and needed to talk to her about the future. This afternoon had highlighted the future wasn't guaranteed. Anything could happen, and he wanted to be with her.

He pulled Chelsea into the cool house, taking a moment to hold her in his arms and breathe.

"I'm safe, Ethan." She clung to him.

He nodded against her head. "I know. Humour me."

"I knew you would come after me," she whispered. "I just needed to stall Johann long enough. I don't think even he had decided what he was going to do after I signed the contract."

He rubbed her back and shuddered at the memory of the butcher's knife. "I'm glad we didn't find out."

"I can't believe you got to me so quickly," she said.

"There weren't many options. Rhys found the development, and we figured that's where he would have gone." He pulled her over to the sofa.

Before sitting, she hesitated. "Can we talk?"

His muscles tightened, and he nodded. "Of course."

"I've been thinking." She let go of his hand and walked to the window, looking at the garden.

Part of him screamed to distract her, to stop her from saying whatever she wanted to say, because it didn't sound great. He stepped forward, and she turned with a shy smile on her face.

He kept his mouth closed and waited.

"The money from the company is more than enough to see me through the first year at Lilydale."

Ethan's breath caught in his throat, but he didn't dare move as hope blossomed.

"I love it here. It's the only place that ever felt like home."

He managed to nod.

"I'm going to stay here and build a business and a home." She stepped towards him. "If you're still interested, I'd like to do it with you."

His muscles unfroze, and he swept her into his arms, relief and happiness making him dizzy. "Yes."

She laughed and the sound filled his heart.

"I love you, Ethan."

"I love you too, Chelsea." He kissed her, tasting the sweetness of her lips, capturing this moment in his memory.

When they broke apart, she was trying to be stern and it looked so cute that he bent to kiss her again. She held up a hand to ward him off.

"But I have one condition."

"Anything."

She frowned. "You shouldn't promise before you know what it is."

"I'll do anything if it means I get to spend the rest of

my life with you."

Her frowned morphed into a smile. "No more doing things for my own good without discussing them with me first." Her gaze hit him and he couldn't look away. "I might not agree with you, but that's my prerogative. I want to be fully informed."

He sighed. "OK. I'm sorry, it's part of wanting to protect you."

"Being informed is a type of protection."

She was right. "Yeah. I can't guarantee I'll always be able to tell you about work, though. In the army it was classified and depending on how Dobby sets up his new security firm, some of that might be classified too."

"All right." A mischievous look crossed her face. "So, how does marrying me in a spring wedding in the gardens of Lilydale sound?"

His heart felt like it would burst. "It sounds like a dream come true."

And he kissed her to seal the deal.

Epilogue

Kylie Reed sobbed in relief as her headlights illuminated the Welcome to Honeybrook sign in front of her.

She'd made it.

After almost four days of solid driving, she was across the other side of the country where no one would think to look for her.

She'd told no one about Chelsea's new venture on the west coast and she wasn't close enough friends with Chelsea that anyone would guess she would come here.

She just hoped Chelsea's invitation to stay a while wasn't a throwaway comment.

Kylie pulled off on the side of the main road outside a lolly shop and took a moment to breathe and wipe her eyes. She flicked on the overhead light and checked her appearance in the mirror.

Dark bags under her eyes. Her short black hair lay flat against her head, instead of its usual spiky array and her mud brown eyes looked lifeless.

She winced. Yeah, she looked haggard, but that could be explained if she said she'd pushed through to make town tonight.

Chelsea didn't need to know she'd barely slept in four

days.

She shuddered and pushed the memory of what had driven her here away. There'd be time to deal with it later.

She skulled the last of the now cold coffee she'd picked up at her final fuel stop and swallowed hard.

She'd be safe here.

Checking the empty street for vehicles, she pulled back onto the road and followed her sat nav off the main road, through a winding street to a double-storey house with a massive garden.

Black remnants of a fire spread over a Japanese pagoda that looked as if it was about to fall down.

Kylie frowned.

What had happened?

She parked behind a hire car and a black four-wheel drive and slowly got out. Perhaps she should have called to say she was coming. Chelsea might already have visitors.

There were a few lights on inside the house, bleeding out the side of the blinds, but the sound of music drew her attention to the large barn. Behind it was the glow of fire and she followed the path through the dark garden to where people gathered around a large bonfire.

She kept back, using the barn as a shield while she scanned the faces. Five incredibly fit-looking men sat on a couple of logs, chatting and drinking beer.

She blinked to make sure she wasn't hallucinating the hotness and her gaze fell on Chelsea who had her arm around one of the men.

Then she noticed two more women who were chatting with her.

It looked like a cosy get-together, one she probably shouldn't crash. She could find a caravan park nearby or maybe a rest stop where she could sleep for the night in her campervan. Then she could call Chelsea in the morning and warn her she was coming.

Kylie turned to go and hit a solid wall. She stumbled

back a step as a hand gripped her arm firmly. She shrieked as fear pierced her.

They'd found her.

"Who the hell are you?" The angry tone was deep and harsh like moonshine.

She struggled to pull away, unable to find words as the man dragged her towards the fire.

Towards safety, not away from it.

That point dulled the fear and she gasped to find her voice as she stumbled into the light. The five men were on their feet instantly.

"I found her skulking by the barn," the man who held her said.

She turned, offended by the term skulking and looked up into stormy blue eyes, a face covered in a dark, bushy beard and his hair tied back in a man bun.

Gorgeous.

Before she could regain her words, he dropped her like she had burnt him, his gaze even angrier than before.

How was that even possible?

But something in them sparked a memory, one deep in the recesses of her mind.

"Kylie?" Chelsea's voice pierced through the haze. "What are you doing here?"

Unease filled Kylie as she turned away, unable to grasp why the angry man seemed familiar. She forced a smile to her face. "You gave me an open invitation." She opened her arms wide. "Surprise?"

Want to find out how Kylie and Noah know each other? Make sure you read Restoring Trust, Book 2 of the Lilydale Cottage series.

Father's Favourites Recipe

I couldn't help working some of my Granny's recipes into this book. Gran had a beautiful garden – not quite as big as Lilydale Cottage – but big enough to play a great game of hide and seek. She hung hammocks from trees and Grandfather had his vegie patch, and there were always flowers blooming. I used to love afternoon tea time when Granny would make a pot of tea and bring out one of her many treats that were always in the pantry.

I think Father's Favourites got their name because they were my Grandfather's favourite treat, but they were also my Dad's favourite too, so the name is appropriate.

I honestly don't know the origins of this recipe. It might have been found on the back of a Weet-bix box, or a condensed milk can, or passed down from a friend. I do know I've been enjoying them for more than forty years.

They're so simple and I always think of my grandparents when I make them.

<u>Ingredients</u>
    9 Weet-Bix crushed to a reasonably fine consistency
    2 Tablespoons cocoa
    1 tin condensed milk (395g)
    1 cup sultanas
    Desiccated coconut (for rolling balls in)

Mix all the ingredients together except for the coconut until they are well combined. For the Weet-Bix, you can blitz them in a food processor, or simply crumble them by hand until they are fine enough to form into balls.

Form into balls (size is up to the individual. If you're like my mum, you'll use a heaped teaspoon to make them. If you're like me, you'll use a heaped tablespoon!)

Roll balls in coconut.

Refrigerate for a couple of hours until they're cold.

Then try not to eat them all in one sitting.

Enjoy!

Thank you for reading!

I hope you enjoyed Chelsea and Ethan's story. Creating Lilydale Cottage was a lot of fun. For those of you who have read all of my books, you might recognise Libby, Chelsea's primary school friend. If you haven't, then you can check out Libby's story in What Goes on Tour, book 1 in The Texan Quartet. If you would like to read Dobby and Mila's story, it's called Rescuing Mila and is book 1 of the Squadron 6 series.

If you want more of Lilydale Cottage, Squadron 6 or any of my stories, make sure you join my new community on Substack.

https://claireboston.substack.com/

Acknowledgements

This book took a long time to write and I want to thank all my readers for their patience. This year bought challenges from moving houses, to starting a new full-time job and settling back into life in WA, after a couple of years living in different states around Australia. With all of that, there never seemed to be enough time to write, but I've been itching to get the story of Lilydale Cottage to you.

Lilydale was inspired by a real life garden in a small town not far from where I live. I don't know exactly what happened to it, but when we drove past one day, the gardens were overgrown, and the grass long and yellow. It had apparently previously been opened to the public and that was enough to spark my story senses tingling. I have photos of it that I shared with my reader group.

I already have plans for the next two books in the series revolving around Lilydale, and a bunch more which revolve around bringing Honeybrook back to life. I love the idea of building a community in this small country town. I also love the idea of building a community with my readers, a place where we can gather and I can share deleted scenes, or stories of all the little personal things that are in my books – things I've taken from real life and which make me smile when I read through. Or you can ask me questions about the stories, or about writing, or whatever you want. At the time Repairing Dreams goes to print, my reader community is in its infancy over on Substack. https://claireboston.substack.com/ I'd love you to come over and join me and help shape whatever the community becomes.

Thanks for reading, Repairing Dreams.

www.ingramcontent.com/pod-product-compliance
Lightning Source LLC
Chambersburg PA
CBHW030019200726
48283CB00012B/686